SHUSAKU ENDO

When I Whistle

A NOVEL

Translated by Van C. Gessel

TAPLING[...]
NEW YOR[...]

First published in paperback in 1980
by Pivot Books

Copyright © 1974 by Shusaku Endo
English translation copyright © 1979 by Van C. Gessel
All rights reserved
Printed in the United States of America

For information, address inquiries to
Taplinger Publishing Company
200 Park Avenue South
New York, New York 10003

Library of Congress Catalog Card Number 79-13183
ISBN 0-8008-8244-X

Contents

Prologue

'Excuse me . . .'

Ozu slowly opened his eyes. At some point he had dropped off to sleep on the bullet train. The cheerless winter sun shone upon the grey surface of Lake Hamana, where two or three boats floated.

'Excuse me . . .' The man who spoke wore an amiable, kindly expression. 'Aren't you . . . Mr Ozu?'

'Um-hmm.' Ozu blinked his eyes, trying to recall the man's name. As he grew older he was becoming more and more forgetful. People occasionally struck up conversations like this with him. He could remember having seen the face before, but however hard he tried he could not recall the person's name or what association he had had with him. These encounters were becoming increasingly frequent.

'I'm Ueda. I guess you don't remember me.' The man looked at a loss. 'We were at Nada Middle School together. . . . I'm Ueda.'

'Ah. You . . . er . . . you . . . uh . . .,' Ozu stammered. But neither the name Ueda nor the face of this man in his middle-school days were filed at any level of his memory.

'I just glanced at you when I passed through this carriage on my way to the dining-car a little while ago. And I knew I'd seen your face somewhere before. Then while I was eating, it suddenly came to me. We were in different classes, but . . .'

'Is that right?'

'We were in the same room when we went on the

school excursion,' Ueda tried to jog Ozu's memory. 'You lost your wallet then.'

'I did?'

'Yes! We all hunted for it. That made us late getting started, and old Rat Hole was really upset.' Ueda put his hand on Ozu's shoulder and turned sideways to let a woman pass by to the toilet.

'Rat Hole. I remember him! The P.E. teacher . . .'

Yes, that had happened, hadn't it? A smile half pleased and half pained at last floated up onto Ozu's parched lips. Rat Hole. The P.E. teacher. The students had given him that nickname because his face looked exactly like a rat crawling from a hole.

'What's he doing now?'

'Oh. I guess you didn't know. He was killed in the war. In China.'

'He was?' Ozu sighed. 'I haven't seen any of the Nada teachers for a long time. . . .'

'Don't you go to many reunions?'

'None at all. I don't get any invitations to them.'

'That's terrible.' Ueda peered into Ozu's face for a moment. 'They must've left your name off the mailing list. I'll let the organizers know. Could I have one of your name cards?'

The train passed Lake Hamana. Smoke flowed slowly from the factory chimneys. In the distance, the white buildings of a housing development stretched out in the afternoon sun.

'Nada's a lot different now from the way it was in our day. It's turned into a first-rate school.'

'So it seems. Back in those days, we got a lot of the students who couldn't make it into any other middle school. . . .'

Ueda said he was getting off at Nagoya and returned to his own carriage. Staring at the name card he had just received, Ozu sank effortlessly into memories of over thirty years before.

Well. Nada Middle School!

It was almost hard to imagine that he had gone to such a school.

He sometimes heard mention of Nada High School* or read about it in the weekly magazines. Unlike the days when Ozu had gone there, it now seemed to be a school that attracted only the most brilliant students. It ranked top in the nation for the ratio of students who were able to pass into Tokyo University. Ozu had even heard of parents who had moved all the way to the Kansai area just so their children could attend that particular high school.

'I just can't believe you went to Nada, Dad,' Ozu's son had said to him many times in the past.

'Why not?'

'For one thing, those guys are our biggest rivals,' his son had said resentfully at the time he was absorbed in studies for college entrance exams. 'I've heard that in one year at Nada they teach as much as in two years at a regular high school. I'll bet it wasn't like that in the old days, was it?'

'In my day . . .? No, it wasn't *quite* like that,' Ozu remembered, shaking his head. 'It was more relaxed then. They divided us up into four classes – A, B, C, and D – according to our grades. The clever ones were in A Class. C and D Classes were for the dim students.'

'Were you always in D Class, Dad?'

'Not always. I made the rounds between B and C and D.'

There had indeed been something relaxed about his Alma Mater in those days.

That cream-coloured building standing in the pine

---

* *Translator's note:* In the pre-war education system in Japan, boys would attend a 'middle school' for five years. From there they either passed directly into the business world or went on for further education to a 'higher school' which corresponded to the modern university. After the war the old 'middle schools' became 'high schools'; thus Nada High School is the descendant of Nada Middle School.

forest on the banks of the Sumiyoshi River near Mikage. To its right stood a wooden judo practice hall. It was there because this school had been built by Jigōrō Kanō, the founder of judo. Judo was a required subject for all students. In Ozu's day, the judo instructor had been . . . what was his name? . . . Mr Gutter.

Ozu closed his eyes and tried to remember the school song. But that song he had sung so often in those days refused to resurface in his aged head. In its place, he abruptly recalled the eight-word inscription by the great Kanō that hung in the assembly hall: 'Might for Right: Mutually Glorifying Self and Others.'

He had not visited the school in a long while.

He had never been to a reunion.

He had heard no word about most of the students who had shared the same classroom with him.

What was the name of the physics teacher? Ozu could not recall the name, but the nickname was still with him – Gas Mask. He had got married in Ozu's third year at the school.

The art teacher, who was called The Shadow because his scalp peeked out here and there through the shadows of his thinning hair, spoke incessantly about Turner in his class. The assistant headmaster, called Shiner because his head shone like the skin of a tangerine, gave lectures about the ancient burial mounds.

During classes, the students in C and D Classes always either engaged in pranks or took naps.

'There's no point teaching any of you!' a teacher sighed one day. 'You don't understand anything I teach you!'

Ozu was one of those students it was pointless to teach. Then there had been Shibusaka. And Satō. And Tsukawa, called 'Monkey'. And 'Cry-Baby'. And . . . .

1 Nada Middle School

'While we were in the study hall, the headmaster came in, accompanied by a new student and a custodian carrying a big desk. Those who had dozed off opened their eyes, and we all stood up as though we had been surprised in the middle of our studies.

'The headmaster signalled for us to sit down. Then he turned to the teacher and said in a low voice, "I'm giving this student to you. We'll put him in the second-year class for now."

'We couldn't see him well for the door, but the new student was a country boy of about fifteen, taller than the rest of us. His hair was done up in a little bob like a choirboy in the village church. His face was sombre yet extremely bashful. . . .'

Flaubert's novel *Madame Bovary* begins with this scene. This afternoon on the bullet train, as Ozu rewound the film of his memory, the scene that slowly floated up like a bubble of water in his head was also of a day when a new student had been brought into the classroom. . . .

It was during art class. Ozu and the other students in the third-year C Class smothered yawns as they listened to the sermons of the aged teacher they had nicknamed The Shadow.

'You see, the English painter Turner . . . no matter what setbacks he encountered, you see . . .' His head tilted backwards, and his tanned scalp was roundly prominent through his thin hair. '. . . He never faltered you see. For example ...'

Unfortunately, Ozu did not have the faintest recollection of what The Shadow had said after that. At such times, Ozu, like his comrades in C Class, had been one of those who yawned and picked his nose.

Those students at Nada Middle School with superior scholastic records were put in the A Class. So-so students were included in the B Class. Those beyond all hope were handed down to the C or D Classes.

'Turner was a man of effort, you see. So if you men would just make the effort ... it's not inconceivable that you could go up to the A Class next year.'

The Shadow intended these to be words of encouragement, but not a soul was listening. If only this class would end even one minute early! If only lunchtime would hurry and come! That was all they could think about.

'Aaah-aaah, aaaah!' Suddenly a student in the centre of the classroom let out a loud yawn like the bellow of a cow.

'Who was that?' The Shadow was furious. 'These impolite noises are ... indecent!'

Just then the door opened, and the assistant headmaster came in with a new student. Just as in the opening scene of *Madame Bovary*. ...

'As you were.' The assistant headmaster gestured with his chin towards the young boy in a drab grey uniform. 'This is a transfer student from Kakogawa Middle School. His name is Flatfish.'

Stifled laughter spread out from the desks throughout the room like ripples on a pond into which a pebble has been thrown. Flatfish? What kind of name is that? This kid's got a weird name and a weird face just like a fish!

The boy stood at one side of the lectern with his back bent, his eyes bleary like a pop-eyed goldfish in a bowl.

'All of you must be nice to Flatfish and help him along until he gets used to the school.' The sharp-eyed assistant headmaster noticed an empty seat behind Ozu. 'Sit back there for now and listen quietly to the lecture.'

From time to time they could hear through the window the grating voice of the commissioned officer assigned to the school as he shouted commands.

Yes. The long war with China was still in progress. An enlisted major had recently been assigned to join the two retired army instructors at Nada.

'Turner, you see . . .'

After the assistant headmaster had left, The Shadow had forgotten all about reprimanding the student who had yawned and had launched once again into the lectures on life that bored his students to tears.

Ozu could not help being irritated as the new student shifted listlessly back and forth in the seat behind him. What annoyed him most was the faint odour that floated up from behind him. It was a strange odour, like a blend of pickled radishes and sweat.

'Hey . . . !'

Suddenly a finger was tapping Ozu's back. When he turned around, the bleary fish-eyed face was peering at him.

'Hey !'

'Yeah?'

'What's he teaching now?'

'Art,' Ozu replied softly so The Shadow would not hear.

Silence prevailed for a time. During the silence, Ozu was irritated by the rustling noises and the strange, indescribable odour.

'Hey !'

Again a tap on his back.

'What !'

'What time is it?'

Ozu did not answer. Even if he is a transfer student, he's got a nerve, tapping me on the back and pestering me with his questions. Of all the gall !

Without warning, a long, plaintive, ridiculous 'cooo-oooh' sound arose from the vicinity of Flatfish's desk. Ozu was not the only one who heard it. The sorrowful 'cooo-oooh,' like the sound of a duck clearing its throat, rumbled twice in succession throughout the room, leaving all the students open-mouthed. They turned towards the sound, suppressing their laughter.

'What was that?' With a fierce expression, The Shadow gripped the edges of his desk with both hands. 'Whoever made that strange noise just now – stand up!'

With bleary eyes, Flatfish clumsily arose.

'You!'

'Yes, sir,' Flatfish answered sadly. 'My belly growled.'

Eddies of laughter swirled around the classroom. Only The Shadow's expression was merciless.

'I didn't make it growl. My belly growled all by itself.'

'Sit down!'

'Yes, sir.' Flatfish quietly sat down. No one could listen seriously to the lecture any longer. While the teacher went on with 'Turner, you see,' the students were sticking out their tongues, screwing up their faces, opening their mouths wide, and peering back at Ozu and Flatfish.

'Turner was a great man, you see . . .'

After school –

The students went out of the main gate of the school and passed through the pine forest, walking homewards like a procession of ants along the road that ran beside the tiny Sumiyoshi River. In those days, all the boys in Kansai dressed in light yellow school uniforms and wore gaiters and heavy clod-hoppers that resembled army boots.

Although their superficial appearance was the same, at close scrutiny it was easy to distinguish the A Class students from those in the C and D Classes. The boys who strutted like roosters, holding their heads high and advancing to the train-stop in strict accordance with school regulations, were generally the gifted students of the A Class. Some of them were looking at English vocabulary cards and committing words to memory as they walked along.

At their rear, the boys who dangled their schoolbags carelessly over their shoulders, cried out to one another in strange voices, and came to a total halt from time to time, were of course from the C and D Classes.

But in just a moment, something unusual will happen.

At the point where the road alongside the Sumiyoshi River, which was generally dry except on rainy days, met the highway linking Osaka and Kobe, the procession of students suddenly slowed its pace. A tiny stand selling bean jam pancakes stood there, and the aroma of sweet jam paste and flour being heated up tickled the nostrils of the hungry students. Since the school prohibited any sort of eating out of doors, they could hardly stop here. If they were caught at this stand, they would be hauled into the headmaster's office, and if worse came to worst would be expelled from school for a day.

So –

When the students reached this spot, they slowed their steps and flared their nostrils wide, contenting themselves with only a whiff of the faint aroma.

Ozu, who was walking a bit apart from the others that day, shared in these emotions. Still a growing boy, he was hungriest at about three o'clock in the afternoon. He too closed his eyes and inhaled the sweet odours.

Someone tapped him on the back. He turned around. It was Flatfish.

'Have you got ten sen?' Flatfish muttered, his eyes bleary as ever.

'Yeah.'

'Then buy some!'

'We can't.' Ozu shook his head. 'If a teacher catches you, you really get it. And some of the seniors are spies. I'd get caught for sure.'

'Yeah, but. . . ,' Flatfish mumbled, looking pained and blinking his eyes, '. . . what's wrong with eating something you wanna eat?'

"Cause it's wrong!'

'What's wrong with buying bean cakes?'

"Cause we're middle-school students!'

'If it's wrong for middle-school students to buy bean cakes, then who can buy 'em?'

Ozu looked at Flatfish's bleary-eyed, fish-like face and did not know how to answer.

When they had passed by the bean cake stand, Ozu noticed another unusual aroma. It was Flatfish's customary body odour.

'Do you . . . take baths?'

'Me? I don't like baths.'

When they reached the highway, Ozu asked, 'Are you taking the train?' He himself took the dilapidated brown train that ran down the centre of the highway to school each day.

'Yeah,' Flatfish nodded.

'I live in Nishinomiya. I take the train to San-chōme in Nishinomiya.'

'Oh, yeah? I'm at Shukugawa.'

'Shukugawa's the same direction as I go.'

But Ozu did not much care for the idea of boarding the train with this foul-smelling boy. One stop before this, a large group of girl students from Kōnan also boarded this train on their way home from school. What sorts of faces would they pull when they smelled the pickled-radish fragrance of Flatfish's body odour?

Those girls in their white sailor school uniforms. Young girls in white sailor uniforms, with round shoulders and rich bosoms. For some reason, Ozu's entire body stiffened when he was on the same train with them. Although they were the same age, the girls became more beautiful each day, while the boys grew increasingly ugly. They sprouted pimples, and their voices changed, and Ozu at times wished he could conceal his scraggy body from the gaze of the girls.

Five or six Nada students had already reached the train-stop and stood waiting for the train.

'I get really hungry at about noon,' Flatfish muttered sorrowfully.

'Don't let your stomach growl!'

With a great creak, a train that looked exactly like a rusty old streetcar pulled up to the station.

Ozu got on the train first, trying to shake off Flatfish. But it was hopeless. Flatfish kept right on his tail, sniffling as he hung from the strap. Three girls in white sailor suits, their skirts arranged primly over their knees, were seated in front of the boys.

'Those bean cakes looked so-o-o good!' Flatfish cried, oblivious of Ozu's embarrassment. 'I really like sweet stuff like that. And like Calpis . . .'*

'Uh-huh.'

Smothering laughter, the girls glanced quickly up at Ozu and Flatfish and then looked down again.

'Tomorrow's the maths test, you know.' Ozu did his best to change the topic of discussion with Flatfish, who was still engrossed in the bean cakes.

'Oh, really?' Flatfish merely blinked and continued, 'Tomorrow I'm going to find a way to buy some bean cakes!'

'Just try it, and see what happens when a teacher catches you. You'll really get it!'

'I won't get caught. . . . I'm going to buy some.'

'When?'

'Let's see. . . . During class,' Flatfish said casually.

This bloke must be a moron, Ozu thought.

The girls were still looking down, but doubtless they were listening to the conversation. Faint smiles of derision quivered on their apple-coloured cheeks.

Flatfish reeled slightly as the train reached a curve. The girls in sailor suits grimaced as they sniffed the mingled odours of pickled radishes and sweat.

* *Translator's note* : Calpis is a sweet drink made of fermented milk.

Ah, yes. That's the way it was.

The bullet train had left Nagoya and was now racing through a stretch of desolate marshland. Peering at the dark, low mountain range, Ozu smiled sadly as he recalled the face of an old friend no longer in the world.

He was a strange one.

What would Flatfish be doing now if he were still alive? Would he be a balding, exhausted, middle-aged man like me?

That next day, he remembered, he brought a cat to school with him. . . .

Yes. The following day was the maths test. Before class began, Flatfish again whispered to Ozu, 'I'm really going to buy some bean cakes!'

'Don't do it! You just can't!'

'I can. I've brought a kitten in a box.'

'A kitten?'

'Yeah. I hid it behind the archery field.'

'What're you going to do with a cat?'

Flatfish smiled a mushy, crafty smile and shook his head.

First period was history; second period was the maths test. The puffy teacher named Blowfish wrote the test problems on the blackboard and passed out answer sheets to the students.

Ozu ran his eyes over the problems. But of the four problems, he could not even understand what two of the questions meant. He glanced around him. Hashimoto, the student on his right, was frantically flashing him the signal asking for answers. Ozu shook his head in refusal. Someone let out a loud sigh.

Just then, a loud *'meow'* sounded outside the classroom window. The students listened quietly for a moment as the kitten howled plaintively for its mother, but soon some of the boys burst into laughter.

'Can't you keep still?' Blowfish reprimanded the class.

Meow! Meow!! Meow!!!

Just beneath the classroom window, the cat bawled incessantly.

'Teacher!' One student stood up, a deadly serious look on his face. 'Please do something about that cat! If you don't, I won't be able to write no answers 'cause of the noise!'

'Yeah!' Others chimed in to support this motion. 'It's too noisy, teacher!'

Mr Blowfish was clearly at a loss what to do. He walked over to the window and, bending his enormous body, peered downward.

At that instant, Ozu felt Flatfish moving behind him. It hardly seemed possible for such a bleary-eyed fellow to be capable of such agility. Before anyone but Ozu had noticed, Flatfish had disappeared from the classroom.

The teacher turned around and surveyed his brats with woeful eyes. Then he said to a student in the first row, 'You there. Go and get rid of the cat.'

'If I do that, I won't have as much time to write my answers. Unfair!'

The boy beside him, a pimply-faced student named Sonoda, raised his hand and said mockingly, 'Teacher, if you give me an A on the test, I'll go and get rid of the cat. . . .'

The students in C Class loved to watch the confusion and consternation of their unfortunate instructors. They longed for the kitten to howl even louder, if that were possible. Or, better still, they prayed that this whole ridiculous test period would be thrown into a shambles and rendered worthless because of the cat. Never were the students more strongly united than at times like this. At no time did they carry out more diligently the educational motto of the school proclaimed by Master Kanō: 'Might for Right: Mutually Glorifying Self and Others.'

Mr Blowfish glared sceptically at the group and said softly, 'Did one of you bring that cat here?'

'What a terrible thing to say!' one boy objected in a peculiar voice. The others joined in, booing.

'Don't blame us for something we didn't do!'

'Oh? Well, all right, all right!' The maths teacher raised his hands to quell the outburst, which was like aggravated bees in a hive. 'Be quiet! Go on with the test!'

'What about the cat?'

'I'll get rid of it. And listen – no monkey business while I'm gone. If you try anything, I'll find out about it.' Mr Blowfish turned around at the door of the class to emphasize his point and then went begrudgingly out into the hallway.

Shouting voices filled the classroom. 'Cry louder! Louder'! one boy shouted to the cat. Some scurried to copy answers from their neighbours and were warned, 'Don't copy *that* one! I've just made up an answer!'

Of all the students, only Ozu was on edge. If the absent Flatfish were not careful he might run into Mr Blowfish in the hall. If that happened, the newly-transferred Flatfish would be severely disciplined.

What is he *doing*?

Just looking at Flatfish, Ozu could scarcely believe that such a bleary-eyed, foolish fellow could be so shrewd and crafty.

The yelps of the kitten beneath the window ceased. The maths teacher was picking up the cat, repeating, 'Shh! Shh!'

'Teacher! Take him *far* away!' one boy shouted in the direction of the window.

Silently the classroom door opened and the face of Flatfish, like a chestnut pod covered with beads of sweat, peered furtively in. He was actually clutching a paper sack full of bean cakes in his hand.

'Got 'em!'

'Idiot!' Ozu said, clicking his tongue. 'What're you going to do if you get caught?'

'I'm not going to get caught!'

'Didn't you run into the teacher?'

'I spotted him walking towards me. But I hurried and hid. It was a close shave.'

The fragrant aroma of bean cakes wafted up from the desk behind. The smell made Ozu's stomach growl.

'Gimme one!'

'Nope!' Flatfish refused coldly. ' "He who labours not, eats not. . . ." But I'll sell you one for five sen.'

Two days after the maths test, Flatfish was beaten in front of the entire class by Mr Blowfish.

Unlike the practice in schools today, students in those days were frequently beaten by their teachers. Nada was not unusual; physical punishment was a matter of course at other middle schools as well. No father came to school to complain that his son had been physically abused. And the day after they were beaten, the students themselves would blithely commit some other act of mischief that would lead to yet another beating. That was the kind of era it was.

On this particular day, Mr Blowfish entered the class-room in a state of agitation.

'Arise!' Sakata, the class leader, barked. The students wearily rose an inch or two from their seats and slumped down again.

'Today . . .' Mr Blowfish placed the answer sheets from the test of two days before on his desk and looked merci-lessly around the room. '. . . I have something to say before we begin the lesson. I've never said that any of you had to get a perfect score on any test. But looking at the results of this last test, the highest score in the class, far from being perfect, is under fifty per cent.'

The boys drew in their heads like baby turtles and

listened to the teacher's sermon. Lectures of this sort were daily fare for the students of C Class, so not one of them listened in earnest. They felt like a man standing beneath the eaves and yawning as he waits for a sudden downpour to pass.

'The students in A Class could answer all these questions in twenty minutes. How does that make you feel? Aren't you ashamed to hear that?'

Not particularly, Ozu muttered to himself. And Ozu was not the only one – all the other boys were thinking the same thing. Gee, teacher. There's no reason to get so upset. . . . Let's just take it easy. That was how they all honestly felt. Let the guys in A Class grind away at the books. We'll do it our way, relaxed and easy.

'But what I'm really upset about today is not the fact that your scores are as poor as ever. I've resigned myself to the realization that the C and D Classes refuse to study and get poor marks.'

Well then, what are you so angry about, teacher?

'What really angers me . . .,' Mr Blowfish paused, 'is that someone here wrote flippant and downright insulting answers on his test paper. Everyone pay attention to this. Flatfish! Come up here to the front!'

Everyone turned around in surprise. Summoned forward by the teacher, Flatfish walked to the lectern with bleary eyes.

'You're Flatfish?'

'Yes, sir.'

'Tell everyone what you wrote on your answer sheet.'

Flatfish was silent, looking as always like a dried fish. Mr Blowfish picked up the answer sheet that was on top of the stack and ordered Flatfish to read it.

'You aren't going to read it?'

'Um . . .' Holding the answer sheet in his hand, Flatfish whispered to Mr Blowfish, 'When you say "read it," do you mean out loud or to myself?'

'Read it aloud!'

'I, er . . .' Flatfish shook his head uncomfortably. 'I'm ashamed to read it. I wrote this for you to read, not to have it shown to everybody.'

'Don't answer back! If you're so ashamed of your answers that you can't read them, why did you write them?'

The eyes of the class members were filled with curiosity and interest as they followed this exchange between Mr Blowfish and Flatfish.

'All right. I'll read it. "Demonstrate the following equations." ' Flatfish's voice was like the faint buzzing of the mosquitoes that cluster at the edge of the eaves. ' "Given a right-angled triangle with sides x, y, and z as in the illustration, x^2 plus y^2 equals z^2." '

'That's the question. Now what did you write for the answer?'

Flatfish lowered his eyes and said nothing. The other boys were also silent, holding their breath.

'I asked what you wrote!'

'Yes, sir.'

'Not "Yes, sir"! How did you answer the question!'

'Er . . . I, uh . . . I answered: "That's right. I think so, too." '

At first Ozu did not understand what Flatfish was saying. It was obvious from the blank stares of the other boys that they were in the same predicament. But in a flash it came to them. In answer to all the questions in the maths test Flatfish had written, 'That's right. I think so, too,' and nothing else.

An explosion of laughter rocked the classroom. Many of the antics of the C Class boys had stirred up the anger of their instructors in the past, but never had anyone written 'That's right. I think so, too,' in response to a test question.

'No laughing!' Mr Blowfish, in a fit of anger the likes of which they had never seen before, quelled the students. 'There are limits as to how far a teacher can be mocked! Flatfish! Brace yourself!' The teacher whacked Flatfish across the cheek with his enormous hand. The sound was like a rice cracker being snapped.

'You will stand there for one hour!'

The C Class students were understandably well-behaved for the remainder of this class. None of the usual spit wads were thrown; none of the questionable pictures were passed around. With lowered eyes, they smothered their yawns and gazed absently at the hieroglyphic-like figures on the blackboard.

From time to time Ozu glanced at Flatfish, who was standing beside the lectern. Even though he had been slapped resoundingly across the face with an open hand just a few moments before, Flatfish was his usual bleary-eyed self. He cut a pitiable figure, like a donkey lashed to a tree on a blazing summer afternoon.

I wonder what's really running through that guy's head? Ozu thought to himself.

As Mr Blowfish drew numbers and triangles on the board, he cast an occasional sharp glance at Flatfish, as though he might be having second thoughts. Even then, Flatfish did not alter his leaden expression.

Finally the long class ended. After the teacher left the room, Flatfish returned to his seat.

'What did you think you were doing?' Ozu asked.

Flatfish looked down and muttered, 'I still don't think my answers were *wrong*!'

2 'At the Age of Seven, Segregate the Sexes'

From then on, Flatfish and the conservative-natured Ozu became curious comrades.

Inwardly, Ozu was half convinced that Flatfish was a total idiot. But the other half of him felt something akin to envy for the cunning, mocking slyness that he himself lacked. These emotions were not confined to Ozu; the entire class began to feel the same way towards this bedraggled, bleary-eyed transfer student.

'You're really weird.' Ozu and Flatfish had started going going home together after school. Ozu narrowed his eyes and gazed at his somehow dingy friend and muttered, 'Are you sure you aren't a little cracked?'

'Don't you call me crackers!' Flatfish objected, pouting.

'Maybe you're not, but nobody gets knocked around by the teachers as much as you. Doesn't it hurt at all?'

'Sure it hurts. But they beat me just about as much at my old school, so I'm used to it.'

'Like today in drill class – what'd you have to do that for? You knew you'd get beaten if you did that.'

'Well, yes. I s'pose I did,' Flatfish nodded, his eyes as bleary as ever. Yet even though he nodded, it was clear from his unchangingly bland expression that he did not feel the least embarrassed or bitter about the beating he had received.

Drill class had been held that afternoon. A retired sergeant-major called Hippo, who always carried a featherless arrow in his hand, had made the C Class students go through crawling drills time after time. The pain in their knees and arms became unbearable as they clutched their rifles and crawled over the gravel-covered practice ground.

'If you continue to crawl around like squashed frogs, I'll make you do it over and over again!' his boots squeaking, Instructor Hippo barked from behind the students. 'The students in A Class have more spirit. You're beyond all hope!'

Why all the noise? Come off it! I can't take this on an empty stomach! the students grumbled to themselves, not daring to say anything aloud. At the conclusion of the crawling drills, the instructor had them take up positions to practise marksmanship. With the armoury or the pine trees as their targets, the boys pulled sloppily at their triggers.

'Attack drills next. Fix bayonets!'

Good grief! Are you going make us run again? Why doesn't the bell ring?

'Attack!!'

As he charged forward with the others, Ozu was conscious of Flatfish at his side, running clumsily along with his shoes thudding heavily. Then he lost track of him. Later, when the students lined up and reeled off their numbers, the transfer student had vanished like a ghost.

'One man is missing!' Instructor Hippo cried first in surprise, then in agitation. 'Where is he?'

Ten minutes later, Flatfish was dragged out from behind the armoury. He had hidden himself there during the attack.

'Yeah, but I was worn out. My legs wouldn't even budge.' Flatfish blinked his eyes and made excuses to Instructor Hippo. But naturally he was whacked across the face with the sergeant-major's bear paw of a hand.

As usual, Ozu boarded the train with Flatfish that day. Ceaselessly on the lookout for the girls from Kōnan, their bodies tensed as they hung from the train straps. But for some reason there was not a single figure in a sailor uniform sitting on this train.

'Why don't you come to my house today?' Flatfish invited Ozu. 'Ebisu Shrine is right close by. And there's stands selling pork dogs and sweets. It's terrific!'

Ebisu Shrine was the oldest and largest Shinto shrine in Nishinomiya, serving as an official government shrine of the highest rank. Ozu could remember his mother taking him and his brother to worship at a shrine on New Year's Day.

'The old man at the pork dog stand charges you by the number of sticks left after you've eaten 'em. But his eyes are kinda bad, and the other day I dropped some sticks on the ground and acted like nothing had happened. He didn't notice a thing.' Hanging from the strap with one hand, Flatfish used his other hand to demonstrate how he popped the pork dogs into his mouth. The famished Ozu could almost smell the aroma of the pork dog sauce and frying oil. Then he shook his head rapidly.

'Oh no. No! Just try stopping at one of those stands in your school uniform. Somebody'll catch you for sure.'

'Then we'll drop our bags and hats off at my house.'

'Your house?'

'Yeah. Nobody's there but my mum and my big sister.'

'Your dad's at work?'

'My dad.' Loneliness appeared in Flatfish's eyes for the first time. 'He died. When I was little.'

'Oh. Does your sister go to school?'

'No. She got married, but her husband's in the army now.'

Rows of houses bathing in the wan afternoon sun stretched out beyond the train window. Ozu thought back to the previous day, when a man from his own neighbourhood had gone off to join the army, surrounded by flag-waving relatives and neighbours. Japan was fighting a quicksand of a war in a country far across the sea.

'Come on, let's go and get some pork dogs. You've got ten sen, haven't you?' Flatfish asked.

'Yes, I have, but . . .'

'If that's not enough, we'll swipe one of my sister's books and sell it at a second-hand bookshop.'

'You really do things like that?'

'Yeah. Sometimes.'

With a dull clatter the train came to a stop, and shouting students from another school got on. These were boys from K. Middle School, and for some reason they did not get along at all well with students from Nada.

'Hey! "Calpis is the flavour of young love"! What a laugh!' One of the boys from K. caught sight of Ozu and Flatfish and shouted even louder, 'Look! The Nada boys are staring at us!' Flatfish gazing at them absently with his bleary eyes became the pretext for picking a fight.

'Ignore them,' Ozu said softly. 'Just pretend you haven't even seen them.'

But when the Nada side withdrew into indifference their opponents became elated with their success.

'What a smell! Those guys must've farted or something. They really stink!'

The other passengers maintained an annoyed silence. Ozu whispered 'Let's get off!' to Flatfish, and the two boys moved towards the opposite door. If this developed into a fight they were sure to lose. Their opponents were three hulking boys, and Flatfish would be no help whatsoever.

When the train came to a stop at the pine grove by the Ashiya River, Ozu flew out of the door. Flatfish followed clumsily.

A trickle of water flowed in the white river bed. A man was riding a bicycle through the pine grove.

'They're following us!' Flatfish whispered, looking behind him. 'What'll we do?'

'What do you mean, what'll we do?' Ozu shouted angrily. 'If we fight 'em, we'll get clobbered. The odds are way against us. Do you think you can handle a fight?'

'Nope. But I'm used to being hit, so it doesn't matter.'

'It may not matter to *you* . . . but it matters to *me*!'

There was a picket fence to their right. The huge mansions of the Ashiya rich lined the neighbourhood. For some reason there was not a soul in sight on the long, white road that ran along the river bank.

'Hey! Hold on, Nada boys!' the three boys who clung to their trail suddenly cried out. 'Stop!'

'What is it?' Having no other choice, Ozu turned around. 'What do you want?'

'Do you think you can spy on people and then just walk away?'

'You're the ones that started the spying.'

'Oh, yeah? If you wanna start something, we'll finish it!' One of the boys, the school bag on his shoulder flapping against his side, ran up to Ozu and Flatfish and tried to block their path. 'Down into the river bed!'

'Oh no! Cowards! There's three of you. Are you going to fight three against two?'

'Well, then, we'll go one against one!' This boy seemed to be used to fights. He set his bag at the base of a pine tree and leapt into the river bed, which was filled with weeds and scattered pebbles. 'Are you coming? One against one!'

Ozu had no alternative but to set down his bag and remove his jacket. He had no faith in his own fighting ability, but having got this far, he had to settle the matter one way or the other. As Ozu was descending into the river bed, Flatfish picked up a rock from the edge of the road and hurled it at Ozu's opponent.

'Ow!' Warding off the rock with his arm, the boy called to his comrades, 'That one's throwing rocks! The dirty louse!'

The other two boys grabbed Flatfish from the rear and pinned his arms behind him. Flatfish struggled, crying out like a squashed frog. Ozu charged at his adversary, but the boy dodged him and kicked Ozu in the knee with his massive shoes. Grappling together, the two boys rolled about on the floor of the river bed.

'Stop this!' a housewife cried out from the opposite bank. 'Someone come. There's some schoolboys fighting!'

Five minutes later –

Ozu lay flat on his back in the river bed, peering up at the afternoon sky. Surprised by the shouts of the housewife, the boys from K. Middle School had hurriedly kicked and beaten Ozu and Flatfish and then fled like a whirlwind.

But the chagrin and misery of having been beaten up left a scar on Ozu's heart, as if it had been seared with a hot iron. The smoke of humiliation still smouldered from that scar.

'Morons!' he muttered, placing both hands under his head and gazing up at the blue sky. 'Next time they're going to get their rotten heads beaten into triangles!' But Ozu was well aware that his own timidity made it impossible for him to take revenge even if they did meet again. That awareness was all the more mortifying.

'Just remember that!'

'Oh, knock it off.' From beside him, Flatfish spoke without warning. In spite of the beatings they had received, his voice was as dull and unconcerned as ever. 'It's nothing to get so steamed up about.'

'You want to just leave things as they stand? You're a disgrace to your school.' The absurdity of discussing school honour in such preposterous surroundings did not occur to Ozu. 'Don't you have any school spirit?'

'There's no such thing as school spirit in a fight,' Flatfish muttered, blinking his eyes.

'Okay, you let it pass. But one day I'm gonna make those guys pay for this!'

'You *are*? How're you going to do that?'

'I'm going to start thinking of a way. 'Cause I like to think.'

Ozu stood up and looked down at Flatfish. The shoulder of Flatfish's uniform was torn and blood was oozing from the back of his hand.

'Hey! You're bleeding!'

'It doesn't matter. Let's go.'

'Haven't you got a handkerchief?'

'Nope.'

'Your uniform is ripped.'

'Yeah. My sister'll blow her top again.'

As they walked along, Flatfish licked the wound on the back of his hand like a dog.

The white road that ran along the river to the station was long, and, as usual, there was not a soul in sight.

'Does it hurt?' Ozu asked, concerned. Flatfish, his eyes bleary, shook his head. Ozu tried humouring him. 'People will notice it when we get on the train. Why don't we buy a bandage at the chemist?'

In the distance the train came to a stop and two girls in sailor suits got out. Dangling their red handbags, they began to walk towards Ozu and Flatfish.

'Oh no! Some girls from Kōnan are coming.' Ozu stiffened and lowered his gaze to the river bed as he walked on. Being painfully conscious of other people, he could never look anyone squarely in the face at times like this.

As they passed the girls, Ozu thought he could feel the whiteness of their sailor uniforms against his skin, and he smelled a fragrance that was somehow sweet and sour.

'Oh, my!' one of the girls cried out. At that moment Ozu did not even dream that the course of Flatfish's entire life was to be determined in that single second.

'Oh, my!'

In the three years he had been a middle-school student, Ozu had never once been spoken to by a girl from Kōnan. But now –

'Oh, my!'

So said one of the girls in white uniforms to Ozu and Flatfish as they passed by.

'This boy's been hurt. He's bleeding!'

Ozu froze in his tracks in surprise and stood stiffly erect.

'Yeah.' Flatfish, being the sort of person he was, hurriedly concealed the hand inside his clothes.

'You'll get your clothes dirty if you do that.' The girl who spoke was sun-tanned, with large eyes. Opening her eyes wide, she spoke to him casually, just as though he were her brother. Things like that just did not happen. In that period, it was considered improper for an adolescent boy to walk together with a girl or even to exchange words with her.

'You've got some gauze, haven't you? You got it at the infirmary today,' she said, turning to the other girl. 'We could give him that.'

'Yes.' Her small, gentle-looking friend reached into her bag and took something out. 'Here it is.' She held the white gauze out to Flatfish. 'You can have this.'

Confused and stammering, Flatfish said, 'Th – th – thanks.'

'Oh, dear, you can't tie it up like that. Here, I'll do it for you.' The girl with large eyes came over to Flatfish, who stood immobile at the summit of embarrassment. Ozu, in total amazement, looked on unbelievingly.

'There you are. Goodbye.' The girls walked off before Flatfish could thank them. The two boys stood motionless for a time without saying a word.

Finally Ozu spoke. 'Hey, you.'

The pure white gauze was wrapped around Flatfish's filthy right hand. The whiteness of the gauze hurt Ozu's eyes.

'That was . . . incredible!'

'. . . Uh-huh . . .'

'No uh-huh's about it. I can't believe it! I bet you're the only one at Nada that's ever had a girl from Kōnan do something like that for him!'

'You think so?'

The figures of the girls were far in the distance by now. They made no effort to look back again.

'What are you gawking at like an idiot? Let's go.'

'Those girls,' Flatfish asked hoarsely, 'what year are they?'

'Dunno. Maybe third or fourth year. But anyway, what did it feel like when she came up next to you and put the gauze on your hand?'

'It was . . . just like I was dreaming!'

'I'll bet it was. I'll bet it was! That was really something else!'

Even after they had boarded the train, Flatfish, with his bleary eyes, was silent.

'Wow, it's really true that an injury can wind up bringing you luck!' said Ozu.

'Uh-huh.'

'Is that all you can say? "Uh-huh"? Boy, there's really something wrong with you!'

That was it. The beginning of it all.

Nearing Kyoto, the train passed the shore of a lake and entered a tunnel. Some of the passengers took their bags down from the overhead rack and got ready to leave the train.

Memories of over thirty years before, accompanied by a bitter-sweet nostalgia, were now coming back to life in Ozu's heart. With painful clarity he recalled Flatfish's unimposing face and his indescribable body odour, long forgotten among memories of his youth now covered over with the dust of many years.

Even we were that age once. Watching as a long-haired young man and a girl who seemed to be his girl-friend moved past him towards the exit, Ozu thought of himself at that age.

What had happened after that?

After that – yes. Hadn't he gone over to Flatfish's house?

Getting off the train at Nishinomiya Ni-chōme and crossing through the vacant, weed-infested lot, he visited Flatfish's house for the first time. It stood on the extreme right of four identical houses. He remembered that when he opened the glass door at the entrance, the aroma of the bathroom had come wafting out.

Flatfish's four-and-a-half-mat room was at the top of a dark staircase. Several bottles filled with earth were lined up on his desk.

'I've got ants in them.' Flatfish carefully pointed out the bottles, as though they were objects of great value. Swarms of ants bustled about in the dirt inside the bottles.

'They're making nests, see?'

'Hey! This room really stinks!'

'That's what my sister said. She got really cross. I've got a mouse I keep secret.'

They heard a woman, apparently Flatfish's sister, coughing downstairs.

Flatfish stealthily took a small cardboard box from his desk drawer. The red-eyed mouse crouched amid half-gnawed cabbage leaves.

'His name is Prince Kari.'

'Isn't Prince Kari the mouse that Dankichi has in the action comic books?'

'One and the same. I bought him at Ebisu Shrine.'

'You've got all kinds of things mixed up in the way you smell, haven't you?'

Flatfish's sister called from the foot of the stairs, 'Come and get some tea.'

'We don't want any tea. We're going to Ebisu now, so give me some money.'

'Moron! Stop talking like that!' his sister said angrily.

'She's always the same,' Flatfish shrugged. 'Hysterical.'

Ozu's memory was vague now about what had happened at Ebisu Shrine. The boys parked their bikes in an unnecessarily large lot and listened to the cries of pedlars selling bogus linaments. Off to one side, two or three stands selling stew and pork dogs were fanned by the wind.

'I'd really like to know the name of that girl from Kōnan,' Flatfish muttered, furtively dropping yet another pork dog stick to the ground. 'I wonder if I could see her again.'

Ozu felt somewhat jealous. 'What'd come of it if you did?'

The old man at the pork dog stand, who had been spreading flour on the meat with his head down, looked up and clacked his tongue. 'I can overlook one or two of those sticks, but you've gone too far. You've already snitched five . . .'

Ozu could remember it even now. Sometimes as they rode the jostling train home from school after that day and the train approached the Ashiya River, Flatfish, his fish-like face the very picture of entreaty, would beg Ozu, 'Hey! Please get off with me!'

'There's a test tomorrow. I've got to get home.'

'It won't take long. We'll only wait for five trains. Even three's okay. If she doesn't get off the third train, I'll give up.'

'What're you going to do if you do meet her?'

Ozu put on a look of begrudging consent as he got off the train at Ashiya with his bedraggled friend.

A grove of pine trees lined the bank of the Ashiya River. Stately mansions, silent even at midday, stretched into the distance on both banks of the river. The fences around the mansions cast clear shadows on the white granite road.

On the surface, Ozu appeared to be accompanying his friend only with the greatest reluctance, but in actuality Ozu himself was also eager to see the girls again. He wanted to see them and get them to do something for him like they had for Flatfish.

Concealed in the shade of the pine trees on the river bank, the two students waited silently for the next train to stop at the station. . . .

The rickety brown train. It looked like an old woman with a child strapped to her back, carrying a stack of packages. Panting, it climbed up the gentle slope and finally it came to a stop at the station with a dull clatter. Three or four passengers got out and went their separate ways.

'Not there,' Flatfish mumbled wretchedly, his eyes bleary.

'I told you so!' Ozu angrily confronted Flatfish. 'There's no point in waiting.'

'But they got off here before . . . so their houses must be around here. And since their houses are here, they have to walk along this road!'

At first glance, Flatfish's logic seemed irrefutable. So the two boys stopped talking and waited vainly for the second train. When the girls did not appear on that train either, the absurd debate began anew.

'Their houses aren't around here. They might've been on some kind of errand when they got off here before.'

'Errand?' Flatfish objected mournfully. 'Like what?'

'How should I know? Maybe they went to a friend's house, or went to study flowers or the piano. Girls this age take flower-arranging and piano classes, you know.'

'Piano . . .?' Flatfish sat down on the river bank and sighed, as though the image of these girls taking piano lessons was the very symbol of felicity.

High school students of today will probably consider the attitude of these youths of more than thirty years ago foolish and antiquated. But the minds of the Japanese of that day were still permeated with the belief that boys and girls should be separated at the age of seven. In those days it was difficult for a young boy and girl even to talk together, much less walk along hand in hand.

They waited for three days. They waited for five days.

But for some reason the girls never got off the train there again.

As they waited thus in vain, Ozu discovered in Flatfish a rare persistence that was not evident in his outward appearance. Finally his persistence was rewarded.

That day, they again watched hopelessly as a third train went by. Angered at his own foolishness, Ozu resolved not to continue this fruitless endeavour.

'I'm going home!' He started down the embankment of the Ashiya River, leaving the reluctant Flatfish behind. Just then, a fourth train appeared sluggishly in the distance and climbed the slope with the familiar dull clatter.

'Wait!'

'No! I can't take any more of this stupidity!'

The train pulled creakily up to the stop. If he ran for it, Ozu might be able to jump aboard as it began to move again. But a tiny grain of hope was still lodged in his heart, and that faint hope slowed his steps.

Three figures in sailor suits came out of the train one after another. Since the sun was in his eyes, it was hard to see at first, but when the girls turned towards him and set out walking side by side, discussing something or other, Ozu knew in an instant that two of them were the girls they were after.

Ozu turned around in confusion. Flatfish, true to form, quickly hid himself in the shade of the pine trees on the bank. Ozu dashed for the pines, too.

The girls must have seen him running away. If they remembered, they must have recognized him as one of the boys they had given the gauze to on the road by the river. But the girls went on walking side by side and talking. They passed by the pine trees where Ozu and Flatfish were hiding as if they hadn't noticed anything.

'See? I told you to be careful!' The voice of one of the girls was audible to Ozu, concealed behind the trunk of a pine tree. There was no doubt – it was the voice of the sun-tanned, large-eyed girl.

It was quiet for a long while. Then, coming rustling towards him like a potato bug crawling out of the earth, Flatfish whispered to Ozu, 'Let's tail 'em!' Ozu saw that Flatfish's forehead was lightly bathed with sweat.

In the student slang of the Kansai area in those days, to 'tail' meant to follow after the girls like a turtle following the tail of a rabbit. Just to follow, without saying a word to them – that was 'tailing'.

The three girls walking together were a considerable distance ahead of them. The white road along the river stretched straight ahead. The shapely, black stockinged legs of the girls were at motion beneath the skirts of their sailor uniforms.

'So we tail them . . .' Ozu swallowed. 'And then what?'

'Dunno. But let's tail 'em.'

'Say something to them.'

'Me?' Flatfish shook his head uncomfortably. 'I couldn't do a thing like that.'

The girls did not seem to notice that they were being followed. At one point two of them stopped, waved, and headed off down a road to the right. The one who remained was the sun-tanned, large-eyed girl. She stopped and readjusted her handbag. Ozu and Flatfish in turn halted quickly. When she started off again, the two boys followed behind her at the same pace. The gap between them remained the same, neither widening nor shortening. That was how students 'tailed' in those days.

When the girl crossed a bridge to the opposite bank of the river, Ozu and Flatfish quickly shrank behind the gate of a mansion off to the side to avoid being seen. At last she entered at an ivy-covered brick wall. The two boys broke spontaneously into a run.

The house was a mixture of Japanese and Western styles, with a European-type structure built onto the wooden residence. High-class residences of this sort were common in Shukugawa and Ashiya.

'It says "Azuma". That's a weird name,' Flatfish sighed as he looked up at the lighted gatepost. Then a smile appeared on his sallow face, as though he had made a great discovery. 'Her name is Something-or-other Azuma!'

They listened intently. But there was not a sound inside the house. It was as silent as an empty house.

Flatfish stroked the wall lovingly with his hand.

'What are you doing?'

'This wall. . . ,' Flatfish muttered to himself. 'My girl might have leaned against it.'

'Moron!' Ozu was truly incensed, though he himself did not know why. Perhaps the impudent words that Flatfish had just uttered had wounded him. 'My girl'! She was not yet anybody's girl!

'Don't say "my girl"!'

'Why not?'

'It's vulgar.'

'Well, what do you want me to call her? "Baby"? That's even more vulgar.' Flatfish stroked the wall with two fingers, bringing them to a stop at the milk delivery box at the rear gate. He opened the box and took out a milk bottle.

'What are you doing? You'll get caught!'

'This milk bottle!' Flatfish whispered intensely. 'She might've put her lips here to drink.'

'Idiot! Maybe she did put her lips there and drink. Or maybe it was her old man!'

'Well, just *maybe* . . .!'

Suddenly a dog barked inside the house. It was the high-pitched bark of a puppy.

'Toby! Toby!' a girl's voice called.

Ozu and Flatfish moved closer to listen to the voice. It was *her* voice.

'Wouldn't it be terrific?'

'What?'

'To live in a house like this and have a dog. We're too

poor to get a dog. I even have to hide my mouse. . . .'

This house indeed seemed like the pinnacle of unattainable happiness to these two boys. Neither of them knew anything yet about life or the meaning of happiness.

3 The Son

Ozu's business trip lasted only two days. But when he returned to Tokyo and headed home after stopping off at the office, he felt as though he had been away for a long while.

'Where's Eiichi?' he asked Nobuko as he removed his shoes.

'This is Friday,' his wife replied, taking his shoes and smiling at her husband's forgetfulness. 'You know he's on night duty at the hospital.'

'Ah,' Ozu nodded. 'That's right.' He wanted to ask something else, but he said nothing. He remembered that the night before he left on his business trip, he had argued over a trifling matter with his son, who had come home for dinner for the first time in some while.

In the past, Ozu had regarded him as a devoted son, but from about the time Eiichi was preparing to enter medical school, Ozu had gradually begun to react against his son's way of thinking. It seemed to him that self-advancement was the primary goal in Eiichi's mind, though Ozu doubted whether the entire medical profession shared that view.

Unlike his older sister Yumi, Eiichi had begun to study furiously when he got into high school. He was able to enter K Medical School because he had worked so hard, but he had lost all his friends. Those who used to come over to the house gradually began to keep their distance.

'That's because they're not like me,' Eiichi often

remarked. 'They've got it made in life because of the contacts their fathers or families have. But Dad can't do anything for me. Friends are friends, but in the end the most important thing is yourself.'

· 'If that's the way you think, your life is going to be very lonely,' Ozu would mutter on such occasions. But an icy smile would appear at the corners of his son's lips.

'You mean life isn't lonely for push-overs like you, Dad? I couldn't stand the kind of life you lead.' Ozu could still remember his son's reply.

The argument the other day was of the same sort. It began as they were discussing the hospital around the dinner table. Eiichi had made a slighting remark about an elderly patient who had no chance of recovery, and Ozu had reproached him. Now Ozu recalled the argument again.

Ozu changed his clothes. His wife poured him a cup of tea in the living-room, and as he looked over the mail that had collected over the past two days, he asked, 'Anything new happened?'

'Not really. The storm door upstairs won't slide properly. I've been trying to get hold of a carpenter, but it's impossible to get one to call.'

'They're short of staff. They've got construction jobs all over the place right now. No reason they should come just for a storm door.'

As he noisily sipped his tea, Nobuko suddenly remembered something. 'There *was* something unusual. We had three strange phone calls.'

'What do you mean, "strange phone calls"?'

'The phone rang, but when I picked up the receiver they hung up.'

'Perhaps it was a wrong number.'

'But I said "Ozu residence", and then it was dead silent on the other end for a moment. It was like they were waiting for some kind of signal or something. It really upset Yumi.'

When Yumi returned home that evening, the family minus the eldest son gathered around the dinner table.

'I didn't think that even doctors had to spend such a long time on the bottom rung of the ladder.' Ozu alone was in good spirits as he brought a cup of *sake* to his lips. 'Most people of Eiichi's age are making a healthy salary by now, but he can't even support himself yet.'

'He can't help that,' Yumi defended her brother. 'That's the way of life he's chosen for himself. He said since you aren't a doctor, he can't use your influence to take over a position at the hospital like other people do. He's got his sights set on getting promotion at the medical school.'

'But it's hard to become an instructor or an assistant professor at the medical school, isn't it? It takes ten or twelve years.'

'That's why he's putting everything he's got into it.'

'It's fine for him to work hard,' Nobuko interjected. 'But I worry about his health.'

'He always says he's going to make it in the world no matter what it takes.' Yumi set down her chopsticks and rose to get a new bottle of *sake*.

'That's the kind of person he is,' Ozu muttered painfully.

'He's not like you at all. He's an intelligent boy.' Ozu's wife looked proud. 'And he studies hard.'

'Some people isolate themselves so they can be successful in life. What good will it do him to become famous at the university if he loses out on everything warm in life?'

'Times are different. Young people now can't survive if they don't push others out of their way. There's really nothing else Eiichi can do.'

Ozu said nothing in reply to his wife. He always sensed that his wife was dissatisfied because Ozu himself had no hope for advancement. Her dissatisfaction was transformed into a compulsion to defend her son by means of remarks like the one she had just made.

'If you're saying that times are bad now, does that mean you think that the war days when we were young were better?'

'That's not what I'm saying. It's just that we took things at a slower pace back then.'

Had those days really been so slow and easy? Those days when cities throughout Japan were scorched by fire; when people fled in droves through the smoke; when inexperienced soldiers like Ozu were daily beaten in their barracks by their senior officers . . .?

'Oh yes, you're always talking about the war days, Dad.' Yumi brought in the bottle of *sake*. As always, she took her mother's side. 'The mood of the times was totally different. You can't even compare it with now.'

The fish-like face and bleary eyes of Flatfish flashed across Ozu's mind again. What would you say if you were alive now?

After dinner, when Ozu was half watching the television, the telephone rang.

'It might be that nuisance caller again.'

'I'll get it.' Ozu picked up the receiver in the hallway. 'Hello? Ozu residence.'

There was no response. The person on the other end was totally silent, as his wife had said. Whoever it was seemed to be waiting in silence for some sort of signal. Finally, with a dull thud, the receiver on the other end was hung up.

On Wednesdays Doctor Ii made his rounds at the hospital. On such days Eiichi and the other workers in the dispensary gathered at the front of the dispensary and waited for the doctor to make his appearance. Those who had patients in their charge were particularly tense on these days. They made one last attempt to pound one week's worth of progress reports and test results on their patients into their heads. They pounded that into their heads and then pondered the most precise words they could use in their report.

Finally the door at the far end of the corridor opened. Doctor Ii, his large body wrapped in a white smock, appeared, accompanied by Doctor Uchida, the dispensary chief.

'Which floor do we begin with today?'

'We will start with the tuberculosis ward on the second floor.'

A young dispensary worker darted forward like a dancing mouse and pressed the elevator button.

At this time of day the hospital wards were unusually quiet. Led by the doctor, the white-smocked procession advanced down the silent hallway, their shoes squeaking.

Mingling with the others, Eiichi stared at the sturdy back of the broad-shouldered Doctor Ii. The self-confidence of the man who held ultimate power in the Second Surgical Department radiated from that back and those shoulders.

One of these days, you're going to become just like that, Eiichi told himself. And he imagined himself in Doctor Ii's place, walking at the head of the white-smocked group, one shoulder slightly raised.

The doctor stepped into the post-operative room of a patient who had had a lung removed by surgery four days before. Maki, the supervising intern, followed quickly behind, carrying an envelope of X-ray photographs. Standing behind, the other members of the group listened intently to the conversation between the doctor and Maki.

'Progress since the operation has been good.' Maki handed the doctor the thermometer suspended from the bed. 'Bleeding has finally subsided. The fever is also down. Blood pressure and mental processes are normal. However, I think we may have to drain the lung.'

The doctor placed his new German-made stethoscope on the patient's chest and nodded. 'It's been four days since the operation, hasn't it?'

'Yes, sir.'

45

'Take some new pictures tomorrow. With the fever the way it is, there's no danger of a tracheal ulceration.'

'Yes, sir.'

The doctor removed the stethoscope from his ears and spoke to the patient. 'You seem to be doing quite well. You'll feel more comfortable in about a week or so. You're doing fine. You can rest assured about that.'

The patient's eyes shone happily. Doctor Ii nodded and left the room.

The group entered a large ward. The six beds were arranged facing one another. The patients, wearing sterile masks, turned simultaneously towards the group. The head nurse had ordered patients who were still infectious to wear sterile masks when the doctor made his rounds.

This time Tahara stood to the side of the pillow of the old man who was under his supervision.

'Are you still finding bacilli in the test results?' Doctor Ii asked.

'Yes. We detected a bacilli count of five in last week's test. Four weeks ago the count was three.'

'What medication is he being given?'

'We're using Isconth and Bethion. But I think we should substitute something else for the Bethion hereafter.'

The faces of the dispensary workers stiffened. Tahara, an ordinary staff worker in the dispensary, was suggesting a change in the medication that the doctor had prescribed for this patient. He was clearly opposing the doctor's orders.

'No. Bethion is all right for now.' In front of the patients, Doctor Ii did not speak in the loud voice he used to call on or scold the staff workers in his classroom. But a clearly unpleasant coloration appeared between his brows. 'If we used one new drug after another like that and built up resistant bacteria in the patient, then we'd run out of ways to treat the problem.' The doctor emphasized these words so that all the staff workers could hear, and then moved on to the next bed.

As they examined the six patients, the entire group was aware that the mood of the Old Man – which was what workers generally called the supervising physician – had soured.

Doctor Uchida, the dispensary chief, turned to Tahara with anger in his eyes. Why the hell would you make such a stupid remark . . .? those eyes were saying. Once a staff worker had clouded the doctor's disposition, there was no way they could return to the sunlight no matter how long they waited. That was common knowledge, but Tahara, whether intentionally or not, had blown it.

This *daimyo* procession spent a good hour and a half making the rounds of four wards and inspecting three other special rooms. It was past noon when they finished.

'Tahara. Just a minute.' Doctor Uchida returned to the dispensary after escorting Doctor Ii back to his office and called out to Tahara. Everyone else stood up deliberately and left the room to have lunch.

Eiichi sat alone in a corner of the cafeteria eating curry rice as he waited for Tahara. He and Tahara were in the same class in medical school, but inwardly Eiichi derided this poor excuse of a man. At the moment, however, he and Tahara had to co-operate on the preparation of a paper entitled 'Chemical Treatment of Post-Operative Tracheal Fistula' to be presented to the doctor. That was why Eiichi also suffered when his partner made stupid mistakes like he had today.

He finished his curry rice, and as he downed his glass of water the stoop-shouldered figure of Tahara appeared at the meal-ticket counter. Eiichi waved his hand and his partner, dragging his feet, made his way to the dirty table.

'You got bawled out, didn't you?' Eiichi asked with a painful look as he tapped the end of his cigarette with his fingernail.

'Yeah.'

'Why did you say that to the Old Man?'

'But . . . everybody knows that Bethion is worthless as an antituberculin drug,' Tahara looked down and answered in a weak voice. 'It wouldn't have any effect on my patients no matter how long I used it. I'd rather use Ethambutol.'

'The Old Man says that Ethambutol is to be used only at the critical stage.'

'I would think that a patient with open tuberculosis is already at the critical stage. But you know as well as I do that the reason the Old Man keeps using Bethion is because he gets research money from the pharmaceutical company that makes the stuff.'

Eiichi lit his cigarette and said nothing. He did not need Tahara or anyone else to tell him that a lengthy series of tests had demonstrated that Bethion was worthless as an antituberculin medication. It was a drug belonging to the Thibion family, and Thibion was no longer used even in Germany, where it was first manufactured. But the dispensary staff blithely ignored the fact that Bethion was still used. Because they knew that the research funds for the dispensary were a beneficence from the pharmaceutical company.

'But . . .' Eiichi grimaced and stared at the burning tip of his cigarette. The two men were silent for a moment, gazing out of the window. 'Listen, Tahara,' Eiichi muttered as he stared at the end of his cigarette. 'Don't do anything foolish.'

'What do you mean by "foolish"?'

'I don't want you mentioning anything about that drug again.'

'But I'm the doctor responsible for that old man. And as his doctor, I would like to see him recover.'

'I know that. I understand how you feel. But, after all, right now we're part of an organization. The dispensary organization. You can't go mucking up the system there.'

'I don't plan to muck up any system. . . .'

'Then don't make any trouble for the dispensary chief, He's got your future in mind. You realize that, don't you?' Eiichi paused. 'But if the Old Man gets mad at you, Doctor Uchida won't be able to do a thing for you.'

'That's what Doctor Uchida has just told me.' Tahara laughed a little sadly and poured some weak tea into his cup. ' "If you act like that you'll never have any hope of advancement," he said.'

'There. You see? 'Cause it'll reflect on your future.'

'But what about the patient?' Tahara said as he brought the tea cup to his mouth.

'Think it over. I won't say another word to you about it.' Eiichi stood up and stretched. 'Well, I think I'll go to the library.'

'You're good.'

Eiichi turned back at Tahara's unexpected remark. 'What?'

'You've got everything worked out.'

'Oh?'

'You're really going to go places in this dispensary.'

Eiichi walked out of the cafeteria without replying. Down the long corridor, nurses and patients in long padded kimonos were clustered at the windows They were probably watching some employees playing volleyball in the courtyard.

You're really going to go places in this dispensary. Tahara's muttered words still rang clearly in Eiichi's ears. They might be words of envy or of sarcasm, depending on how he took them.

Exactly right. I plan to go places, Eiichi repeated to himself, imagining Tahara's face. What's wrong with that? As he spoke, Doctor Ii's confident manner of walking flashed before his eyes. Twenty years from now, the figure making rounds and leading along the staff workers would be his.

'Doctor Ozu of Surgery. Doctor Ozu.' The loudspeaker called out his name. 'Please contact the operator. Doctor Ozu of Surgery. Doctor Ozu.'

Eiichi picked up the receiver of the local line at the end of the hallway.

'This is Ozu.'

'There's a call for you,' the operator's voice responded inside the receiver.

'Who's it from?'

'Nurse Keiko Imai in Internal Medicine.' He sensed embarrassment and hesitation in her voice. 'She says . . . she absolutely *must* speak to you.'

'Please put her on.' Eiichi stifled a feeling of displeasure and gripped the receiver.

'It's me,' Keiko's voice soon came through.

'What do you want?' Eiichi said coldly. 'I'm busy right now.'

'Doctor, please see me tonight.'

'Tonight? I can't get away tonight.'

'Just ten minutes is all I ask.'

The haggling continued. Eiichi finally hung up after agreeing to see Keiko at five o'clock that evening.

Stubborn woman. He thought of Keiko's tearful face. When she cried she looked like a monkey, and that face was so ugly it disgusted him. He no longer felt any sort of attachment to this nurse. Now I've got to see her again tonight, he thought. He went to the nurses' station in the second ward without returning to the dispensary.

As he was skimming through the test records of his patients, Doctor Uchida came in. 'Come here a minute.' The doctor beckoned Eiichi outside. 'What a mess. For Tahara, too. The Old Man was really out of sorts.'

'I gave Tahara a few words of warning myself in the cafeteria a while ago.'

'Oh? And what did he say?'

Eiichi hesitated a moment and then replied, 'Well, he's got a really stubborn streak in him.'

'That's true. Men like him have got to be watched.'

'I'm very sorry.'

'I'm not referring to you.' Smiling wryly, the dispensary chief tapped Eiichi on the shoulder. 'You have nothing to worry about. The Old Man appears to trust you. And we certainly have high hopes for your future.'

'Yes, sir.' Eiichi bowed his head and watched as Doctor Uchida descended the stairs.

The patients had a rest period from one to three p.m. It was silent throughout the wards of the hospital.

Opening a book in the library, Eiichi's heart was heavy as he thought of his relationship with Keiko Imai, whom he would have to meet tonight.

His affair with Keiko had gone on for six months. He had had affairs with other nurses before that, but none had given him as much trouble when he broke off the relationship as had the relentless Keiko.

From the library, he stopped by the second ward once again and had a look at his patients. As the rest period came to an end, a disorderly clamour returned to the ward.

Eiichi shared responsibility for five patients, of whom three were cases of chest tuberculosis. Two of these men awaited surgery. One was soon to be released from the hospital.

Eiichi, in all honesty, was no longer interested in tuberculosis patients. Because of antibiotics and early detection, the number of patients was decreasing and the method of treatment was prosaic. It was not a field with a future. He had therefore set his sights on the field of cancer. The university planned to build a cancer centre in the near future. His colleagues in the dispensary eagerly awaited the construction of the centre. Surgery in the future would be concentrating on cancer, the heart and the brain.

One of his present patients was an old man with lung cancer. He was a high-ranking official in a certain large corporation. They would probably have to operate in a short while. But of course they told the old man that he had tuberculosis. Eventually they would have to tell his family the truth.

Eiichi went into the old man's room on the corner of the third floor. A young woman was intently arranging some flowers in a vase. It was the patient's daughter.

'Hello.' Eiichi smiled and looked around the room. 'How are you feeling?'

The drowsy old man tried to sit up in bed.

'Don't get up.'

'I'm about the same. But this afternoon I coughed up some blood.'

Eiichi placed his stethoscope on the patient's chest. The daughter, who had been standing back with both hands clasped behind her back, said worriedly, 'Doctor, he says the pain has reached his arms.'

'That could be neuralgia.' Eiichi looked deliberately cheerful and cocked his head. 'There's nothing to be worried about. The pain won't last long.'

'It isn't cancer, is it?' Lying on his back, the patient studied Eiichi's expression. 'I had a friend who died of lung cancer. . . . He always complained of pains in his chest and arms. . . .'

'The pain that accompanies lung cancer isn't this mild,' Eiichi replied without letting the smile disappear from his face. 'So don't worry yourself needlessly. Just leave everything to us.'

A look of relief and trust appeared on the daughter's face. Now there's a good daughter, Eiichi muttered inwardly. Then Keiko's eyes appeared before him and he quickly lowered his gaze.

'Doctor, will I have to have surgery?'

'That's the reason you were hospitalized, isn't it?'

'If the surgery is successful, will I be able to work the way I used to?'

'Of course. You can play golf and do anything you want.' Eiichi had got used to lying to cancer patients. Lying to them was part of a doctor's job.

'Take care.' After he left the room, Eiichi gave no more thought to the fate of this old man. Here one could not afford to sympathize with the fate of each and every individual.

That evening, he met Nurse Keiko Imai at a tea room across from the hospital. The tea room was crowded almost to capacity with men and women returning from work. Keiko was waiting for him off in one corner, staring at the door. When Eiichi walked over to her, she lifted her face and smiled sadly.

'I'm sorry,' she apologized.

'It doesn't matter. But I don't have much time. The dispensary chief wants to see me,' Eiichi lied so that he could cut the conversation short. He sat down.

After the waiter had taken their orders, Keiko was silent for a few moments.

Keiko looks so fresh in her white uniform; why does she turn into such a drab when she changes into her street clothes? Eiichi thought miserably. Quite frankly he had lost all interest in and affection for Keiko. His sole wish was to get out of this tea room as quickly as possible.

'Well, what did you want to talk to me about?'

'Why haven't you seen me lately?' Keiko clenched her lips and stared bitterly at the coffee cup that had been set before her.

'What do you mean, "why"?' Eiichi was openly displeased. 'I've told you time and time again. I have a lot of surgery patients and I'm very busy.'

'That's a lie.' Keiko shook her head violently. 'Nurse Sekiba in Surgery is a friend of mine. There was only one operation this week.'

Eiichi faltered for a moment. 'I have no idea what Miss Sekiba has to say. But in the dispensary we have all kinds of work besides surgery. We've got reports to write, and we have to prepare for the research seminars in the dispensary.'

'You've had research seminars before, and you still had time to see me.' A tear trickled down Keiko's cheek as she stirred her spoon around in her coffee.

'Oh, come on.' Eiichi lowered his voice, conscious of the surroundings. 'This is nothing to cry about.'

'If you don't want to see me any more, why don't you come right out and say so?'

Driven by an impulse to bring the whole matter to a close, Eiichi said, 'I thought you were more open than this.'

'What is that supposed to mean?'

'Don't you think you're being just a bit too selfish? You phone me without giving a thought to my position. You have no idea of the embarrassment that caused me, have you?'

'I'm sorry . . .,' Keiko looked down and answered softly. 'But I'm so unhappy.'

'That's ridiculous. There's nothing to be unhappy about. Isn't it enough that we enjoyed each other?'

'I don't want that kind of love.'

'Don't be silly. I didn't get involved with you intending to fall in love. Everybody's doing it, you know.' The words 'I hate the way you pester me' rose to the top of his throat, but Eiichi swallowed them. This woman thinks we're lovers just because we've slept together three or four times!

'Anyway, to settle all this, I don't want you bothering me any more.'

'I know about it.' Keiko had been sitting with her head down, but suddenly she looked up at him with eyes full of hatred. 'I know!'

'Know what?'

'That you've been seeing Doctor Ii's daughter lately.' Keiko's words were suddenly shamelessly catty. 'That's true, isn't it!'

In confusion, Eiichi impulsively looked away. 'Rubbish! Who started a rumour like that?'

'It doesn't matter.'

'I remember dancing with her at a dispensary party. But I wasn't the only one. Everyone else did, too. I don't like you exaggerating the whole thing.' Eiichi kept his head down and avoided Keiko's eyes as he hurried through his explanation. 'And most of all, that's a rude thing to say about Doctor Ii's daughter.'

'Well, forgive me, but then I'm only a nurse. I'm certainly no match for a doctor's daughter!'

'Don't talk like that!' At his voice, an intimate couple behind them turned to look at them. Eiichi lit an unwanted cigarette to disguise his embarrassment.

'Someone saw you walking with her in Shibuya.'

'In Shibuya? Oh, that. Doctor Ii ordered me to go with her to buy him a trunk.'

'And you're always happy to bow and scrape when someone high-up orders you, eh?'

Eiichi stood up angrily. 'I'm leaving. I can't afford to waste my time at a place like this.' He took the bill from the table and walked over to the cashier. Keiko followed relentlessly. Ignoring her, Eiichi paid for the coffee and went out.

'I'm sorry!' Keiko again apologized pathetically, walking quickly to keep up with his long strides. 'I didn't mean to say that.'

'It's a little late for that now.' Eiichi's voice was cold. 'I don't want to see you again. Goodbye.'

The signal at the intersection changed from red to green, and people began to move across the road. Eiichi moved into the throng of people and realized that Keiko was no longer following him.

Well, that's the end of that! he muttered to himself But I wonder who told her about me and the Old Man's daughter.

He thought of the pale, happy face of Doctor Ii's daughter. It was true that he had first got to know her when he had helped her pick out a travel bag for the Old

Man to take to a medical convention in New York. On the way back, they had stopped for tea. But, then –

But, then, it was also true that it had occurred to Eiichi how much it would benefit his advancement if he got to know the Old Man's daughter better.

When Eiichi returned home that evening, his parents and sister had finished dinner and were sipping tea in the living-room.

'Welcome home. Have you had dinner?'

'I ate at the hospital,' Eiichi replied with characteristic brusqueness. In the bathroom he washed his hands with painstaking care and then gargled. Because he was a doctor – or rather, because doctors are that way – a concern with cleanliness was almost a mania with him.

'We've got some candy your father brought home. Won't you have some?' his mother called, sensing that Eiichi was going straight from the bathroom to his own room on the second floor. Mother and daughter were both aware that Eiichi had been avoiding his father recently.

'Sure, I'll have some.'

When Eiichi stepped into the living-room, Ozu noticed that drops of water still glistened in his son's hair. Before he set out on his business trip, he had noticed that Eiichi had lost some weight.

'I'll bet the night shift wears you out,' he said to Eiichi, trying to discern his mood.

'No, not really,' Eiichi answered absently, picking up the evening paper and starting to read.

'This candy is delicious.' Yumi tried to piece together their shattered conversation. 'Sweet things are good for you when you're tired out.'

Eiichi did not answer his sister. He tossed some of the candy his father had bought into his mouth.

'Did you have any operations today?'

'No.'

'I'll bet you're exhausted when you have an operation, aren't you?'

'It depends on the operation,' the son answered his father wearily.

'I suppose you have a lot of cancer operations?'

'They're not limited to that. Since we're on the bottom rung, we have to help out with everything.'

'But now that anaesthetics are so advanced, it must be a lot more comfortable for the patients. When I was in the army, a week after I went in, there was a fellow who had his appendix removed. They didn't use any anaesthetics in the army, and apparently it was very painful.'

Eiichi kept his eyes on the newspaper and did not answer. Are we going to hear about the war days again? His father reverted back to 'those days' at every opportunity. He spoke of those days as if they were the only period in his life. That always put Eiichi in an ill humour.

'In those days, you see, there really wasn't anything you could call medicine.'

Nobuko alone interceded with a muttered agreement.

Since Eiichi was silent, Ozu turned his thoughts elsewhere. When we were in the army we were beaten every day, so we became insensitive to the pain at some point. Young people today don't know what endurance is.

The phone rang in the hallway.

'Maybe it's that caller again.' Yumi stood up uneasily. 'I hate it! I pick up the receiver and they don't answer. Why do they do that?'

'You mean you can't guess?' her mother said worriedly. 'It's some pervert . . .'

'Ridiculous.' These phone calls just might be Keiko's way of harassing me, Eiichi thought to himself. That stubborn woman was certainly capable of such a thing.

4 *Though We Endure*

The war spread to Europe the year Ozu and Flatfish entered their fourth year at the school. Hostilities were no longer limited to the struggle between Japan and China.

The number of students in the A Class planning to take entrance exams for the Naval Cadet School and the Military Academy suddenly ballooned. When they had completed their fourth year they were qualified to enter a higher school.

Of course, Ozu and Flatfish had no interest whasoever in qualifications or in the activities of the tireless A Class.

'There's no way we could get into the army or navy schools.'

They had given up all hope of entering not only the army and navy academies, but also the difficult high-grade schools. Their teachers, too, seemed to hold out little hope for these inferior pupils.

'At least try to get promoted to the next grade. We're not saying you have to make it into the one or two first-class high schools. There's probably not even much chance that any of you could get into an average high school. Go on to a private college that matches your abilities. It's better to be the head of an ass than the tail of a horse,' their teachers muttered in tones half of encouragement and half of despair. But the drill instructor and the military officer assigned to the school were another story altogether.

'In this time of emergency . . .,' Drill Instructor Hippo lined up Ozu, Flatfish and the other members of C

Class, '. . . good-for-nothings like you are human trash! Many of the men in A Class are thinking of changing the school of their choice and attending an army or navy academy. But none of you are giving any thought to that! Oh no! Rather than think, you prefer to spend each day in idle loafing. Drones, that's what you are!' He often made caustic remarks of this sort.

'Nauseating old buzzard!'

'I'd really like to bash him over the head!'

The students muttered slanders against Instructor Hippo when drill practice came to an end and they were ordered to dismiss. But none of them actually had the courage to bash the retired sergeant-major over the head.

Still, Flatfish one day performed another of his outrageous acts. It happened when the siren sounded to signal the end of noon recess.

Flatfish and Ozu were lying on the lawn beside the archery field discussing the Azuma girl. Since that one day, they had not run into her for a long time. But though they had not seen her – or rather, *because* they hadn't seen her – Flatfish's and Ozu's attachment to her persisted.

'I hung around her house the other day, but I never saw her.'

'You just don't give up, do you?' Ozu was weary of Flatfish's persistence, but strangely he felt no jealousy. Instead he felt sympathetic towards his bedraggled friend who loved the same girl he did.

'Let's go back to class.' Ozu rose, and he and Flatfish started slowly towards the school building. As they passed the armoury and peered through the open door from which a padlock dangled, they saw the figure of Instructor Hippo inside, writing something in his notebook. The instructor examined the condition of the students' guns from time to time.

'It's Hippo,' Ozu whispered.

'Yeah,' Flatfish nodded with bleary eyes. As Ozu looked on, his hands abruptly reached out and closed the door.

That was not all. With a click, his hands fastened the padlock.

'Hey!' Ozu cried in horror. 'What're you doing?!'

'Hmm!' Flatfish himself was surprised. 'What have I done?'

'What've you done? You've fastened the padlock! Hippo can't get out. He's locked up in the armoury!'

The school building had swallowed up most of the students. Only Ozu had seen what happened.

'Gee . . . my hands did it on their own. They moved all by themselves and locked him in without knowing what they were doing.'

'What're you talking about? Let's get out of here!'

The two boys scampered off as fast as they could go. Ozu's shoulders were heaving as they flew into the school building. 'You've really done it now!'

'I have?'

'You bet you have! He'll be locked up in the armoury until somebody goes to rescue him. If they find out you did it, you'll get expelled!'

'Don't say anything to anybody!'

'I won't. . . . But you are *really* something else!'

During the next class period, Ozu heard almost nothing of the lecture on Japanese grammar. He had difficulty enough understanding the teacher's explanations under ordinary circumstances, even if he listened. But today was different, as though his mind were elsewhere.

Even Flatfish, who customarily fidgeted about in the seat behind him, was quiet today. He shrank down in his seat and waited for class to end.

Just as the interminable lesson was almost over, a messenger came into the room and said something to the teacher.

'Did one of you,' the teacher turned to the students, 'lock the door of the armoury?'

The students stared blankly at the teacher.

'Someone locked the armoury door while the Drill

Instructor was examining the firearms. They tell me the Instructor pounded on the door for help for an hour.'

Laughter rocked the classroom.

'What do you find funny?'

'You, teacher!' someone shrieked. 'You're laughing too!'

'I am not laughing!'

'I saw you laugh. Anyway, it's a punishment from heaven.'

'And why is it a punishment from heaven?'

'Heaven's punishing the Instructor for always calling us drones!'

'What are you talking about? Does this mean that one of you is the culprit?'

Whistles and jeers rolled across the room like waves. 'Why do you always blame us?'

'Yeah! Maybe somebody in A Class did it!'

'That's enough!' With a perplexed expression, the teacher waved his hand. 'If you won't admit to it, then that's good enough for me . . . .' He turned to the messenger. 'Please tell the Drill Instructor that it wasn't anyone in this class.'

The messenger nodded and left the room. With a faint smile, the grammar teacher said, 'Listen, you've got to stop playing so many tricks on the Drill Instructor and the major. It'll look bad on your records when they send them on to the high-grade schools.'

Ozu breathed a sigh of relief and turned around in his seat. Flatfish's eyes were as bleary as ever. His face was a blank, as though nothing at all had happened.

That year and the year that followed, the world situation changed abruptly. The German troops that occupied Poland did an about-face and began a blitzkrieg against Belgium and Holland, then in the twinkling of an eye occupied Paris.

'Fantastic!' One morning, someone brought a colour photograph of a German Messerschmidt into class. The students gathered round and peered at it with wide eyes. The glorious victories of the German forces were printed in bold characters in the newspapers each day. Ozu and his friends read the accounts and their hearts leaped. It did not occur to them that someday their own country would be engaged in a fight to the death because Japan had joined forces with Germany.

'Japan is now the leading power in Asia. Germany now controls Europe.' The windows of the assembly hall rattled with the applause of the students when a gaiter-clad newspaper correspondent just back from China lectured at the school. At that time, the students at the middle school had not yet heard the words 'militarism' or 'fascism'. Neither were they told of the resistance Japanese troops were meeting in China, nor of the true intentions of Chancellor Hitler and his Nazism. So they had no idea that they would soon be tumbling down the precipice of a dark valley. The clear-sighted students of A Class entered military academies, while the slipshod C and D Class students glanced at them from the corners of their eyes and then welcomed the summer of their fourth year.

The situation at home became very constricted. Women were forbidden to have permanent waves. In public places members of the Women's Patriotic League passed out leaflets saying 'Luxury is Our Enemy!' But summer vacation was summer vacation. On the day of the last distasteful examinations, cicadas were chirping in the pine trees of the school garden, and huge summer clouds floated in the warm blue sky.

Ozu and Flatfish and the other students flew from the school buildings, filled with a sense of freedom.

'It's vacation!'

'Yeah!'

'What shall we do?'

'Let's go to the seaside!'

They stuffed their swimming trunks into their bags. There were a number of places to swim in the Kansai area. The sea was not dirty as it is now. You just had to stretch out your foot to be on a beautiful beach.

'Why don't we go to the beach at Ashiya and drink some cider?'

'Maybe we'll see *her*.'

'Maybe we will.'

The two boys knew, of course, that their chances were slim. Since that day, they had never again seen the girls on the train. One of the main reasons for this was that an extra hour of classwork had been added to their schedule when they entered the fourth year, so now they boarded the train at a different time from the girls.

Instead of taking the National Railway, they set out for the Ashiya beach on the Hanshin Line, which ran closer to the seashore. Swarms of people were already swimming in the sea, which brightly reflected the sun. Several reed huts lined the white beach, and there the boys put down their bags and undressed. In no time, Flatfish was guzzling down a bottle of cider.

'You're really filthy when you're naked. You ought to at least try washing once in a while.' Pity was written on Ozu's face as he gazed at the emaciated body of his unimposing friend. But Flatfish was unperturbed.

'Once I'm in the water, that'll take the place of washing.'

Then they flung out their arms and dashed towards the spot where the white-capped waves broke upon the shore.

'Hey, watch it! You're getting sand on my head!' a sunbather shouted at Flatfish.

When they reached the sea, they splashed each other for a while and then began swimming the breaststroke.

Summer holidays! Ozu thought. A feeling of pleasure surged through his body. No more nauseating classes for a season. No need to listen to the soporific voices of his teachers; no tests to torture him. The members of A Class were apparently spending their vacation grappling with preparation for entrance examinations, but he was happy to leave such things to them.

Flatfish, swimming alongside Ozu, suddenly burst out laughing.

'What are you laughing at?'

'Eh?'

'What're you laughing at?'

'Can't hear you!'

They swam for a while longer and then returned to the beach.

'You're really weird. What do you think you're doing, giggling while you're swimming?' Ozu asked.

'I'll have you know I was performing a physics experiment.'

'Physics? You! What kind of physics?'

'You've heard of rockets, haven't you? They say Germany's got rocket planes.'

Before vacation began, their physics teacher had indeed mentioned rockets as a piece of gossip. Of course Ozu had had next to no interest in such a tiresome topic. . . .

'Therefore,' Flatfish said with a serious expression, 'I performed a rocket experiment.'

'How'd you do that?'

'I tried farting in the water while I was swimming. And it really made me go faster!'

The sand on the beach was as hot as searing metal. A man was playing with his dog at the edge of the water. Children were piling up sand and building little mountains.

'Hey!' Ozu suddenly turned to Flatfish. 'What school are you going to try for?'

'My family's poor,' Flatfish said with some sadness. 'So I may not be able to try for any. My uncle'd probably agree to pay for my schooling if I were a good student. . . . But with my grades, there's no way.'

Ozu said nothing and looked out at the ocean and the summer clouds. If Flatfish did not continue his schooling, in three years he would have to take a draft examination.

But looking at that meagre body, it was impossible to imagine Flatfish in a military uniform.

'Well then,' Ozu said softly, 'you'd better study a little.'

'I don't like studying.'

'. . . I don't either.'

They were silent for a while. The warm sun soon dried their wet bodies.

'Oh!' Flatfish suddenly cried out.

'What is it?'

'It's *her*!' Flatfish was staring down the beach to their right, his mouth wide open in stupefaction.

It was her. She was wearing a black swimsuit and a white bathing cap. She was just about to step into the water with the friend who had been with her on the road beside the river at Ashiya.

'It really is!' Something that was either a gasp or a sigh escaped from Ozu's lips. 'It *is* her!'

Flatfish was already up and running down the beach. Ozu followed. They came to a stop and looked on enviously for a brief while as the girls frolicked in the water. They wanted to say something to the girls, but neither youth had the courage to speak.

Pure white clouds like cracked ice floated on the horizon. Blending in with the sound of breaking waves, the voices of the people playing on the beach were blown in on the wind. Ozu closed his eyes and inhaled the breeze. Here there were no boring lectures, no examination jitters. Nor were the footfalls of war audible.

The swimming caps the girls wore appeared beside one another at a break between the waves. The two girls were swimming out towards the open sea.

'Let's go!' Flatfish threw himself into an approaching wave. Ozu followed suit.

Seaweed clung to their legs, and they swallowed some of the salty water. The two girls were surprisingly good swimmers and they headed towards the open sea with no difficulty.

Ozu, who was not a particularly confident swimmer, grew more nervous the further he got from shore, and suddenly he changed direction. Flatfish, unaware, continued to follow the girls. When Ozu got near enough to the shore to stand up, he looked back and saw the two girls clinging to a buoy that floated far in the distance.

Flatfish was still swimming.

That guy . . .

Is he okay? He can't swim as well as me. He's giving it all he's got even if he can't swim. He's trying to reach the buoy.

Do you really like her that much?

A rather large wave swallowed Flatfish up. His close-cropped head floated on top of the wave and then sank.

What's he doing? The idiot!

Ozu had not yet realized that Flatfish was starting to drown. But when he saw Flatfish shoot up and begin to flap his arms about wildly, Ozu thought, 'Damn!'

He's shouting something. He's shouting 'Help!' The next wave buried Flatfish, but again his head and arms broke the surface of the water.

The girls set out from the buoy. They had heard Flatfish's cries and were trying to help him.

Ozu shouted to a man rowing a boat. 'My friend – he's drowning!'

'What? Drowning! Where?'

'Over there!'

The girls reached Flatfish at that moment, but they had difficulty manoeuvring his floundering body.

'I'll be right there!' The boatman pulled his oars swiftly, heading towards the three bobbing and sinking heads.

As Ozu looked on, Flatfish was dragged up onto the beach, one of his arms around the boatman's neck. Behind them came the girls, pushing the boat ahead of them as they swam.

'You shouldn't head out for the open sea when you can't swim well enough,' the boatman grumbled as he left Flatfish in Ozu's care. 'A few seconds more and he'd have been a goner.'

'Yes, sir.'

The girls came up beside the outstretched body of Flatfish. Ozu turned beet red and apologized, 'I'm sorry.'

'We're just glad he's okay.' Their voices were still tense with excitement, even though Flatfish appeared to be reviving. 'I didn't know what to do,' said the Azuma girl. 'He was really thrashing around!' Then suddenly surprised, she cried, 'Why, I've seen you before!'

'Yeah.' Flatfish's eyes were bleary. 'You gave me some gauze.'

'Oh, I can't believe it! Every time we see you you cause us trouble.' The girls laughed gaily. The wetness of their black swimsuits clearly outlined the swelling of their breasts.

Ozu took courage and spoke. 'You don't go by train much these days.'

'What do you mean?'

'We wanted to thank you for the gauze but we never see you.'

'At school they told us to get on the train at different times. And besides . . ,' the girl who wasn't named Azuma – Ozu knew only her last name – teased the boys, 'when we get in the same carriage . . . you Nada boys stink.'

'Stink?'

'Yes. You're all sweaty and smelly. It's awful. Isn't it, Aiko?'

Aiko Azuma smiled broadly but did not reply.

'We're not the ones that stink . . .' Ozu started to say, but clamped his mouth shut. Flatfish was the one who stank. Please don't confuse me with Flatfish, he muttered to himself.

'And why do you always make strange noises and swing from the straps in the train? It's really annoying!'

"We never did that,' Ozu replied falteringly.

'Liar. And what about the time you and this bloke hid

along the bank of the Ashiya River? We know all about
it. You followed Aiko home and then prowled around her
house, didn't you!'

'Did not!'

'Besides which, you stole a milk bottle!'

Ozu blushed a bright red and lowered his eyes. The
girls were turning their noses up at them. They didn't know
the least bit about male psychology. The boys made a
racket on the train and followed the girls merely to get
their attention. Ozu could still see before him the tiny head
of Flatfish as he paddled frantically for the open sea
though he could barely swim at all. . . .

'Let's go.' Aiko seemed to have grown tired of the
conversation and urged her friend along.

'Okay. Goodbye.' They stood up, brushing off the sand
that clung to their white legs. The sky was blue, and from
the sea they could hear the voices of the swimmers.

'Wait!' Flatfish sat up and implored. 'Let us buy you
some cider.'

'We don't want any of that,' they refused curtly. 'We
don't want to ruin our stomachs.'

Resignedly, Ozu and Flatfish watched the tiny figures
of the girls frolicking in the sea. Though they would have
liked to talk to them further, Ozu was painfully aware
of the fact that the girls did not have the slightest interest
in them. It may have been his first taste of the pangs of
love. But if this feeling could be called love, it was
certainly a strange sort of love. For Ozu felt no jealousy
towards Flatfish, who was madly infatuated with the same
Aiko. Rather he felt a sort of kinship with Flatfish as they
shared the same joys and sorrows.

'Well, anyway,' Ozu blurted out in a voice that was
either a gasp or a sigh, 'you did a good job of swimming
out there.' Unlike the area close to the beach, the water
where Flatfish had almost drowned appeared deep, with
rough waves. 'I bet you were frantic.'

'Uh-huh.'

'But girls really are cold, aren't they? Those two don't have the faintest idea why you swam all the way out there.'

Flatfish, his face pressed against the beach, did not reply. Splotches of sand clung to his slender back. His thin, ungainly back seemed to wear a sad expression. Ozu was painfully aware of his friend's distress.

'But at least we've found out her name,' he tried to encourage Flatfish. 'We got something out of it. Aiko Azuma. What a weird name.' He tried writing the name in the sand with his finger. 'Nothing'll come of it anyway.'

'Why not?'

'Girls all get married as soon as they get out of school. They find some swell from Ashiya or Mikage, or else a a soldier. All the girls from Kōnan are like that. But it's going to be a long time before either of us can earn a living.'

With his chin propped up on both hands, Flatfish listened in silence to Ozu's words. 'Goodbye,' he muttered sadly.

'Are you leaving already?'

'Not me. The girls've come out of the water and they're heading for the dressing-room. They're gonna leave.'

'What are you going to do?'

'Let's follow them.'

'You'll just make them cross.'

'I don't care. Let's follow them.'

Ozu understood how Flatfish felt. They could not suppress the desire to follow the girls, though they knew they would be scorned and hated for it.

For almost ten minutes they stood beside the reed dressing huts that cast black shadows upon the white sand. It had taken no time at all for the boys to change into their clothes.

Several evening primroses were growing beside the dressing huts. Flies were swarming on a watermelon rind that someone had tossed away.

When Aiko and her friend appeared, dressed in Western-style clothes and carrying their bags, they glanced quickly at the boys and said, 'So long.'

'Er . . . where are you going?'

'Home, of course.'

'We'll go with you.'

'No! Leave us alone, and don't go following us!'

The road along the river was brightly lit by the sun. Aiko and her friend chose the shady spots to walk along. A grasshopper chirped from the dry reeds in the river bed. All the mansions along the road were silent in the early afternoon.

Ozu and Flatfish were growing desperate. Since the girls did not look back even once, they knew it was a bad idea to be following them. But the knowledge only increased their persistence. Their minds were operating like that of a boy who deliberately torments a girl he likes.

If the girls walked faster, Ozu and Flatfish abruptly quickened their steps. If the girls slowed down, the boys also slackened their pace. They constantly maintained the same distance between them.

The road was white and the shadows of the mansions fell blackly upon it. Two workmen were enjoying an afternoon nap beneath the pine trees at the river bank.

'You don't give up, do you?' Aiko's friend could not stand it any longer and turned and called.

Ozu and Flatfish stopped, stubbornly silent.

'What do you want?'

'We're not doing anything wrong,' Flatfish answered in a subdued voice. 'You don't have to get so upset.'

'We'll tell on you!'

'To who?'

'Your teachers at Nada!'

'Who cares?'

'You two are indecent!'

'Indecent?'

'Everybody knows it's indecent to chase after girls in

times of emergency like this.' She turned to Aiko and said audibly, 'Let's run!'

When the girls dashed off, Ozu and Flatfish set off after them at a trot. Their hearts welled with excitement, like that of a hunting dog pursuing a rabbit.

'Hey!' Flatfish called out as they ran. 'What's indecent about us talking to you? What's wrong with being together? We won't do anything bad!'

The girls ran to a bridge and started over it without answering. Aiko's house stood just on the other side of this bridge.

Suddenly, a young man in a pure white uniform appeared from the dark shadows of a mansion on the opposite bank. He wore a cap and a short sword dangled from his waist.

Ozu and Flatfish knew at a glance that the white uniform belonged to the naval academy that was so far from their grasp.

The young man stopped and smiled at the two girls who were running towards him. He greeted them, and they discussed something together with great familiarity. The girls turned round; they were obviously telling the young man about Ozu and Flatfish.

What's this? What's going on? It took a moment for the boys to grasp the situation. They could not understand why the two schoolgirls should know this dashing naval cadet.

The young man in the white uniform shifted his eyes towards Ozu and Flatfish. His expression was fierce. Against his heavily tanned face, those eyes were piercing.

Ozu and Flatfish froze with their mouths wide open. They had no choice but to turn and retreat ignominiously, like a brow-beaten mongrel.

Dressed in his white summer uniform with a short sword at his side, the naval cadet disappeared down a shaded side street, flanked on either side by the girls. The heat became unbearable and the chirping of the cicadas from the garden of one of the mansions became noticeably louder.

'Who the hell was that?' Flatfish spat and sat down by the trunk of a pine tree beside the river. 'Does he think he can mess around with girls just because he's a naval cadet? These are times of emergency, you know.'

Anger was something Ozu had seldom observed in Flatfish and he was rather amused by it. 'Well then, we're in the same boat.'

'No, we aren't.' Flatfish shook his head. 'We aren't soldiers. But that guy's a soldier, so he's in a different position.'

'Maybe he's her brother.'

'Whose brother?'

'*Hers*!'

'Do you really think so?' Relief tinted Flatfish's eyes. 'Well, it's okay if it's her brother.'

'Do you really like Aiko that much?'

'I'm nuts about her.' Embarrassed, Flatfish looked down into the river bed. 'Every time I hear a song, I think of her.'

'Oh, give up! She doesn't even *like* you. It's hopeless no matter how much you love her.'

'I've got it!' Flatfish stood up suddenly. The firmness of his expression stunned Ozu. 'I'm going to try for the naval academy!'

'Naval academy? You?'

'Yeah, me! I'll become a naval cadet just like that creep. *Then* she'll give it some thought.'

'Give what some thought?'

'Marriage!'

'Marriage to you?'

'Right!'

Ozu was shocked and could think of nothing to say. For one thing, to a student at middle school, marriage was an event as distant as a dream. And he could not even begin to imagine Flatfish getting married.

'Do you think you can pass the navy physical,' Ozu muttered pityingly, 'with a body like that? And the academy exam is as hard as at the best higher schools!'

'I'll run every day. That'll build me up.' Still, Flatfish did not seem to have any inspiration for dealing with the academic examination.

But in actuality, when the summer holidays ended and the new school term began, though his eyes were still bleary and he still smelled of sweat, Flatfish appeared at school with a tanned face. He reported that he had trained faithfully by running around his neighbourhood every single day. Listening to Flatfish, Ozu thought of his friend's tiny head being tossed about by the waves as he swam desperately for the open sea. And he knew that what Flatfish reported was true.

'I sent her a love letter today,' Flatfish confessed to Ozu. 'I told her I was going to prove to her that I could get into the naval academy.'

But no answer to Flatfish's love letter came from Aiko. Once again Flatfish's face took on a piteous expression.

5 *The Approach*

Eiichi liked to climb up onto the roof of the ward and look down at the arrangement of white buildings that made up the hospital complex. After lunch today, he climbed to the roof and looked around, leaning against the railing. White smoke was flowing from a large chimney which stood beyond the ward buildings. Nurses and doctors in white uniforms and examination smocks, and patients in long gowns walked through the plaza, in which trees and flowers had been planted.

The brownish buildings of the university stretched out behind the research laboratory. Eiichi could see students playing catch on the recreation field.

Eiichi had grown accustomed to this scene over the ten years since he had entered the medical school. In a sense, his life had got started there, and there he would have to live out his future. To put it strongly, for Eiichi the world was this hospital, and here his fate would be determined in its entirety.

'I really like the hospital in the evening,' Tahara had told him once. 'In the evening there's a light burning in every one of the hospital windows. It makes it look like a gigantic boat floating on the sea at night. And behind each one of those windows, children are being born, and people are dying. They're all waging a battle against disease, the enemy of mankind. At times like that I always think that a doctor is someone who helps these people.'

Eiichi chuckled inwardly at Tahara's sentimental words.

'There are limits to that help,' he taunted Tahara. 'A doctor can't get too involved in his patients' problems.'

'Why not?'

'If you're going to diagnose and treat your patients properly, you can't dote on them. There are times when you have to be totally callous.'

'I know that, but . . .,' Tahara muttered with some sadness. 'In the end, a doctor can't help but feel love for his own patients.'

'But a doctor can't afford to get all wrapped up in his patients, to coddle them. Frankly, I think it would be more appropriate for a doctor to think of his patients the way a jeweller thinks of the watches he repairs.'

'But patients are people!' Tahara shook his head. 'Not watches. A patient doesn't suffer from the disease alone. There is life at the core of this! And if we don't take that life into consideration when we treat the patients . . .'

Tahara's unsettled expression angered Eiichi. 'A doctor can't bear that much responsibility on his own shoulders! A doctor isn't a priest or a columnist giving advice to the lovelorn. When a patient comes into this hospital, I'm not interested in anything but his illness. If I had to start thinking about their lives beyond that, I wouldn't be able to make up my mind about the proper treatment. . . . It's just too much to handle.'

'You're strong,' Tahara responded enviously. 'I'll never be strong like you.'

It did not matter to Eiichi whether he was strong or not. In his eyes, men like Tahara were excessively sentimental and timid.

At any rate . . ., Eiichi looked down at the hospital from the rooftop and once again muttered to himself, . . . someday I'm going to make it in this world. At all costs. At all costs. . . .

The afternoon sun left orange-coloured blotches on the

white laundry drying on the rooftop. When Eiichi threaded his way through the laundry and opened the heavy metal door, the odour of disinfectant that permeated the entire hospital came wafting out.

As Eiichi walked past the nurses' station, the head nurse, who had the telephone receiver to her ear, turned towards him. 'Ah. Doctor Ozu has just come in,' she said to someone. 'Doctor Ozu, it's Doctor Uchida calling. He'd like to see you right away.'

'Doctor Uchida? I wonder what he wants.' Fearing a reprimand over some matter concerning his patients, he hurried across the sunlit courtyard to the dispensary. Doctor Uchida was sitting alone in his revolving chair.

'Ah!' The doctor tossed his cigarette into a crumpled tin can and stood up. 'Would you mind going over to the examination room in Opthamology?'

'Opthamology?'

'That's right. The Old Man's daughter has come in for an examination. It seems she has a piece of iron or something in her eye. She came in without warning, and I got hold of Saeki in Opthamology, but . . . I'd like you to stand by and make sure there are no slip-ups.'

'Yes, sir.' Nodding, Eiichi started out of the dispensary office.

'If circumstances permit, take her home.'

'The Old Man's daughter . . .?'

'She might have trouble getting home if they bandage her eye. I thought of asking Tahara to do it, but he's just not very sharp. So I'd like you to take care of it, unless some of your patients have special problems.'

'No . . . no problem there.' As he walked down the corridor Eiichi thought of the face of the young woman he had accompanied to a department store to buy a bag for Doctor Ii's trip to America. She told him she had graduated from the university just two years ago. When they had completed their errand, they had stopped for tea at a parlour, and she had told him about the vacation she had taken in Switzerland when she was at school. With a droll expression, she had confessed light-heartedly to Eiichi that she liked skiing and jazz better than anything else in the world.

When he reached the opthamology examination room, Eiichi buttoned his gown and softly opened the door. He could hear the voices of Doctor Saeki and the young woman conversing behind the single-panel screen.

'Well, I don't think there's any damage to the eyeball, but as a precaution I'll give you some medication for it. You don't have any allergies, do you?'

'No, I don't.'

'You probably won't need to keep this bandage on. But just for tonight, don't watch too much television or the like.' Doctor Saeki stood up and gave the name of the medication to the nurse. The young woman bowed and, leaving the room with the nurse, discovered Eiichi behind the screen.

'Oh!'

'I stopped by to see you.' With a smile, Eiichi turned to Doctor Saeki. 'I'm Ozu of the Second Surgery Department. Doctor Uchida asked me to pay my respects.'

'That's very kind of you,' Saeki said with some sarcasm in his voice, 'to come all this way.'

In the corridor, Eiichi turned to the opthamology nurse who accompanied them, 'Thank you. I can take over from here.'

'But the medicine . . .'

'I'll handle the prescription. Otherwise, we'd have to make Doctor Ii's daughter wait at the pharmacy. . . .' He picked up a phone in the corridor and called ahead to the hospital pharmacy to have them rush the preparation of the medicine. Eiichi was always shrewd when it came to such matters.

'Would you like to stop by your father's office? Of course, Doctor Ii has gone over to the Ministry of Public Welfare today, so he won't be in . . .'

'I think I'll just go straight home now.' She tilted her head, awkwardly adjusting her eye bandage.

'Well then, I'll get the medicine for you right away. How do you spell your first name?' Eiichi ascertained that her name was Yoshiko and hurried to the pharmacy.

You can't let any opportunities pass you by, he repeated to himself. Doctor Uchida wanted me to see her home just because she's the Old Man's daughter. But I can use this opportunity to promote my own advancement, too!

'There's three days' dosage here.' When he returned to where Yoshiko was waiting in the empty corridor, he held out the container of medicine and explained, 'There's some medicine to put in your eye and some to take internally.'

'Am I that bad?'

'Not at all,' he laughed and shook his head. 'If it'd been me, I wouldn't have given you any medicine at all. The important thing is not to use your eye today. Don't watch any television – like Doctor Saeki told you.'

'Oh blast,' she chuckled. 'There was a programme I wanted to see tonight.'

'What was that?'

'Sammy Mercy's going to be on. I'm really wild about the way he plays the trumpet.'

'Well, you could listen to the sound without watching the picture.' Then immediately he offered, 'I'll get you one of his records instead.'

'Oh!' She looked at Eiichi in surprise. 'You don't have to do that.'

'I'd like to. Why don't we go and buy one right now? I haven't got anything to do today.' From experience, Eiichi knew it was best to drag a woman off without giving her time to think. If he had said something ordinary like 'Let me see you home,' she would have known it was nothing but apple-polishing by one of her father's disciples.

He set out ahead of her. A nurse he knew by sight came out of a room across the corridor. She stopped when

78

she saw the two of them, then bowed silently and started past them.

'Say!' Eiichi called to the nurse, removing his examination smock. 'I'm sorry, but would you drop this off at the nurses' station in the Second Ward?'

'Yes.'

'And tell the head nurse I won't be back in today.'

The nurse nodded and went on. In Eiichi's mind, the patients under his supervision no longer existed.

They caught a taxi in front of the hospital and headed for Shinjuku.

'Your father is really amazing.' Eiichi looked over at Yoshiko, who sat beside him with her knees pressed together. 'We young men can't even begin to follow his example. Besides examining patients and performing surgery, your father has lectures and conferences crammed into his schedule. And he performs every one of those things with such vigour!'

No daughter disliked having her father praised, Eiichi calculated inwardly. Tonight she would probably tell her father everything he said. He must weigh his words carefully.

'I call your father Superman.'

'How dreadful!' Yoshiko laughed aloud as she gazed at the scene out the window. 'He *is* very busy. Mother always complains about that. She says he can't sit still for a moment.'

'Is he like that at home, too?'

'Yes. He hates to be idle. Even on Sundays, he'll call up someone at the dispensary to play golf or tennis. And at his age . . .'

'Is that so?' Eiichi felt a little uncomfortable. 'Who from the dispensary plays with your father?'

'You mean you don't know about it?' Yoshiko answered innocently, lightly touching the eye bandage with her finger. 'He plays golf with Doctor Uchida or Doctor Kanda. For tennis he goes with Mr Yoshikawa or Mr Kurihara.'

Since Uchida, Kanda and Yoshikawa were all men of authority in the dispensary and many years Eiichi's senior, he could understand their association with the Old Man. But Kurihara . . .

So he's weaseled his way into the Old Man's home?

Kurihara had entered the dispensary a year ahead of Eiichi. His father was the president of a large pharmaceutical manufacturing company. Eiichi had heard that when Kurihara's father was hospitalized with a stomach ulcer two years ago, Doctor Ii had treated him as a special patient, performing all the examinations and surgery himself.

'Does Mr Kurihara often visit your home?'

The taxi proceeded, impeded occasionally by the traffic signals on the streets near Shinjuku. Eiichi thought of Kurihara's composed, son-of-a-bourgeois face, and his own mouth twisted up when he spoke.

'Yes. He says he's very good at skiing, and he promised to take me along sometime.'

'That's nice.'

That's nice, he answered, but he had difficulty concealing his inner displeasure.

There's plenty of young men in the dispensary . . ., Eiichi said to himself. But if the Old Man's letting Kurihara come to his home . . . perhaps he's considering Kurihara as a match for his daughter.

Eiichi became morose and was silent for a while. The S.O.B.s who have fathers to back them up always come out ahead. Then there's me – I haven't had a jot of help from my has-been of a father. I have to make it all on my own.

'Have you played tennis with Mr Kurihara?'

'Yes.'

He imagined Yoshiko and Kurihara in white athletic

outfits, holding rackets.

They got out of the taxi at Shinjuku. In the record department of K. Bookstore they purchased the record they were looking for.

But Eiichi, who had been buoyant until a few minutes ago, was now suffering from wounded pride. Unbeknownst to those like Eiichi who stood at the bottom of the ladder, there were some people in the dispensary who were on friendly terms with Doctor Ii and his family. And there was a chance that sometime those people might form a clique that would control the destinies of those like Eiichi below them.

Eiichi sat across from Yoshiko in the tea room of the large bookstore, smiling only with his face. 'Do you like the trumpet?'

'Yes, I'm crazy about it. I'm sure I would've taken it up if I'd been a man.'

Men and women just like Eiichi and Yoshiko sat on either side of them, coffee or fruit-juice set before them as they discussed one thing or another.

'Do you ever go to concerts?'

'Sometimes. But I get the dickens at home if I'm out too late.'

'With Kurihara or someone?' he asked nonchalantly, bringing his coffee cup to his lips.

'He's taken me a couple of times. But he says he likes classical music better. He has a terrific record collection!'

Pondering his feelings of displeasure, Eiichi quickly calculated his future moves. The soundest course of action would be to join the ranks of those who had access to Doctor Ii's home, he thought. Another method would be to boot Kurihara out of the way and make this woman his. But he must not rush things now.

'How long,' she suddenly asked, 'do I have to wear this awful bandage?'

'If there's any inflammation, you'll have to wait until the swelling goes down. But since Doctor Saeki says there isn't any damage, I imagine you could take it off in a couple of days. But give him a call first.'

'Oh, thank goodness! You see, next Saturday I'm meeting a prospective husband.' She spoke the words like a little child and then laughed like a child. 'I have to meet him. A friend set it up. Do you think it's all right for me to meet him when I've already decided to turn him down?'

'Well, Yoshiko,' he said, calling her by name for the first time, 'does that mean there's someone else you like?'

'Oh no! I'm too spoiled to begin with.'

The tea room was beginning to get crowded, so they stood up to leave. Eiichi offered to see her home, but she shook her head, saying she had another errand to run and would get a taxi herself.

After parting from her, Eiichi realized with regret that he had done nothing today to make any lasting impression on Yoshiko. He had thrown away precious time in the taxi and at the tea room in hackneyed, commonplace conversation. He had wasted a well-deserved opportunity.

This is the sort of thing . . ., he repeated to himself, . . . that's going to leave you in the same wretched position as Tahara . . .

Three or four quiet, drab days of Indian summer passed in the dispensary. There were no major operations and no sudden changes in the condition of his patients. But within Eiichi's breast, a change had begun to take place. He started to be irritated by the presence of Kurihara, whereas before he had scarcely been conscious of him.

Kurihara did not seem to be a particularly outstanding member of the dispensary staff in the eyes of Eiichi and his fellows. His complacent features marked him as the son of a wealthy family. He was gentle and beaming and on good terms with everyone, but there was just nothing striking about him. Eiichi could not remember ever having heard him make an exceptional pronouncement at research sessions or dispensary meetings. Dispensary workers of his sort commonly worked for a short time at the university and then took over their father's jobs, managing local clinics or private hospitals. Since Kurihara had a large pharmaceutical manufacturer backing him up, Eiichi and the others assumed that he would be working for that company in the future.

Since his last meeting with Yoshiko, Eiichi had been annoyed by sonny-boy Kurihara. Eiichi had a hunch that Kurihara was going to be one more obstacle standing in the way of his future, though Kurihara himself did not know it.

Now, wait! Eiichi muttered to himself each time he caught a glimpse of Kurihara in the dispensary or at the nurses' station. Just because this guy's got to know Doctor Ii's daughter doesn't mean he's going to become the big cheese around here in the future. . . .

But merely uttering these words did not extinguish the uneasiness in his heart, and his displeasure was undiminished.

Just when it seemed the quiet, Indian summer days would go on indefinitely, an unexpected incident occurred.

That morning, when Eiichi went to the nurses' station, the head nurse called him out into the hall. 'Oh . . . Doctor Ozu,' the head nurse stammered, seeming to find the words difficult to speak. 'It's about one of Doctor Tahara's patients. . . .'

'The old man?'

'Yes. I've been ordered to change his medication. We're to stop using Bethion and start using Ethambutol.'

'Change his medication? Who told you to do that?'

'Doctor Tahara. But I'm sure Doctor Ii is the one who decided to use Bethion. Do you think it was done with his permission?'

Eiichi was quiet for a moment.

'If it wasn't, I'll get in trouble for it later,' the nurse said.

'Okay. I'll look into it. Please don't mention this to any of the other doctors until I find out about it.'

He recalled vividly the time when Tahara had contradicted the Old Man during his examination rounds.

That idiot. . . . Such stupidity . . .!

Tahara was not in the dispensary. Eiichi went to the library to look for him. He found Tahara in a corner with his head buried in a book.

'Hey!' He hauled his unimposing friend over to a dark stairway.

'What is it?' Tahara's tie hung askew over his slightly soiled white shirt.

'Did you order the nurses to use Ethambutol?'

'Yes, I did.' Tahara peered up at Eiichi and nodded.

'Did you get Doctor Uchida's permission?'

'No.'

'Don't you think it would have been better to get his permission?' Eiichi suggested modestly.

'But the patient,' Tahara shook his head with uncharacteristic firmness, 'is my responsibility. So I changed the drug on my own authority.'

'When the Old Man and Doctor Uchida find out, they won't buy that.'

'I don't care. Bethion isn't doing a thing for his illness . . .'

'That's beside the point.'

'That *is* the point!' Tahara groped in his pocket for a cigarette but could not find one. Eiichi held out one from a pack he had just bought and lit it for Tahara with his lighter.

'Listen, above all else, I'm a doctor. It hurts me to have to go on giving a worthless drug to a patient. Whether the Old Man ordered it or not. . . .'

'But what'll you do if the Old Man or the chief find out?'

'I'm prepared for whatever happens,' Tahara laughed forlornly. 'Ever since that day I've done a lot of thinking on my own. I guess it would be an exaggeration to say I've anguished over it.'

'You can't go making decisions on your own. We are just staff workers in the dispensary of the Second Surgery Department.'

'That's why the Doctor had to be told that Bethion is no good. In front of everybody.'

'I know that.'

'But nobody said a thing. And I got hell from Uchida.' Tahara stared at the burning tip of his cigarette and spoke the words as though to himself and not to Eiichi. 'That's why I have no choice but to handle it this way.'

'You must reconsider.'

'No. I've made up my mind.'

'Oh? Well, if that's how you feel, I won't interfere. We came to this dispensary together, and we've been collaborating on that report, so of course I worry about you. But I wash my hands of it.'

'I won't make any trouble for you. This is my problem.' Tahara threw his cigarette to the floor and crushed it out with his unpolished shoe. Then his hunch-backed figure disappeared into the reading room.

Eiichi left the library, wondering whether he should keep quiet about this matter or report it to the dispensary chief. If he reported it, he would be squealing on Tahara. But if he said nothing, he would probably get in hot water for winking at something he knew was going on.

I don't want to come out of this a loser.

He returned to the hospital. Deep in thought, he nodded to the men who were cleaning the building with disinfected rags.

That's it!

An idea came to him. That's it . . . I'll consult with

Kurihara. I'll unload the responsibility for this thing on that affable soul.

This was his way of taking a little revenge on Kurihara. The man was his senior, after all. There was nothing unusual about consulting with him.

Around noon was the most active time at the hospital. In the corridor of the outpatient examination ward, patients waited like sheep for their names to be called. An infant in its mother's arms was crying; nurses were bustling about. Eiichi saw scenes of this sort daily.

'When will Doctor Kurihara be through with his examinations?' he asked an outpatient nurse.

'He has two more patients waiting.'

'Then would you tell him I'm waiting in the hall?' Puffing on a cigarette in the corridor, Eiichi gazed absently at the patients. A middle-aged man was reading a magazine or newspaper, patiently awaiting his turn; a young man with a bandaged neck was immersed in troubled thought.

'Excuse me.' Eiichi turned towards the voice. An elegant woman in Japanese dress looked into his face with a smile. 'Is this the room for pre-surgery examinations?'

'Yes, it is.'

'Thank you very much,' she said politely. She sat on the edge of an empty sofa and closed her eyes. Her expression was weary and her colouring was poor.

After Eiichi had waited for about fifteen minutes, the door to the pre-surgery examination room opened and the slightly hefty Kurihara appeared.

'Did you want something?'

'Yes,' Eiichi nodded uneasily. 'There's something I'd like to discuss with you. Are you going back to the dispensary?'

'I planned to, yes.'

'Then we can talk on the way there.' He lowered his

voice as he walked beside Kurihara. 'Actually, it's about Tahara.'

He explained the sequence of events to Kurihara.

'Tahara refuses to be swayed. So I don't know how to deal with the matter.'

'But . . .' Kurihara stopped walking. The narrow eyes in his chubby face blinked and peered at Eiichi. 'Why are you telling me all this? Shouldn't you be telling Doctor Uchida?'

Kurihara was clearly puzzled. He had no idea why Eiichi, who up until now had not been that close to him, should come to him to discuss this matter.

'But if I tell Doctor Uchida about it, Tahara will get a lot more than a reprimand.' Eiichi deliberately looked sad. 'Tahara and I have been together since our schooldays. And since we're working on a report together, I'd like to see this thing settled privately.'

'But this is something that's bound to come out in the open. What a mess. If, as you say, he's set on this, he's not likely to change his mind even if I have a talk with him.'

'Probably not. But since you're my senior in the dispensary, I'd like you to give it some thought.'

'There's nothing I can do.'

'Couldn't you intercede with Doctor Ii?'

'Why me?'

'Well, I heard that you visit the Doctor's home frequently . . .' Eiichi did not miss the good-natured smile that danced across Kurihara's cheeks.

'How come you know about that?'

'Actually, the Doctor's daughter mentioned something about it the other day when she came by for an examination. She was looking forward to you taking her skiing sometime.'

'The Doctor has been very kind to my father. . . . But I don't think it would do any good even if I did bring this up. That's just the way the Old Man is.'

'I'd like you to give it a try anyway. I really don't know what to do. I gave it some thought, and I decided the only thing I could do was ask for your help.'

'Well, don't set your hopes too high,' Kurihara answered, his hand thrust into his examination smock. Eiichi bowed and walked away.

That was well done . . .! Eiichi inwardly evaluated the success of his venture as he walked back to the second ward. Hereafter Kurihara could assume only two possible attitudes. He could be silent, or he could report the matter to the dispensary chief. If he were silent, he would be taken to task as Eiichi's senior for covering up something he had been aware of. If Eiichi happened to be questioned, he could excuse himself by saying, 'I reported it to Doctor Kurihara.'

If, on the other hand, Kurihara reported everything to Doctor Uchida, the matter would reach the ears of Doctor Ii, and Tahara would be dealt with appropriately. Then those who sympathized with the unfortunate Tahara would turn eyes of reproach upon Kurihara for squealing. No matter what the outcome, the person who would suffer most in this matter was Kurihara. But the good-natured sonny-boy did not suspect a thing.

I'm rotten, I really am . . ., Eiichi derided himself with a thin smile upon his lips. But I don't have a father to back me up like Kurihara does. I've got a man wallowing in mediocrity for my father. There's no other way for me to get ahead!

That afternoon, Eiichi examined his patients and ascertained that there were no pressing problems. When he performed examinations, he was a doctor faithful to his duty, an attending physician upon whom his patients could depend to the very end.

'Doctor, when I get better, I'd like you to come and stay at my resort house in Itō,' the old man with cancer, his eyes fixed on his daughter, told Eiichi when the examination was over. 'And I'd like you to come and work in the clinic at my company.'

'We'll discuss that when the time comes,' Eiichi laughed. 'Right now, let's concentrate on getting you well as quickly as possible.' But Eiichi knew better than anyone else that this patient did not have long to live.

When Eiichi returned to the dispensary, both Doctor Uchida and Kurihara were absent. Tahara's seat was also unoccupied. The other staff workers were concentrating on their own tasks with melancholy faces. Not a word was spoken, but everyone seemed to have heard about Tahara.

In a while, Doctor Uchida returned alone. Catching sight of Eiichi, he screwed up his face and shook his head. Eiichi gathered from that expression that the matter had ended with the worst possible results. Undoubtedly Tahara would be packed off to a tiny clinic or hospital some- where . . . .

Eiichi was on the night shift that evening. If there was no sudden alteration in the condition of the patients, it was the responsibility of the doctor on night shift to accompany the night nurse in making the rounds of all the wards when the lights were extinguished at nine o'clock.

'Everything all right?' The faces of the patients danced up one by one in the blue light of the nurse's flashlight. Occasionally the television would still be on in a room.

'Please hurry and get to sleep.'

'I can't sleep. Could you give me some sleeping pills?'

Eiichi listened to conversations like these between the nurse and the patients and then returned to the night duty room. The room contained nothing but a bed like those in the hospital rooms, and a crude clothes closet.

After washing his hands, Eiichi opened his bag and took a drink from his pocket whisky flask; then he began to read a book.

There was a knock at the door.

'Who is it?' he asked cautiously.

'Tahara.'

He opened the door. A weary Tahara stood before him.

'Where've you been? I thought perhaps something had happened to one of your patients.'

'Sorry.'

'What do you want?'

'I'm sorry I troubled you this morning. I've been talking to Doctor Uchida about a number of things until just now.'

'And?' Eiichi poured some whisky into a washstand cup and offered it to Tahara. 'Drink this. I'll drink out of the bottle. . . . So, what did he say?'

'I have to leave the dispensary,' Tahara replied lifelessly.

'Leave the dispensary?'

'Yeah. And he said there's a job opening for a dispensary director at a private clinic in Fukushima Prefecture, and why don't I try for that? He consoled me by saying it would be good to have real experience in the provinces and then come back to the dispensary here. . . . In short, I got canned. Just like I thought I would.'

'What did you say to him?'

'What could I say, except that I understood? They'd already made up their minds, anyway.'

The two were silent for a few moments. Eiichi took a drink of whisky from his flask. 'I don't know what to say.'

'Don't worry about it. I knew it was up to me to handle on my own after I disregarded your advice. But I'm really sorry about that report we were supposed to collaborate on.'

'That doesn't matter. . . .'

'But I don't regret what I did,' Tahara muttered, drinking down the whisky in his cup with one gulp. 'I think I would have been much more unhappy if I'd continued to use Bethion on that patient.'

'Everybody has their own way of living.'

'That's right,' Tahara nodded. 'At the hospital in Fukushima, I want to be a doctor who works for his patients. It wouldn't matter if my whole life were buried in oblivion doing that. I'd prefer that to being a doctor who works for his own benefit.'

'A doctor who works for his own benefit, huh?' Eiichi curled his lip slightly. 'Well, give it all you've got.'

6 Graduation

Now that many long years had passed by, Ozu's memory was hazy about what events – with one exception – had passed between the boys and Aiko from the end of the summer vacation to New Year's.

The one thing he did remember was the second love letter that Flatfish wrote. No. To be exact, Flatfish did not write it all by himself. He had plagiarized certain passages from 'How to Write Letters', a supplement to a women's magazine his sister was reading, and interpolated passages from popular songs, revised by Ozu.

' "If the moon was a mirror, I'd like to see your face reflected there." ' This passage was taken from the popular song 'If the Moon Was a Mirror.'

' "I write this letter as the rain subsides this evening. The garden is filled with the gentle fragrance of the leaves of the trees, and inexplicably my thoughts turn to you," ' and other such foppish phrases were lifted from the supplement to the women's magazine.

Come to think of it, the letter had opened with 'My Dearest Madam : Dispensing with the formal preliminaries' and ended with 'Respectfully yours'. Flatfish had copied these phrases from somewhere, and at the time the two boys did not see the absurdity of writing 'My dearest Madam : Dispensing with the formal preliminaries' in a love letter.

During noon break, after everyone had left the classroom, Flatfish copied the letter out several times until he had a perfect copy. Then he went with Ozu to deposit it in the mailbox.

The address scrawled on the enevelope read :

Miss Aiko Azuma
Ashiya Village
Muko County
Hyōgo Prefecture

The envelope made a light tapping sound as it was swallowed up by the mailbox. The two boys gave a sigh of relief.

'I wonder if she'll read it.'

'Of course she will.'

'Even if she doesn't read it, she wouldn't think of throwing it away.'

'Of course not.'

But Flatfish stroked the mailbox with his hand several times to compose himself.

Ozu could hardly wait to get to school the next day.

'Have you had a reply?'

'Not yet.'

'We posted it yesterday, so she should be getting it today. It'll probably take her a day to read it and write an answer. So you ought to get a reply in a couple more days.'

But five, then six days passed. And again, as with the first letter, there was no letter for Flatfish from Aiko Azuma. Each morning when he saw Ozu, Flatfish shook his head with bleary eyes.

Ozu, being the sort he was, experienced both pain and relief at the same time. If Aiko had answered Flatfish's amorous epistle, Ozu would have been heartbroken.

'I haven't received an answer from you. But if it's difficult for you to send me a reply, please hang a white cloth on the pine tree by the statue of Jizō on the banks of the Ashiya River by five o'clock next Monday. If there is a white cloth hanging there, I'll know your answer is "Yes." ' In words to that effect – but more awkwardly expressed – Flatfish sent another letter to Aiko. That Monday evening Ozu and Flatfish got off the train at the Ashiya River stop and raced down the river bank to examine the pine tree.

Nothing was hanging there. No white cloth, not even an old rag, dangled from its branches.

In their fifth year, the students were given a sheet of paper by the teacher in charge and told to write down the names of the schools to which they wished to apply.

The members of A Class and B Class wrote quickly, since they already knew the schools they were aiming for. But Ozu and the others in C Class had a difficult time deciding just what schools they should try for.

In those days, Tokyo First High School and Kyoto Third High School were known as the 'Insurmountable Barriers'. Next in line were Sendai Second High, Okayama Sixth High, and Kumamoto Fifth High. These superior schools were naturally beyond the reach of the members of C Class. With resignation, Ozu wrote down Himeji High School as his first choice and entered the name of P. Private University as his second.

The next day it was apparent that the teachers had discussed the boys' choices among themselves in the teachers' lounge. In the morning class, The Shadow, with his perpetually severe face, said, 'Unlike the members of A Class, you have all been rather self-effacing in your choice of schools. Truly it is better for a man to be the head of an ass than the tail of a horse. No matter what the school, if you do your best, you can become great. Even the English painter Turner . . .'

But Mr Blowfish, somewhat perplexed, called from the lectern, 'Flatfish. You haven't written anything except the Naval Academy as your first choice. Are you serious about this?'

'Yes, sir.'

'But listen. The Naval Academy is as hard to get into as one of the big-name schools. We'd be lucky if a third of the

A Class could get in there. I think it's hopeless for *you*!'
Flatfish's reply was inaudible.

'What did you say?'

'Yes, sir. I said, "Where there's a will, there's a way." '

Everyone laughed aloud. Only Ozu, who knew what was
in Flatfish's heart, and Mr Blowfish did not laugh.

' "Where there's a will, there's a way." But you don't
have any will. Those words are meant for people who will
make an effort.'

'Yes, sir.'

'Won't you try for an easier school like everybody else?'

Flatfish looked sullen and gave no answer. Mr Blowfish
sighed. 'Of course, it's up to you what schools you want to
try for. . . .'

During the break between classes, Flatfish said to Ozu,
'You know, I'm not just trying to get into the Naval
Academy because of *her*. As I told you once, my uncle
said he'd pay my way. But I don't want to be such a
burden on him. And the Naval Academy doesn't cost anything, you know,' he explained.

Ozu knew from the start what the outcome would be.
He supposed that there was probably a ninety-nine per cent
chance that both he and Flatfish would fail their entrance
examinations.

But luck and miracles do exist in the world. Maybe the
test administrator at the Naval Academy would have bad
eyesight and misread a score of 20 as 80. There was a
possibility that Flatfish's random answers on the tests might
accidentally be correct. Their only hope was to depend on
this one per cent of luck and miracles.

'Do you think you'll do okay on the physical exam?'

'My eyes are the only things that're any good.'

'You can't get by just with good eyes. You've gotta put
on more weight.'

'I know. I'm eating five bowls of rice every day.'

The entrance examination for the Naval Academy was divided into two parts. The first part was held in August at the examination centres in each prefecture. A physical examination was administered. By means of this stringent test, those with poor vision or illnesses, and those who did not meet the standards for height and weight, were eliminated.

Those who passed the first examination were given an academic test in December. These tests covered Western mathematics, Japanese and Chinese literature, physics, chemistry, and almost every other academic discipline, so the students who took this examination had to be familiar with many more general areas of study than those who took high school entrance exams.

Flatfish's unimposing body at last seemed to start fleshing out, perhaps due to his accelerated intake. Having such a meagre body to start with, he could not help but suffer by comparison with the physiques of the A Class members who planned to take the Naval Academy examinations. Ozu closed his eyes and tried to imagine Flatfish dressed in the smart uniform and cap of a naval cadet, with a short sword dangling at his side. But no matter how hard he tried, it was unthinkable. . . .

August came at last. A year had flown by since that day in the middle of summer vacation when Flatfish had almost drowned in the sea at Ashiya.

On a day as sultry as that day a year ago had been, with the morning sun blistering, Ozu graciously accompanied his friend to the examination site at the prefectural middle school.

Perhaps because it was wartime, or because there were many others who wanted to test their strength, there were so many examinees passing through the gates of the school that Ozu felt weak in the knees. Forming a column, the best students from all over Kobe, dressed in khaki uniforms, advanced with measured steps towards the athletics field. Even the A Class students from Nada Middle School stood apart and viewed this overpowering procession with frightened eyes.

Flatfish'll never make it! It seemed to Ozu that every one of the other examinees had more ability and more of the sort of physique befitting a naval cadet than Flatfish did.

'Hey!' Ozu strained his wits to help his friend. 'You mustn't go to the bathroom!'

'Why not? I've really gotta pee bad.'

'Idiot! If you pee, you'll just lose that much weight!'

'Oh, really?' Flatfish nodded appreciatively. 'Wait here a minute.'

'Where are you going?'

'You've given me a great idea. I'm going to guzzle down some more water. That'll put even more weight on me!' Darting between the other examinees, Flatfish did in fact run for the drinking fountain. At last he hitched his pants up around his waist.

'Ow! It hurts! My belly's sloshing around!' He returned with drops of water still on his lips.

A ponderous bell sounded. The examinees formed a line on the sunlit athletics field and were swallowed up in the weather-worn wooden school building.

'When they give you the lung capacity test, take a deep breath and don't let any air out.'

'Got it.' His eyes bleary, Flatfish disappeared into the building at the rear of the line.

It was an incredibly hot morning. Cicadas were dinning in the cherry tree at the corner of the school building. In the shadow of the tree, the friends of the examinees waited with great patience. Strangely, they could not hear a sound coming from the dilapidated wooden building.

About a half an hour later, five or six examinees appeared at the door of the school. Two or three others followed behind them. All wore expressions of embarrassment.

One boy spotted his waiting friend and ran to him. 'No good. I failed!'

'How come?'

'It was my eyes. The eye test.'

'If you flunked that, does that mean you can't go on?'

'They said, "You can go home." '

But the two boys did not seem greatly disturbed by this failure. The boy might have felt humiliated if he had failed in the academic exam, but failure because of nearsightedness left few wounds on his heart. It was almost as if he had come to take the Naval Academy exam merely to test his strength.

After some twenty nearsighted boys had been sent out of the school, a period of silence followed. The voices of the brown cicadas dinning on the shining trunk of the cherry tree grew noticeably louder.

I wonder what he's doing right now? Ozu imagined the unimposing naked body of his bleary-eyed friend being measured for height and climbing up on the scales. Right this minute, Ozu thought, they might be telling him, as they had told the nearsighted boys, 'You can go home.'

But, oddly enough, Flatfish did not appear among the successive groups of boys who had failed.

Maybe . . ., thought Ozu, and even though he was not the one being tested, his heart begin to pound, . . . maybe he's been crafty enough to fool the examiner. . . .

It was nearly noon. Suddenly the examinees appeared from various doors. Over half of them had already failed today. Those who passed today's tests were to receive detailed internal examinations the following day.

'I'm going to try for an accounting school.'

'The physical exams aren't as hard there!'

Among those voices of self-derision, Ozu by chance overheard this conversation :

'There was a really weird guy who took the test!'

'Oh, yeah. You mean the guy who peed? He must've been straining too hard!'

'What happened to him?'

'I dunno. I just saw the examiner giving him the devil.'

It's Flatfish! Ozu realized at once. No doubt about it. It's Flatfish!

Almost all of the examinees had gone out through the schoolyard in a line. Those who went through the gate with their chests happily thrown out had doubtless passed the test today. Those who went out sulking and dragging their feet had failed. Yet still Flatfish had not come out of the school building.

The poor guy. . . . Ozu could almost see the unsightly figure of Flatfish peeing all over the examination floor because he had drunk too much water. He could imagine how ashamed Flatfish had felt with the mocking eyes of everyone upon him as he was rebuked by the examiner. It had all been for Aiko. He had done it all because he wanted to be loved by Aiko.

Ozu stood alone for another five minutes in the school-yard. Finally the awkward figure of Flatfish appeared from the school building. From a distance, he threw his arms up in the air and shouted, 'I passed!'

Ozu's eyes opened wide. 'What? Passed? You?'

'Yeah!' An unaffected look of joy had appeared on Flatfish's normally expressionless face.

'I don't believe it. You're lying.'

'It's no lie!'

'You didn't come out for so long, I was sure you'd flunked. Then when I heard somebody'd peed in the exam, I was sure it was you.'

'That . . . *was* me. I peed all over the place. We had this grip-strength test, and I put everything I had into it . . . and out it all came!'

Ozu goggled his eyes at Flatfish. 'Then your trousers must still be wet.'

'Naw. We took the test in the raw. Took off everything. So I didn't ruin my trousers.'

'Tell me all about it.' It made no sense at all to Ozu. How in the world could this fellow whose body was poverty itself, and who peed in the middle of the examination, have passed the rigorous first day of testing?

Flatfish began his explanation in a whisper.

In the examination hall, the examinees were lined up from one to one hundred and from one hundred to two hundred.

'Strip!' the examiner, a non-commissioned officer, ordered sternly.

'Do we . . . take off our underpants too?' someone asked.

'Yes! Leave nothing on!' the answer came back.

Flatfish had been fighting back the urge to urinate for several minutes. He had drunk enough water at the fountain to burst his stomach. And then, when he was forced to strip off all his clothes and reveal his scraggy body in all its pristine nakedness before one and all, the urge to urinate became all the more unbearable.

He *must* endure until the weigh-in. As the first boy in line climbed up on the scale and was told, 'Good! Fifty-three kilogrammes,' Flatfish stamped his feet one after the other.

When Flatfish's turn came, the non-com examiner glanced at him and muttered to himself in Kyushu dialect, 'That's one helluva swollen gut.'

Flatfish was afraid that the examiner had found out about his water drinking. But then the examiner said softly, 'Good. Forty-nine kilogrammes.' Flatfish breathed a sigh of relief.

The accident occurred ten minutes later. In the grip-strength test, he was supposed to grasp the metal handles of the grip-strength scale and announce the number on the indicator needle to the examiner. Flatfish grunted and turned beet red.

As he strained, all sensation left the lower part of his body. In an instant, urine was gushing past his knees and onto the floor. . . .

'What's going on here?' the examiner shouted. The volume of his voice drew the eyes of all the examinees towards them. 'You're pissing on the floor!'

Flatfish's knees folded under him. He wanted to dig a hole and disappear into it. The urine began to flow along the floor in a stream.

'What are you doing!' the examiner screamed. 'Aren't you going to clean up this mess you've made?'

Flatfish pulled on his trousers and ran swiftly from the hall. He found a bucket and a rag in the lavatory down the hall and returned with them.

'Excuse me. Excuse me.' As he threaded his way between the examinees, they stepped back and stared at him as though something unclean had approached them.

With a scowl, the non-com examiner looked on as Flatfish mopped up the floor with his rag. Behind them, the laughter of the other examinees could be heard.

Then it happened.

'Stop!' a voice called. Flatfish turned around. A middle-aged officer in a white naval uniform came up to Flatfish. The officer turned a stern face towards the other examinees. 'You laughed at this student's accident! Men who mock the mistakes of others are not qualified to enter the Naval Academy. Not one of you tried to help this student. There is no excuse for laughing at the errors of others!' His voice was soft but piercing and the examinees became dead silent. The officer shifted his eyes towards Flatfish, who was still crouching on the floor like a squashed frog, wearing only his trousers. 'I can only admire the spirit of a man who grips the machine so intently that he loses control over his bodily processes. Sergeant, give this man passing marks on the grip-strength test!' After he had announced this in a voice loud enough for the other test administrators to hear, he wheeled about and walked away.

For a time, all was silent around Flatfish.

'Good. You pass the grip-strength test. Move on!' the non-com laughed and urged Flatfish on. 'But first take the bucket back to where you got it.'

'Yes, sir!' Carrying the bucket with him, Flatfish looked

around for the officer who had helped him out, but he was nowhere in sight.

'Hmm!' Hearing this story, Ozu expelled something that was midway between a sigh and a gasp. 'Sounds like that old officer had some good left in him.'

'You bet. He made me think it wouldn't be so bad to join the navy.'

It suddenly occurred to Ozu that Flatfish might actually get into the Naval Academy. Perhaps this fellow could devote his life to Aiko Azuma, just as he had that day at Ashiya, swimming amid the high waves for all he was worth.

'What happens in the physical tests tomorrow?'

'They take X-rays. That's no problem.'

'You just might pass.'

'You bet I'll pass,' Flatfish replied nonchalantly. 'There's an academic exam in December. If I pass that, I'll be a naval cadet! Then I can put on my white uniform and short sword and go to Aiko's house!'

Though the summer vacation was not yet over, Ozu was able to find out that six of the fifteen members of A and B Classes who had taken the physical exam at the same location had failed. From the C Class only Flatfish had taken the test – but he had passed.

Their elation was a fearsome thing.

When the new term of their fifth year began, the news that Flatfish had passed the preliminary examination for the Naval Academy (even though it wasn't the academic exam) when several from A Class had failed it, came as a surprise to all the members of C Class.

' "Where there's a will there's a way." No matter what you are engaged in, you must have the will. Those who have no will never find a way.' The Shadow was quick to praise Flatfish in front of the class. 'It should be quite evident from all this that if any of you made the effort, you would not be inferior to the students in the A Class. In the same manner, you see, Turner . . .'

Certainly everyone felt the need to reappraise Flatfish. For none of them had even considered the possibility that Flatfish might pass the physical exam for the Naval Academy, under whatever circumstances, with a scraggy body like his.

'When I get in the navy,' Flatfish, in his usual vein, talked to everyone as though he had already passed the December exam, 'I think I'll become a pilot. The future of the navy isn't in battleships. It will be the age of aerial warfare.'

It was common knowledge that Germany had demolished the nations of Europe with its superior Messerschmidts, but everyone agreed with Flatfish's remarks. At any rate, the value of his stocks in class zoomed upward.

Ozu watched as Flatfish made a complete about-face in his life.

There were scenes Ozu had never beheld before. Between classes, Flatfish began memorizing English vocabulary words from a collection that the students called 'Akao's Little Word Book'.

'The Iwakiri maths text is a little too hard for me. The one with charts has cartoons in it, so it's more interesting. For grammar, I'm reading the Hōsaka text.'

Ozu listened in amazement as these words flowed from Flatfish's lips. Never had he heard anyone in C Class discuss something like the textbooks needed to prepare for an examination.

'Have you *really* started studying?'

'I haven't any choice. If I don't have a go at it, I'll never pass the test in December.'

Until now Ozu and Flatfish had been on the same level, but now it even seemed to Ozu that Flatfish had suddenly become a grown-up.

'You've . . . changed.'

'Well, they say love changes a person. If I wasn't in love with Aiko, I certainly wouldn't be studying. I think it's pretty weird myself!'

'Do you really love her that much, this Aiko?'

Aiko Azuma. They hadn't seen her again since that day on the beach. Even so, her face appeared more vividly than ever in the imaginations of Ozu and Flatfish. She, of course, had no notion that she had been the cause of this marvellous transformation in the life of one young man.

Autumn deepened. The gingko trees along the road that ran beside the railway tracks scattered countless leaves onto the walkway. The poplar trees in the schoolyard turned to yellow. The ears of the eulalia along the banks of the Sumiyoshi River withered white.

December came. At the eleventh hour, Ozu followed Flatfish's example and had a look at 'Akao's Little Word Book' and bought a textbook called *The Study of Mathematics Through Charts*. But he realized he had no chance of getting into Himeji High School, his first choice.

December the eighteenth. At Sannomiya Station, Flatfish boarded a train bound for Hiroshima. There he would take the academic examination for the Naval Academy.

Even though it wasn't his own problem, Ozu could not help being on edge for three days after Flatfish's departure. He imagined the examinees sitting in front of their test papers in the silent examination hall. He pictured the bleary-eyed Flatfish there among them. Here in the classroom, Flatfish's desk was the only one vacant. When the teacher took the roll-call, he smiled painfully and nodded, 'Ah, he's gone to Edajima, hasn't he?'

The winter vacation was at hand, but during the holidays there were supplementary lectures that interested students could attend. This was a sort of paternalism on the part of the teachers, who wanted to help the students prepare for the imminent examinations.

At last, on the first day of supplementary classes, Flatfish appeared in the classroom.

'Hey! How was it?'

A mob surrounded Flatfish.

'No good. I got all dizzy in the head. The three days just flew by.'

'What about the test?'

'I dunno. I don't even want to think about it.'

Flatfish looked tired and emaciated. Staring at that face along with everyone else, Ozu saw that his friend had exhausted energy he did not have, and he realized the desperation with which he had struggled.

'I might not make it,' Flatfish confessed quietly to Ozu when they were alone. 'The maths and grammar problems were really hard. I wrote down something, but I'll bet the examiners are really strict.'

'Still, luck's been with you so far,' Ozu encouraged him. But luck alone was of no avail in an academic exam.

Flatfish never attended another supplementary lecture. Ozu could picture his face as he sat at home, dejected.

Three days after the supplementary lectures commenced, Ozu boarded a train alone and started for home. At one of the stations along the way, three or four passengers got on. One was a naval cadet dressed in a dark blue uniform. He reached for the train strap with a stern look on his face.

Ozu had seen that face before. It was the naval cadet who had talked with Aiko and her friend that summer vacation after they had gone swimming at Ashiya.

Ozu began to have trouble breathing, as though a gigantic hand was pressing down on his chest. But the cadet merely stared out the window and seemed to have no recollection of Ozu.

When the train reached the station at Ashiya River, the cadet held his body stiffly erect as he got off the train.

An ill-boding premonition flashed through Ozu's mind. Even he did not know the reason for this foreboding.

Flatfish has flunked, was the thought that came to him in that moment.

January the second.

His premonition had been accurate. Flatfish appeared at his home unexpectedly.

'I failed.'

Standing in the entranceway of his house, Ozu took the telegram from his bleary-eyed friend.

'Sorry. Try again.'

To Ozu's eyes, the words of the telegram, which had been forwarded by the superintendent of Flatfish's dormitory, seemed like nothing more than a formation of lifeless figures.

'Let's go outside.'

Ozu did not know what to say to console Flatfish. At that moment, he would not have minded using all the money he had received as a New Year's gift to heal the wounds in his friend's heart.

'I've got some money. I'll treat today.'

'Uh-huh.' But there was no energy in Flatfish's voice.

'Cheer up! You can always take the Naval Academy test again. You ought to be pleased that you passed the physical. If you just take a year off and study . . .'

'I can't,' Flatfish shook his head feebly. 'I can't cause my family any more trouble. I don't have a dad, and my sister's back at home. I can't goof around forever.'

'But won't your uncle pay for your tuition?'

'If I did well in my studies, I could ask him for it, but . . . Aw, it doesn't matter. After I get out of Nada, I'll get a job.'

'A job?'

'Yeah. There's nobody but me to support my mum and sister. . . .'

Even though it was New Year's, the streets were virtually deserted. Because of the war, a Japanese flag hung from every house.

'Let's go to Ebisu Shrine!' Ozu nudged Flatfish, who was walking with his head drooping. 'Hey! You can eat all the pork dogs you want. I really do have some money!'

Flatfish smiled timidly. 'I'd rather go to Ashiya.'

'To her house?'

'Yeah.'

There were uncommonly few passengers on the train, too. A man whose face was flushed with New Year's *sake* was softly humming a song and beating time with his hands.

'But if you get a job you'll lose your student draft deferment.' Ozu finally voiced his greatest concern for Flatfish. 'You'll get drafted.'

'But . . . there's nothing I can do about it.'

'If you aren't careful you'll get sent off to the front lines.'

'If I thought about that I wouldn't be able to do anything. I'll worry about it when the time comes.'

They got off at the Ashiya River stop. As they crossed over the bridge they looked down at the river bed desolated by winter. Large stalks of bamboo still decorated the gates of many of the homes in the area.

When they reached Aiko's house, Flatfish stopped at the gate and stared intently at the house.

'She might be there.' Then suddenly, 'Should we ring the bell?'

'Huh? You're gonna . . . ring the bell?'

'This is the last time I'll see her. I just want to say goodbye.'

From the time Flatfish rang the bell to the time the door was answered, Ozu considered running away several times. But Flatfish stood resolutely stiff.

A maid appeared and surveyed them suspiciously. Then she declared flatly, 'The young lady is not at home. She has gone to Kyoto.'

Three months later.

Ozu remembers graduation day.

In the assembly hall, beneath the inscription 'Might for Right : Mutually Glorifying Self and Others' penned by

Jigorō Kanō, the founder of Nada Middle School, the headmaster and a representative of the parents congratulated the students. Seated in unbroken rows, the students were feeling uncharacteristically sentimental, and they mulled over their memories as they listened silently to the addresses.

Ozu, who by some miracle had been accepted at P. University, stole a glance at the profile of Flatfish beside him. Naturally there were students in the C and D Classes who had failed to enter higher schools and who would spend some time studying and then try again. There were also those like Ozu who had slipped into prep schools of private universities with less demanding admission standards. However, the only boy who would not be entering any school and who would be going to work at a company was Flatfish.

After the ceremonies the students returned to their classrooms, brandishing their diplomas. Outside the windows the sky was clear, the wind cold.

'This is where we say goodbye,' Mr Blowfish said softly. 'It's funny. They say that the students that cause the most trouble are the hardest to forget. Maybe that's why I can't help caring more about you than I do about the students in the A and B Classes.'

'Is that true?' someone interrupted.

'What do you mean? I'm telling you how I sincerely feel.'

'Are you sure you're not just glad to get rid of us?'

'Well, I do feel a little that way,' Mr Blowfish grinned. 'You've all been a real pain in the neck.'

Everyone laughed. But it was a refreshing laughter as they recalled each of the pranks they had perpetrated in this classroom over the past five years. They had no fond memories of their lessons. Their recollections were rather of angering and frustrating their teachers.

'Please make sure that no one else like us is allowed into Nada from now on.'

'Right,' Mr Blowfish nodded. 'But from a teacher's point of view the students that do nothing but study and then go on to a higher school aren't very interesting. I'd hate to see Nada turn into a first-rate, boring school. Anyway, I don't want any of you to forget your Alma Mater. Come back and see us now and then.' He placed both hands on the desk and bowed his head briefly, then left the room.

'Let's go,' Ozu called to Flatfish, and they went out of the school building.

'I guess I won't be seeing this classroom again,' Flatfish said, his eyes bleary. 'And I won't see you any more, either.'

'Of course you will!' Ozu said, shaking his head. 'I'll come and see you at your company every once in a while.'

'But it takes a long time to get to Akō.' With assistance from his uncle, Flatfish had secured a job with a salt manufacturing firm in Akō.

'There's always Sundays.'

'I'd really like it if you could come.'

As usual, they went out the school gate and walked along the bank of the Sumiyoshi River with the other students.

'Hey, look! They're doing it. They're doing it!' Flatfish caught sight of today's graduates surrounding the bean cake stand on the river bank and furiously buying up the bean cakes. He shouted happily, 'The teachers'll give you hell!'

'No they won't!' someone replied. 'We've graduated from Nada. We're on our own now. Starting today!'

7 A Certain Woman

The going-away party for Tahara was held at a tiny eel shop near the hospital. It sounded good to call it a going-away party, but in reality it was a gathering to bid farewell to a colleague who had been thrown out of the dispensary.

Dusk had turned to dark by the time Eiichi finished his work at the hospital and set out for the eel shop. Lights were starting to flicker up in the small buildings and shops along the road.

Five or six dispensary workers were in an upper room of the shop awaiting the arrival of the dispensary chief and Doctor Ii. An air of melancholy filled the room. Several of them had glasses of beer, but the conversation still tended to fragment, and the group remained in low spirits.

'But the air is good in Fukushima, and there's no pollution. And you'll be able to ski, you lucky devil!' someone said in an attempt to lift Tahara's spirits, but the conversation did not progress beyond that point. They were all only too aware of the reason Tahara was being sent out to the provinces.

Doctor Uchida and Kurihara finally arrived about a half an hour late.

'Sorry we're late. Sorry,' Uchida apologized to everyone. 'Unfortunately Doctor Ii won't be able to come. Another commitment suddenly came up. He sends his best regards to everyone.'

It was unusual for the Old Man to be absent from the going-away party of a member of his own dispensary who was moving to a distant locale. Everyone looked down in silence for a few moments.

'Well now. Tahara here, in spite of his youthfulness, is going to be one of the directors of the dispensary in Fukushima. We'd like you to study the administration of hospital care in the provinces and the problems of medical care in farm villages at first hand.' Doctor Uchida poured a glass of beer for Tahara. 'Then when you come back here, we'd like you to put that research into practice.'

From his seat in the corner of the room, Eiichi studied Tahara's face. He noticed the tearful smile that passed across his friend's face as the dispensary chief addressed him.

'Kurihara.' Distressed by everyone's silence, Uchida turned and spoke to Kurihara, who was seated beside him. 'You're a good skier. You must go up to the North-east quite often.'

'Not that often. . . . But I've been to Mount Zaō a number of times.'

'Well, the next time you're up that way, I want you to take Tahara out on the town and give him plenty of encouragement.'

'Yes, I'd planned to do that.' Kurihara narrowed his eyes against his large face and nodded. He did not seem to notice that the younger dispensary workers were glaring at him reproachfully.

What are you talking about? the dispensary staff was thinking at that moment. Everyone knew that Tahara had been expelled because Kurihara had reported the medication incident to the dispensary chief. Kurihara's action had been unavoidable, but he should have done more to defend his subordinate.

But he still tries to look as though he has absolutely no responsibility for what happened. . . . The young dispensary workers felt like apologizing to Tahara for their own powerlessness. Eiichi sensed that this feeling took the form of hatred for Kurihara. He chuckled scornfully to himself. . . .

Under normal circumstances, at the conclusion of a gathering like this, the young workers would say, 'Doctor Uchida, why don't you take us somewhere else now?' And, taking advantage of his kindness, they would usually set out for a second and third round of festivities. But tonight when the party broke up, each said goodbye in his own way, waving a hand and quickly departing. Tahara smiled feebly and thanked everyone, then disappeared alone down the stairs to the subway.

'Ozu.' Starting off after Tahara, Ozu was stopped by the voices of Doctor Uchida and Kurihara. 'If you don't have anything else to do, why don't you come along with us?' The dispensary chief tossed his cigarette onto the pavement and crushed it out with his foot. 'How about it?'

'Fine.'

They strolled leisurely for a while and then climbed the stairs to the second floor of a building where there hung the sign 'Chanson Snack'.

The only other customers were an affectionate couple seated at the counter.

Kurihara peered into the room. 'The stall in the corner is free,' he informed Doctor Uchida.

When they were seated, Uchida ordered a Campari soda. Kurihara and Eiichi ordered whisky and water. Seedy chanson music poured from a speaker on the wall, increasing the gloom of the establishment.

'Now, about the way we handle matters from now on. . . .' Doctor Uchida gulped down his Campari Red soda in one motion and spoke to Eiichi. 'The younger workers probably consider our action heartless, but it was the only thing we could do to preserve order in the dispensary.'

'I understand that.'

'Yes. I thought you would. But you were working on a report with Tahara, weren't you?'

'Yes.'

'Then it presents a problem without him there, doesn't it?'

'It does, but I was planning to go on gathering the data by myself.'

'Oh, really?' The dispensary chief nodded and thought for a moment. 'I haven't discussed this with Doctor Ii yet, but how would you feel about assisting Kurihara with his work? Of course it would be with a view to completing the report he's working on now . . .'

'Doctor Kurihara's report?'

'Yes. We'll be building a cancer centre at our hospital eventually, but there's a lot of preparation that has to be done first. Kurihara is tackling the relation between anti-cancer drugs and surgery. Would you be interested in doing research in that area?'

Eiichi swiftly analysed Doctor Uchida's words – or rather, their implications. So Doctor Ii had ordered Kurihara to form the link between his father's pharmaceutical company and the new cancer centre.

'When will the cancer centre be completed?'

'We're aiming for next year. Of course it must be our dispensary and nobody else that controls the central administrative authority. That's something we must attain. We'd like your help in this. We'll put in a good word for you with Doctor Ii. . . .'

When they went their separate ways, Eiichi descended into the subway. As he waited on the platform for the train, he mulled over what Doctor Uchida had said.

We'll be getting a cancer centre in our hospital. Doctor Uchida and Doctor Ii plan to have their own dispensary and no other department take control of administration. That was why they made so much of Kurihara, who had a large pharmaceutical manufacturer backing him up. They must be soliciting a vast amount of research funds in exchange for using the anti-cancer drugs produced by that pharmaceutical company.

That means Kurihara is going to become more and more indispensable to the Old Man. The thought was indescribably depressing. To Eiichi there seemed to be two categories of people : those who become successful through the influence of their parents with no effort on their own part, and those who, no matter how hard they try, remain the dregs of humanity because they have no one to back them up.

Like Tahara, thought Eiichi. What if he'd had backing like Kurihara? If that had been the case, he would never have been tossed out of the dispensary like an old pair of sandals and shipped off to the provinces.

I wonder if this means I'm going to have to spend the rest of my life working under Kurihara? He estimated the thickness of the wall that blocked his path. The obstruction seemed stronger than he had ever imagined. The only way to break it down was to obtain the same kind of backing that Kurihara had.

A woman . . . The thought came to Eiichi with painful clarity as he clung to the subway strap. Marriage. I have to find a woman who can help me get ahead. The innocent face of Yoshiko Ii flashed before his eyes once again. If I could just marry his daughter! But that was next to impossible at this stage of the game. Who would even think of the doctor's daughter in connection with a single shabby dispensary worker?

It was already late when he returned home, and his parents seemed to be asleep. His sister Yumi opened the door.

'Would you like something to eat?'

'No,' he answered sullenly. He felt like taking his anger out on someone. 'Gimme some water.'

'You've been drinking again, haven't you?'

'What's it to you? Give me some water!'

'There was a call for you,' Yumi said, studying her

brother's face. 'A woman called Keiko. A nurse.'

Eiichi looked glum and said nothing.

'She wants you to call her.'

He went into the living-room and drank the water his sister brought him in one gulp.

'You're hopeless when you're irritable.' Yumi remained standing. 'Did something go wrong at the hospital?'

'Leave me alone. Go to bed.'

The phone in the hallway rang.

'That must be her – the nurse. . . . I think she might be the one who's been making those strange phone calls. Has something happened between her and you?'

Eiichi went out into the hall without answering. When he picked up the receiver, he heard Keiko's voice say, 'Hello?'

Eiichi hung up the receiver without a word.

The following day, Doctor Ii made his rounds.

As usual, the men in their white examination smocks gathered around Doctor Ii in the corridor of the ward, which had abruptly become silent. Swallowed up in one room, then spat out, they moved on to another.

Tahara was no longer a member of that group. A dispensary worker named Umemiya had taken over the patients Tahara once treated.

Doctor Ii nodded confidently as he listened to the complaints of each patient. Casually placing his stethoscope on their chests, he talked with them, selecting words that guaranteed recovery.

Even when he removed the stethoscope from his ears and spoke to the company manager with lung cancer whom Eiichi supervised, Doctor Ii said, 'When you get well, I'd like to play a round of golf with you.'

A light of hope flickered suddenly in the eyes of the emaciated patient. 'Will I recover enough to play golf?'

'Certainly! That is, of course, if you follow my instructions and take care of yourself. . . .'

Eiichi stood respectfully to one side listening to this conversation, making mental notes of these remarks that one should say to an incurable patient.

But when they had gone out into the corridor, the Old Man whispered, 'Doctor Uchida, it's about time we told this patient's relatives the truth. . . . Who's in the next room?'

'It's a new patient who arrived yesterday,' Kurihara shuffled the charts in his hands and answered hurriedly. 'She was sent to Surgery from Internal. They couldn't locate a tumour in the manual examination, but she had a positive reaction on the D.K.I.K. Her relief photographs indicate some pathological change.'

The doctor nodded gravely and stopped at the door of the private room. The name card read 'Aiko Nagayama'.

When the group entered the room, the patient sat up. adjusting her gown at the breast.

'Please relax,' the doctor said affably. 'How do you feel after your first day in the hospital?'

'I slept like a log, thank you.' A sad smile appeared on her slightly pale face. She was an elegant woman, with large eyes.

'Would you draw up your knees please?' Kurihara and the head nurse helped her facilitate examination of her abdomen. She blushed when her gown was opened and her chest exposed to the gaze of all these young doctors. But Doctor Ii paid no attention and leaned over her.

'Does this hurt?' he asked.

'Yes.'

'Have you had problems with your stomach before?'

'No. I just suddenly started losing weight.'

'I see . . .'

There was silence for a few moments. The Old Man knit his brows as he studied the stomach X-rays.

'Let's run two or three tests. There's nothing to be

worried about, of course. At worst it's a stomach ulcer.'

But everyone knew that was a lie. The photographs clearly indicated an abnormality.

At the end of the rounds, when the group was seeing the Old Man off at the door of the ward, Doctor Ii suddenly turned around. 'Mr Ozu.'

The Old Man seldom spoke to people of his lowly station at times like this, so Eiichi feared that he had committed some sort of blunder during the rounds.

'Yes, sir,' he answered, confusedly making his way to the front of the group.

'Listen,' a good-natured smile appeared on the doctor's energetic face, 'I wanted to thank you for taking care of my daughter when she injured her eye. She asked me to thank you for everything you did.'

'It was my pleasure. How has she been?'

'She's just like nothing had ever happened.'

Eiichi had not known that the usually stern face of the Old Man was capable of looking so cheerful when he spoke about his daughter.

The doctor and the dispensary chief walked out of the ward side by side and headed for the research laboratory in the main building.

The dispensary workers shook their arms as though a great burden had been lifted from their shoulders, lit up cigarettes, and went their separate ways. They had thirty minutes of free time before noon.

Well, now! Eiichi thought, savouring the joy welling up within him. So she hasn't totally forgotten me!

Take advantage of every opportunity. If he folded his hands and sat back now, that would be the end of his association with her. It seemed a far better idea to consider what Doctor Ii had said to him as a golden opportunity.

He reached for the red telephone in the corridor. After a moment's hesitation, he looked in his notebook and dialled a number.

A maid answered. After a pause he heard Yoshiko's voice.

'My goodness!' She was surprised by the unexpected call. 'How have you been?' She thanked him for the day at the hospital. 'And I love the record!'

'You haven't been back to the hospital since then, so I've been worried about you. How is your eye?'

'That medicine did the trick completely.'

This exhausted their topics for conversation, and Eiichi was afraid he would have to hang up then, but Yoshiko came to the rescue. 'I've started golf lessons.'

'Golf?'

'Do you play?'

'No, I don't. I've thought of taking it up, but it's not something that a poverty-stricken doctor can afford . . .'

'Don't be silly. They lend you clubs at the practice range. I borrow mine from a friend.' She thought for a moment. 'Would you like to play with me? Yes, let's! This coming Saturday. . . ,' she invited him innocently.

Eiichi replaced the receiver and licked his lips. I'm really glad I called her, he thought, relishing the pleasurable sensation he felt when he had accomplished something. . . .

On the Saturday of their date, he headed for the golf practice range, which lay in a grassy area. Through the window of his taxi he caught sight of Yoshiko standing at the entrance dressed in slacks and a cap. He waved and she lifted one hand lightly in response.

'This is incredible,' he muttered, gazing at the crowds of men and women swinging clubs on the green lawn.

As Yoshiko had told him, the range lent out clubs. Ignorant of the game, he bought only a pair of gloves, and following Yoshiko's instructions, he borrowed a number one wood and stepped out onto the practice range.

'I'll get a coach.'

'A coach?'

'Yes. They have professional instructors here.'

A few minutes later, a tanned young man came up and greeted Yoshiko. 'Well for starters why don't you practice the stroke I taught you last time and get that down pat.' He looked at Eiichi. 'You can try it, too.' The young man demonstrated the grip, the placement of the feet, and the manoeuvring of the club; then he said, 'Now, both of you try it that way.'

Eiichi did not relish the prospect of looking like a clod in front of Yoshiko.

'That's very good, miss,' the young man praised Yoshiko. Then, cocking his head, he said to Eiichi, 'I'm sorry, but you're squeezing yourself up like an accordion.'

'An accordion?'

'Yes. Your head's too low. Just hold it naturally. I'll put this up here, and you swing without moving your body up and down.' He rested his club on Eiichi's head. Yoshiko looked at him and laughed.

Eiichi was thoroughly depressed to find that the handling of the clubs, which had looked so simple at first, was unexpectedly difficult. Yoshiko was able to hit the balls she placed on the ground, but he was generally swinging at the air. And the young coach was ignoring Eiichi and concentrating his teaching efforts on Yoshiko.

'Why have you given up?' Yoshiko teased Eiichi, seeing him standing with his club between his legs. smoking a cigarette.

'I just can't seem to get the hang of it.'

'Don't let it worry you. It's normal for every beginner to miss the ball,' the young coach was quick to encourage him. 'Once you get rid of the accordion, you'll have a good style.'

Eiichi gripped his club once again and stood before the

ball. As he stared at the white ball, it suddenly changed into a white tennis ball, and the face of Kurihara swinging a tennis racket popped up before his eyes.

Shit!

For the first time, he felt a comfortable resistance from the wood and heard an exhilarating sound.

'Nice shot!' the young coach shouted. 'That's the feel. You've got it now!'

Eiichi smiled wryly and nodded. There was no way Yoshiko could know what he had been thinking as he had stared at the white ball.

'You can tell from the sound of the club when you've connected just right,' he added.

They hit two baskets of balls and then relaxed in the parlour of the practice range.

'You're quite the athlete,' Yoshiko said. 'You hardly missed one of the balls in the second basket.'

'I'm not any good.' Eiichi forced a smile. ' "Slice", is that what you call it? Even the ones I happen to hit head off to the side. The young man warned me I'd be picking balls out of the rough if I were on a course.'

'But you're much better than I am.'

'About how many times have you come to the practice range?'

'Only five or six. Mr Kurihara brought me the first time.'

'You learn everything from Mr Kurihara, don't you?'

Eiichi's tone of voice was unintentionally sarcastic, but Yoshiko answered innocently, 'Why, only skiing and golf.'

'I suppose Mr Kurihara is closer to you than anyone else in the dispensary, isn't he?'

'Well . . . hardly any of the others come over to the house.'

This girl still knows nothing of the evil in the world, Eiichi thought. She's probably never experienced love or been betrayed by a man.

'But it takes a lot of nerve to call at Doctor Ii's home. As far as we're concerned you're a woman from another world.'

'Why? How dreadful!' Yoshiko knit her brows and looked at him seriously.

'Well, you've never had any real hardships in your life. And you'll probably get married to a young man from a well-to-do family – somebody like Kurihara – and live happily ever after. We beggarly dispensary workers can't even imagine a life like that.'

'I wouldn't like a life like that! Of course I don't want to be unhappy, but I'd pity myself if I ended up treading the beaten path to happiness.' Folding her hands, she rested her tilted head upon them and laughed pertly.

'Well then, what sort of person would you like to marry?' Eiichi asked casually, lighting a cigarette and lowering his eyes from hers.

'What sort of person . . .? I'd like someone who's a gamble.'

'A gamble?'

'Yes. Somehow I'm just not interested in a person who already has it made.'

Eiichi thought he had heard those words before. Ah, yes. This was one of the things that young girls who know nothing of the world and have never tasted the agonies of existence often say about marriage.

'Is that funny?' Yoshiko asked, noticing Eiichi's thin smile.

'No. Not really.' Eiichi quickly became serious. 'I was just thinking how well you've thought things out.'

'Oh, I'm talking about things I don't know anything about!'

He gazed at her as she blushed slightly, and it occurred to him that he would probably be able to seduce this sweet young thing in no time at all.

That day they said goodbye at the practice range. But Eiichi made a point of asking her for another date.

When Eiichi went to the dispensary the following day, Kurihara, who perhaps because he was his senior seldom struck up conversations with Eiichi, came up to him and said, 'I hear you went golfing with Doctor Ii's daughter.'

'Yes.' Eiichi was a bit uneasy. 'She called and asked me to. . . .'

'Oh . . .?' Kurihara said nothing more about it. But Eiichi noticed the faint tinge of displeasure that passed across Kurihara's large, sonny-boy face. 'Anyway, as Doctor Uchida told you, we'll be doing research together now . . .'

'I'm looking forward to that.'

'You know the woman who was hospitalized the other day? It looks like it might be stomach cancer. . . .'

'I see.' As Kurihara spoke, Eiichi pictured the face of the middle-aged woman with large eyes he had seen on the day the doctor made his rounds. Her name was Aiko Nagayama.

'I'm thinking of using her as a case for our research. She's my patient, but would you like to give me a hand with her?'

'Certainly.'

Kurihara nodded with a superior air. 'Well, let's do some pictures of her stomach tomorrow. You give her a good examination prior to that.'

After checking the rooms of his own patients, Eiichi did as Kurihara instructed and knocked on the door of the woman's room. There was no answer, so he softly opened the door. A potted plant stood on the window sill. The woman was sleeping with her head turned to one side.

'Oh!' Eiichi's movements awakened her, and she sat

up in bed, adjusting the collar of her gown.

'How are you feeling?' Eiichi shifted his eyes to the flowers in the pot at the centre of the room. 'These have bloomed nicely, haven't they?'

He took out his stethoscope and put it in his ears. 'We're going to take some pictures of your stomach tomorrow, so please don't have any breakfast.'

'Er . . . what's happened to Doctor Kurihara?' she asked uneasily.

'Doctor Kurihara will be coming too, of course. Starting today, the doctor and I will be handling your examinations.'

'Am I that bad?'

'Oh no. Doctor Kurihara is very busy, so I'm giving him a hand down here. My name is Ozu.'

Hearing the name Ozu, she looked at Eiichi mysteriously. 'Is the stomach camera painful?'

'Not really. Of course women don't very much enjoy having people peeking into their stomachs.'

She laughed like a mother being teased by her son.

'You mustn't be embarrassed in a hospital. You have to be brave.' These were words the Old Man had once spoken to a young woman patient. Eiichi repeated them verbatim to this woman. 'How much weight have you lost?'

'I think twelve or thirteen pounds. I didn't even notice it myself. . . . Everybody told me how thin I'd become.'

He shifted the stethoscope. 'People close to you usually don't notice you've lost weight. Did your husband mention it to you?'

'No,' she shook her head. 'I don't have a husband. He died . . . a long time ago.'

'I see. . . .'

This sort of conversation really had no meaning. It was just a matter of the doctor asking questions to put the patient's mind at ease during his examination.

'What sort of illness did your husband have?'

'It wasn't an illness.' She smiled somewhat sadly. 'He died in the war.'

Eiichi removed the stethoscope from his ears. He belonged to a generation to which concepts like 'war' and 'died in the war' seemed like happenings in a far-off world. He always rebelled instinctively against people of his father's age who came up with tales of the war in some context or other.

There was a faint aroma of perfume when she readjusted her gown after the examination. He had not noticed it before, but this patient seemed to have applied perfume to her bed gown.

'My father was in the war, too.'

'In the navy?'

'No, the army. Ever since I was a kid I've heard so many stories about the war that I'm sick of them. It just doesn't seem real to me.'

'I suppose not. . . .' Another smile appeared on her cheeks. 'My younger sister says she hates to hear me talk about nothing but the war. . . . "The war ended a long time ago!" she says.'

'I'm with her.' Eiichi toyed with the stethoscope in his pocket. 'Now, no breakfast tomorrow. After we do the stomach camera, you may develop a slight fever, but it's nothing to worry about.'

When he went out of the room he could no longer remember what this patient's face looked like. The only things that concerned him were the charts that reported the state of her illness. After looking over her charts at the nurses' station, he picked up the extension phone and called Kurihara at the dispensary.

'I've just examined her.'

'How is she?'

'Just like it says on her charts. Are we using the GFT stomach camera tomorrow?'

'Yes, that's what I had in mind.'

'Then I'll put in an order for the secretion restrainer. Should I have them prepare some Opistan along with the Atropin and Puscopan?'

'Well, since it's a woman . . . she may be oversensitive, so do you think you ought to use Opistan?'

Kurihara's tone was relentlessly that of a superior giving orders to an inferior. Eiichi realized that no matter how perfect a report came from their collaborative efforts, the credit would eventually go to the senior member, Kurihara. That was standard practice in the dispensary.

I won't let that happen, he said to himself as he hung up the phone.

When he returned home earlier than usual that day, his father's shoes were neatly arranged in the entrance-way.

'Oh, thank heavens!' His mother appeared from the kitchen. 'Your father isn't feeling well and came home early from the office. He says he threw up.'

'Hmm.'

'Have a look at him!'

'Have a look? It's probably nothing.' Though Eiichi was a doctor, it annoyed him to have to examine a member of his own family. Whenever his sister caught a cold, he would tell her to buy some medicine and go to bed.

'Your father wants you to take a look at him. Please . . .'

Eiichi changed his clothes and reluctantly entered the room where his father was lying down. His father was lying on his back in his *futon*, reading the evening paper.

'I hear you threw up.'

'Yes. At work, all of a sudden I got this pain in my stomach. Just after lunch.'

Eiichi sat next to his father's pillow, moving to one side the pan that was there. There was newspaper in the pan, but no vomit.

'What did you have for lunch?'

'I had a client with me, so we ate in the employees' cafeteria together.'

'Did your client feel ill?'

'I don't know. He left right after that.'

'Did anyone else at the company throw up?'

'No. I was the only one.'

Eiichi pulled back the covers and placed his hands on his father's abdomen. Ozu looked on with satisfaction at every move his son made.

'It's a little swollen.'

'It's nothing, is it? I'm at that age . . .'

'Of course not,' Eiichi smiled mockingly. 'If it were cancer you'd have different symptoms. Don't eat anything tonight, and get some sleep. I don't think you'll need any medicine. . . .'

'Can you tell just by feeling whether it's cancer or not?' Ozu asked, catching his son's sleeve as he started to leave.

'About thirty per cent of the time. Of course, from weight loss or the complexion . . .' He suddenly thought of the woman he had examined today. 'Just today I was examining the stomach of a new woman patient who appears to have stomach cancer. I couldn't be sure just by touch, but one of her symptoms was a sudden loss of weight.'

'Can you do anything for her?'

'Well, if the cancer is confined to the membranes of her stomach, there's a chance of total recovery. But it's probably spread. . . .'

'How sad. I don't suppose you've told her, have you? Is she an old woman?'

'She's the same age as you. A widow. She said her husband had died in the war. Well, you get some sleep.'

His father seemed to want to continue the conversation but Eiichi turned away and went back to the living-room.

'How is he?' His mother was stacking up the dishes.

'It's just a little stomach upset. He'll be fine,' he answered brusquely.

'Could I make him some hot rice cereal?'

'Don't give him anything to eat.'

He switched on the television but soon turned it off again. The smell and the atmosphere of this house disgusted him.

8 The New Employee

After Eiichi left the room, Ozu closed his eyes and tried to sleep. It pleased him that his son had examined him just now. Lately Eiichi had hardly spoken to him at all, but it was gratifying to know that his son was at least concerned about him when he was ill.

There's some good in him after all, he thought.

Ozu closed his eyes and placed a hand on his still uncomfortable stomach and gradually began to feel sleepy. In his drowsy state, he again recalled the figure of Flatfish.

Let's see . . . how many months after our graduation from Nada did his letter come . . .?

He remembered that for a period after their graduation they did not correspond with each other. Then a letter came during Ozu's first summer vacation from the P. University prep school. It was postmarked Akō, where Flatfish was working, and a snapshot was enclosed. It pictured the doleful face of Flatfish; his hair was slicked down and he wore a slightly baggy suit.

'Every day I get lectures about the penurious spirit of the Osaka merchant. I'm going to save up a lot of money and become rich, too.' So Flatfish had scrawled on the back of the picture. And his letter related the sort of training Flatfish had received at his company over the past two months.

His first day at work, Flatfish and two other new employees had been called into the office of the president.

'All right.' A gold-plated watch set before him on his desk, the fifty-year-old, sparsely-whiskered president gave them a short lecture. 'Now about the spirit of our company here. It's based on the fact that we waste nothing. That means you don't throw anything away. It means you save. I built up this company on that spirit. And so I want each one of my employees to work with that aim in mind.'

The president looked at Flatfish. 'Do you understand this?'

'Nope.' Flatfish's eyes were bleary.

'Take a look at this.' The president pointed to his own three-piece suit. 'How many years do you think I've worn this suit?' he asked.

'Two years,' Flatfish answered.

'One year,' 'three years,' the other two employees answered in turn.

'Wrong!' The president shook his head. 'Ten years. Remember this if you buy a suit in monthly instalments – if you brush the suit carefully every night after you get home, you can wear it decently for ten years. I won't allow any of you to have a new suit made for the next ten years. Without that kind of resolve, you'll never save up any money.'

'Yeah, but . . .' Flatfish pouted his lips. 'When the trousers wear out, they get shiny.'

'When that happens, you get some flour and sprinkle it on the trousers and then beat them with a wet towel, and the shininess will disappear. Now take these shoes – I've worn them for seven years. If you watch the way you walk and you aren't slothful about taking care of them, one pair of shoes will last you seven or eight years. That frame of mind is the spirit of our company.'

The ideals of the president – Stinginess is the Spirit of Our Company – had permeated the thinking of his employees, and no sooner had Flatfish and the others entered the company than they were obliged to recite the

following words each morning :
1. There is no such thing as garbage.
2. Before throwing something away, think of some use it can be put to.
3. He who laughs at a penny will weep for a penny.
4. Dust accumulated makes a mountain.

In the office, which was nothing more than an old dark shop that the company had appropriated, the employees were forbidden by strict order of the president to throw away a single page of newspaper, a single pamphlet, or a single envelope that was brought from outside.

'If you hold on to pamphlets, you can write memos on the back,' the president constantly instructed his employees.

'Now take the mail that comes in to our company – if we turn the envelopes over, we can use them for the mail we send out. If you find little pieces of rope on the street, bring them in. We'll find a use for them. That's what we call the Way of the Merchant!'

Telephone calls to clients were seldom allowed at the company.

'If you've got business within walking distance, then walk there. If it's so far away you can't walk it but there's no hurry, send a postcard. Only use the phone when there's no alternative.'

As he listened to these lectures from the president, Flatfish for some reason suddenly thought of his old classmates at Nada Middle School. If he wanted to match up to those who had gone on to higher schools, Flatfish had no choice but to become wealthy. And the miserly mannerisms of his company president greatly aroused Flatfish's interest.

'So now I'm going to become stingy, save money like the president, and become successful,' Flatfish had scrawled in his letter to Ozu. 'I don't think money's everything, but it seems to me that when you don't have money, other people make fun of you, and you can't stand on your own two feet. The sooner I can get set up on my own, the better my chances that *she* might look in my direction. I still haven't forgotten her. I think about her every day. I don't suppose I'll get to marry her, but if I do see her again sometime, I'd like to be the kind of person she couldn't look down on.'

In his next letter, Flatfish wrote of the utter admiration he had developed for the president.

'He says that when he takes a client out, he always goes to a *sukiyaki* restaurant. Can you figure out why?'

If there were, say, five for dinner including the clients, he would make reservations for three at the *sukiyaki* restaurant. Then the president would have a new employee like Flatfish secretly buy enough meat for two at a butcher's shop and bring it along. When the waitress wasn't looking, he would quickly add the meat to that supplied by the restaurant.

'That way you can feed five for the price of three. And the president laughed, because he could use all of the restaurant's soy sauce and sugar he wanted for free. I was really impressed.'

As he read through these letters, Ozu was relieved to learn that Flatfish was thriving in his new environment. He seemed to be the sort of fellow who could get along well no matter where he was. Of course it did not occur to him that Flatfish himself could seriously be caught up in the spirit of stinginess at his company.

So when he finally saw Flatfish again after a long interval, Ozu received one shock after another.

The day Flatfish finally returned to Osaka from Akō for the Obon Festival, Ozu went to meet him at Sannomiya Station. As the train pulled up to the platform, Ozu worried about how Flatfish would regard him in his P. University uniform.

On the opposite platform hung a placard with large lettering that read, 'Hail the Departing Soldiers!' Beneath the placard, a man in a suit with close-cropped hair was being seen off by his family as he waited for his train to arrive. It was clear at a glance that he was going to war. Watching him, Ozu began to feel as though he were doing something wrong by being a student, and he lowered his eyes.

Flatfish's train finally came slowly alongside the platform.

'He-e-e-ey!' Ozu caught sight of Flatfish sticking his head out from the train and waving his hand.

The unimposing face had not changed a bit. In his second-hand suit and red shoes, Flatfish looked to Ozu like a child dressed in adult apparel. His hair was needlessly parted and slapped down on either side with scented ointment. Certainly this was just the sort of outrageous joke that was typical of Flatfish.

'I didn't recognize you. Honest! You look like a pop singer.'

'Really?' Flatfish raised his hand proudly to his tie. 'I thought I'd surprise my mum. I'm buying all this in monthly instalments.'

'Do you go to work every day dressed like that?'

'Are you kidding? If I did that, I'd get hell from the president. A merchant can't wear snazzy duds. When you work, you wear work clothes.' Flatfish glanced at Ozu's prep school uniform. 'Still, I like that better,' he sighed.

The two left the station and went into a tea room across the way. It tickled Ozu's pride to be able to go freely with other adults to the tea rooms that had been forbidden them in their middle-school days.

After they were seated in the booth, Ozu took a pack of Gold Kite cigarettes from his pocket and tapped one with the tip of his finger. 'How about a smoke?' He wanted Flatfish to see that since middle school he had got used to smoking cigarettes.

Flatfish grinned broadly. He took a yellowish-brown pack of cigarettes from the pocket of his suit. It was a pack of Beacon cigarettes, a brand even more expensive than Gold Kites.

'What's this? You're pretty extravagant, aren't you?' Ozu was surprised. 'In your letter you said you were all gung ho for the Spirit of Stinginess. . . . But you're not sticking by it at all!'

'Wrong! This is the way a true miser does it.' Flatfish shook his head. 'The president taught me this. If you buy cheap cigarettes like Gold Kite, you smoke them all without a thought. But if you buy expensive cigarettes, you hold off and hardly smoke any. Besides, it looks good to pull them out in front of people. That's killing two birds with one stone.'

He showed the inside of the pack to Ozu. Not one cigarette had been touched.

Suddenly Flatfish cried out, 'Don't throw the dead match away! You've got to save them carefully in a box. Nothing in this world is useless. Like those spent matchsticks – if you save them up, you can use them to kindle a fire under your bathtub.'

Ozu smothered a smile at these words, which were so like the teachings of the president. He gazed at his friend's face, but Flatfish's expression was deadly serious.

Just then they heard the bustling of a crowd outside the tea room. Through the window they could see members of the Women's Defence League wearily carrying paper flags imprinted with the Rising Sun.

'Somebody's going to war,' Flatfish muttered. 'They're getting recruited from all over the place.'

'Yeah . . .'

'It's awful. We might be going sometime, too.'

Ozu nodded silently. But he could not yet picture himself as a soldier. His situation was different from that of Flatfish. A great gulf was beginning to open between Ozu, who as a student had a draft deferment, and Flatfish, who did not.

'I wish the war would end.'

'Let's talk about something else.' Ozu wanted his meeting with Flatfish, whom he had not seen for some time, to be more cheerful. 'Your miser stories are a lot more interesting!'

'Yeah. Should I tell you about the president's test? He'll grab a new employee unexpectedly and give them a weird test. He says you can tell right off whether a person's going to be rich someday just by looking in their wallet.'

'What kind of test is it?'

The clamour of the crowd was gradually fading into the distance. A new customer came into the tea room.

'Show me your wallet.'

'Wallet? Mine?'

'Yeah.'

When Ozu took his wallet out of his trouser pocket, Flatfish peered into it with bleary eyes.

'Nope. No good!' He shook his head, a sober look on his face. 'You're never going to be rich.'

'Why not?'

'There's five ten-sen notes. And you've got three fifty-sen notes, haven't you?'

'Well . . . what's wrong with that?'

Flatfish returned the wallet and replied softly, as though he were teaching his friend an important lesson. 'This is what the president always says. People spend small change too easily. When you have small change, you spend it like mad. So when you get five ten-sen notes, you change them for a fifty-sen coin. When you get two fifty-sen notes, you get a one-yen note. When you've got ten one-yen notes, you put them in the bank. Without that approach, a guy'll never make money. . . . It's really true.'

'You're really sold on your president, aren't you?'

'Yeah. I think he's a great man. He really puts all he's got into it. When somebody gets that involved in something, you can almost taste it.'

Personally Ozu regarded the president as a money-mad penny pincher, but he did not dare express his opinion. He was somewhat relieved that his friend, who had not been able to continue his schooling, was satisfied with his present situation.

'Then it's been good for you, hasn't it? Going to work at a company?'

'Yeah. I think so.'

When they got up to leave, Ozu tried to pay the bill, but Flatfish said, 'Let me take care of it.'

'If you do that, you'll be violating your Spirit of Stinginess!'

'Today's an exception. A long time ago you treated me to a pork dog at Ebisu Shrine.' Then Flatfish looked on accusingly as Ozu threw his empty cigarette pack into the waste basket. 'You're hopeless. If you were to keep that empty pack, you might be able to use it for something. Nothing in this world is useless.'

Several months passed. Sugar and matches were put on the ration, restaurants were allowed to do business only between the hours of five and eight, and the military drill period at Ozu's P. University was lengthened. The hues of the war picture gradually deepened. But the life of a student was still the life of a student.

Life at the prep school had initially been difficult for Ozu to adjust to, but as he became accustomed to it he made new friends. These new friends taught him to cut classes and instead play mah-jong at someone's apartment or shoot a round of billiards. He picked up the habit of smoking and learned to rub oil on his uniform cap to make it glisten like leather.

So little by little the bleary-eyed figure of Flatfish faded from his memory. He became slack at writing letters and correspondence from Flatfish's end also came to a stop.

One clear day in September, the freshmen at the P. University prep school set out for Amagasaki to put in labour service at a munitions factory. For a year or two it had been the policy at P. University to send students to render this service about once every two months.

The students, dressed in military drill uniforms, spent half a day carrying heavy materials from the warehouse at the direction of the plant workers.

'What do they make us do this for?' they all grumbled. 'Making students do this isn't going to help the country!'

When they were bathed in sweat and had swallowed a goodly amount of dust from the warehouse, they were finally released from this unaccustomed physical labour.

When they were let out, Ozu and four or five of his friends headed for a train to go to someone's dormitory to play mah-jong.

Boarding the sunlit train noisily with the others, Ozu glanced casually around the car and then caught his breath in surprise.

Aiko Azuma was seated in the centre of the train bench.

She had changed completely. Her figure was no longer that of the young girl in the sailor uniform who had carried her bag as she walked along the bank of the Ashiya River. She was dressed in a pure white kimono, with her hair done up in a permanent, and she was saying something to an older woman who stood holding the train strap. Unaware that she was being observed, Aiko sometimes nodded, sometimes peered out of the window with sad eyes.

'What's the matter?' one of Ozu's friends prodded him. 'You are going to play mah-jong, aren't you?'

'Yeah.'

But Ozu's gaze was fixed on Aiko. He was stunned at how beautiful and grown-up she had become. In his memory, she had been just another schoolgirl, no different from the rest of them. But seeing her now after such a long time she had changed utterly, like a chrysalis transformed into a butterfly.

When the train reached Kotōen Station, the older woman with Aiko motioned to her and took down a bundle from the rack. Unaware of Ozu's presence, the two women stepped past him and moved towards the door.

'Watch your step here,' the old woman cautioned Aiko. 'If you were to fall, you might hurt that little baby you're carrying.'

Aiko smiled and nodded gently, then disappeared out of the door. The door closed.

'That little baby you're carrying.' The words lingered in Ozu's ears. 'That little baby you're carrying.' Was she already married then? Ozu felt as though he had been beaten over the head with a bat.

For several days Ozu debated with himself whether to tell Flatfish. Though he realized Aiko was bound to get married eventually, it was a shock to run into her now that she was actually some other man's wife. So it was obvious how Flatfish would feel if he were to find out about it, and then learn further that she was pregnant.

But the fact was that Ozu knew about it. And since he knew about it, it would be best to tell Flatfish now.

'Well, I've got something to tell you. Now don't be shocked. I ran into Aiko the other day. She didn't notice me, but . . .'

When he dropped the letter containing these words into the mailbox, it made a dull thud inside the box. That dull thud reminded Ozu of the time Flatfish had dropped a love letter into the mailbox in the same manner.

A reply was unusually long in coming. Three days, then four passed, but not even a postcard came from Flatfish. Ozu felt the full force of Flatfish's grief being transmitted to him. Because it was Flatfish, undoubtedly he would merely stare at Ozu's letter with bleary eyes. Ozu could imagine that scene very clearly.

Why is it . . ., Ozu suddenly thought one day, that I'm

always worrying about him? . . . I'm a student at P. University now, and I've got my own life to live. . . .

And yet Ozu could not resist the feeling that the bonds linking him with Flatfish were somehow very strong. Even though he sometimes forgot all about Flatfish, and correspondence between them had ground to a halt, he felt that some pretext or another was always bringing them together again. . . .

When ten days had passed, a letter finally came from Flatfish. Ozu was surprised that the cheap brown envelope had been sent by registered mail.

He didn't need to send it registered mail. . . .

When Ozu opened the envelope, a money order for ten yen dropped out. And in the letter:

'I'm sorry to ask this of you, but would you buy something for her with this? My boss won't give me time off to come there, so please do this for me. And tell her I'm praying that she'll have an easy delivery. It's okay if you buy something for the baby. Please?'

Ozu decided that the ten yen had come from Flatfish's hard-earned savings. He must have withdrawn it from the savings he had been accumulating since his conversion to stinginess.

Moron! . . . he wanted to say to Flatfish as he looked at the ten yen figure. Hasn't this gone far enough? She doesn't care anything about you. Why are you spending the money you've saved so carefully on Aiko?

Yet even as he berated Flatfish, Ozu felt a stab of pain in his chest, and he recalled Flatfish's tiny black head being buffeted by the waves at Ashiya as he frantically pursued Aiko.

'That guy's really a pain in the neck!' Ozu clacked his tongue as he sat alone in his room. 'This is it. After this, I'm not listening to any more asinine requests. . . .'

Ozu had no idea what to buy with the money order. Flatfish had said he could buy something for the baby, but baby clothes were rationed now, and without coupons a department store would not sell him any. Everything was becoming scarce.

He grew weary of thinking and decided to give the registered letter to Aiko as it had come. It was only ten yen, but if he explained to Aiko how hard Flatfish had worked at Akō to save the money, she would certainly understand how Flatfish felt.

On Saturday afternoon he turned down the invitations from his evil comrades and took the train to the Ashiya River stop.

Just as in the past, there were few people on the road beside the river, and the large mansions and Western-style houses lining both sides of the river were silent. But conspicuous among these houses were some that had replaced their metal gates with new wooden ones. Ozu realized that this had been done in response to the official request that any sort of iron be turned over for the construction of armaments. And unlike former days, Ozu was walking along the road alone.

The short journey held many memories of his experiences with Flatfish. The river bed where they had grappled with the other students, the spot where they had first met Aiko, and the bridge where the naval cadet had appeared – each of these places stirred an indescribable nostalgia in Ozu's heart.

When he reached her house he felt a bit self-conscious but he resolutely pushed the bell. The maid he had once met opened the door and thrust her face through the gate.

'Is Miss Aiko here?' Ozu asked, swallowing his saliva. The maid looked puzzled at his enquiry.

'May I ask your name?'

When Ozu gave her his name, she said, 'She's married now. . . . She lives in Nigawa.'

'Nigawa – is that near Takarazuka?'

'Yes.'

A look of wariness flashed across her face when Ozu

asked for the address, but she told him, 'It's Tsukimig-aoka in Nigawa.'

Ozu bowed and quickly turned away. She called to him from behind, 'Er . . . the name is Nagayama.' Amused perhaps at his haste, the maid lowered her eyes and smiled.

Idiot – that Flatfish! Ozu grumbled to himself as he walked along the road. Putting me to all this trouble. It's mortifying!

Taking up all my time like this . . . Ozu began to lament the fact that he had wasted his Saturday afternoon not on his own love-life, but on that of Flatfish – and on an unrequited love at that. But he could not suppress the feeling that from somewhere or other a bleary-eyed fellow was whispering, 'Please don't say that!'

At dusk, he got off the Hankyū line train at Nigawa Station. There were only three buildings in front of the tiny station – a bakery, a bookstore and a vegetable stall. Ozu could see no other shops. Surrounded by pine trees, the elegant Western-style homes stretched along the banks of the white bed of the river, which was smaller than the Ashiya River. Ozu had only been here a couple of times before, but each time he felt as though he had come upon a group of alpine summer cottages in some foreign country.

At the Kimura Bakery he asked directions to Tsukimigaoka.

'Ah, the Nagayamas' home?' The owner of the bakery knew the address of the family that Aiko had married into. 'You take this road to the right. There's a big pond down that way. If you ask when you reach the pond, you'll be able to find it.'

He walked a short way down the road as he had been instructed and caught a glimpse of a pond in the middle of a grove. When he drew closer he saw that it was a rather large pond, with a sign reading 'Boats for Rent'.

Aiko's new home was a Western-style building with a

high wall. Ozu stifled the same urge to flee that he had felt earlier and put his finger to the bell.

The door opened. It was Aiko. She wore a girlish *obi*, and a black ribbon was in her hair.

'Oh!' There was surprise in her voice. Ozu forgot himself for a moment and gazed at her face, which seemed much younger than when he had seen her before.

'I remember you. You went to Nada, didn't you?'

'I'm sorry to bother you.' Unsure of what to say, Ozu bowed his head repeatedly like a grasshopper. 'I saw you on the train the other day. You were on the train from Amagasaki with an older woman, and I got into the same car. So I wrote a letter to Flatfish, and Flatfish asked me to give this to you.'

Aiko peered at Ozu and did her best to suppress her laughter as she listened to this unintelligible explanation.

'I didn't follow that very well. Now who is Flatfish?'

'A friend. He nearly drowned once in the sea at Ashiya . . .'

'Oh, my!' She giggled, perhaps remembering. 'Please come in for a moment.'

'No. Yes.' Ozu looked pained and stood stiffly at attention. 'If it wouldn't be any bother, I'll come in for five or ten minutes.'

'Please.' She lowered her eyes a bit. As he removed his shoes in the entranceway, Ozu worried that he might have holes in his socks.

'Umm . . . I'll only take five minutes of your time.'

In the parlour near the entranceway were several sofas covered with white material. There was also a hanging scroll with an inscription that Ozu could not read, and a large clock.

'Is this . . .,' he asked with great trepidation, ' . . . your husband's home?'

'It's my husband's parents' home,' she answered with a gravely serious expression. When she said the word 'husband' Ozu felt as though Aiko were suddenly many years older than him.

'We didn't know that you'd got married.'

'Oh . . .?'

There was a pause in the conversation and Ozu, not knowing what to say, pulled the ten-yen money order from his pocket. The money order was wrinkled and worn by now.

'Flatfish asked me . . . to give this to you. Flatfish is working for a company now. He's in Akō.'

'But why?' she tilted her ribboned head and asked with wonder. 'Why would Mr Flatfish do this?'

'He . . . er . . .' Ozu was at a loss for words. He did not know how to explain it. 'He said in his letter he'd like me to buy something for your baby. But since I didn't know what to buy, I just brought the money.'

'But . . . *why*? I don't understand at all.'

Ozu closed his eyes and blurted out in one breath, 'A long time ago, in the sea at Ashiya, he swam through some big waves even though he couldn't swim very well. Do you remember that? And Flatfish . . . pushed himself to do it because he wanted to talk to you. For years he's been saying that he'll never forget the gauze you gave him once.'

At the end of his speech Ozu opened his eyes. Aiko was sitting with her hands on her knees, gazing at him with total bewilderment on her face.

'But . . .,' she finally opened her lips and muttered, 'I . . . I really can't accept this. I know hardly anything about either of you.'

'But . . . won't you please take it? He said in his letter that I had to give it to you no matter what.' He placed the money order on her lap. It slid from there to the floor.

They were silent for a moment. Ozu stared at that spot on the floor.

'Thank you very much,' Aiko muttered, suddenly bending her head and reaching out to pick up the money order. 'When the child comes, I'll get something for it. . . .'

Then they were both silent again. Unable to endure the stillness, Ozu asked, 'When is your baby due?'

Aiko, relieved, smiled and answered, 'Another six months. It's still a long way off.'

'I imagine your husband is very happy.'

'Well, he . . . he's in Kure. I don't know if he'll be able to be here when I have the baby.'

'In Kure . . .?'

'He's in the navy.'

Then that time . . . Ozu started to say, but in spite of himself he kept his mouth shut. He recalled the figure of the naval cadet in the pure white uniform who had appeared at the edge of the bridge over the Ashiya River.

'In that case,' he suddenly stood up, 'I'd better be going.'

'Could you wait for just a moment?' She vanished from the parlour.

Well, I've given her the money. But I'll never do anything like this again! he inwardly warned Flatfish.

Aiko returned with a small fountain pen in her hand. 'Er . . . would you send this to Mr Flatfish, please? I really don't have anything to give him. My father bought this pen in Shanghai for me when I was a student at Kōnan.'

The pen was tiny and black. Ozu put it in his pocket and nodded.

When he reached home, Ozu took the pen from his pocket and placed it in a box. The pen, she had informed him, was of German make. It seemed to have been well used, for the flow of the ink was rather poor. But it was unquestionably an item that Aiko had treasured and used in the classroom at the girls' school or in her own study room for many years.

Before placing the pen in the box, he tried to imagine

what Flatfish's feelings would be when he received it. And he pondered Aiko's reasons for giving it to Flatfish. He was sure that this pen, for which she probably had no further use, would hereafter become one of Flatfish's most prized possessions.

About a week after he posted the pen, a letter in the customary scrawl arrived from Flatfish. He wrote that he would treasure the pen for the rest of his life. He also asked Ozu to forgive him and promised that he would not trouble him any more. When he had finished reading the letter, Ozu felt he had fulfilled all his obligations to his friend.

Thus autumn came to an end. But Ozu and his friends did not yet realize they were on the threshold of a momentous change in their lives.

One morning early in December, Ozu was shaken from sleep by his mother.

'Wake up! Wake up!'

'If it's for school . . .,' he poked his sleepy head out from under his *futon*, 'I'm going to go in the afternoon. Let me sleep some more.'

'That's not it! Japan and America are at war!'

He scrambled from his *futon* and snatched the extra-edition newspaper his mother held out to him. 'December 7, Predawn: WAR BREAKS OUT IN PACIFIC BETWEEN JAPAN AND AMERICA' – the bold black characters stabbed at his eyes.

'Wow!' he shouted. 'We did it!'

'What will happen? Do you think you'll be called up?' His mother studied his face uneasily. 'This is terrible.'

'What do you mean? Japan'll thrash America!'

He shovelled down his breakfast and bolted from the house. Perhaps at school someone would have more news.

At Umeda Station a naval marching song was playing over the loudspeakers. After the march, a news broadcast caused a great stir among the passengers. At the conclusion of the news, a spontaneous cry of *'Banzai!'* rose from the crowd.

144

Ozu went to school, but he couldn't find out anything else. And there seemed as yet to be no decision on the matter of greatest concern to the students – the cancellation of their draft deferments.

'At last the time for a confrontation between the spiritual civilization of Japan and the material civilization of a foreign country has come!' the professor of philosophy declared before his class, his voice rising to a crescendo. 'The conquest of the modern age may well be at stake in this war. This morning it occurred to me that the mission of Japan is to deal the death blow to the foreign culture that has already reached a stalemate in our country!'

But Ozu and his friends were less interested in this difficult rhetoric than in the successive reports of military conquest.

9 *The Photograph*

That evening Eiichi, who was on night duty, had dinner at the grimy Chinese restaurant across from the hospital and then returned to the dispensary.

The cluttered desks of each worker lined the now vacant room. Empty whisky bottles and cups were strewn among the test tubes, books and medicine bottles.

Eiichi put a cigarette in his mouth. Discovering he had no matches, he glanced around to see if someone had left any behind. It was then he noticed a tin of pipe tobacco sitting on Kurihara's desk.

It was a tin of American pipe tobacco. He remembered having seen Kurihara occasionally smoke a pipe as well as cigars.

Eiichi casually picked up the empty tin and glanced at the writing on it. Then he opened the lid. A single tiny photograph had been tossed into the tin. It was covered with a thin layer of tobacco dust.

A woman wearing an overcoat stood with the sea behind her. She was looking towards the camera, squinting at the sun and smiling. On the back of the photograph, 'In memory of our drive in Shimoda,' was written with a girlish hand.

Eiichi stared at the photograph for a few moments.

Seems like I've seen her somewhere before. . . .

He was sure he had seen her somewhere. But he could not remember where. At first glance he had thought it was Yoshiko. He was relieved that the face was not hers.

Eiichi started to put the photograph back into the tin, then took it out again and placed it in his pocket. He picked up the tin and, turning out the lights in the room, went out into the deserted hallway. He tossed the tin into a wastebasket at the far end of the hall.

I wonder if Kurihara'll notice the tin is gone tomorrow? Eiichi thought. But suppose he does: if he keeps his composure, then the girl in the picture means nothing to him.

He was not conscious of doing anything particularly wrong. It was really nothing more than a little prank. And he had no special curiosity about or interest in the girl in the picture.

But when he climbed the stairs of the ward and glanced into the nurses' station, he suddenly thought, Hmm, isn't that girl a nurse here at the hospital?

'Any changes in the patients?' he asked the young nurse who was filling out the daily logs for the ward.

'No. None.'

He could hear voices and the sounds of televisions coming from the rooms on either side of the hallway. Aluminium trays were piled up on a dinner cart.

Do you know which section this nurse works in? He considered taking the picture from his pocket and asking the unsuspecting young nurse who was writing the ward log. Even nurses from different sections were bound to run into each other at the dormitories.

'Well, I'll be in the night shift room.' Reconsidering, he took his hand from his pocket. 'If anything comes up, call me there.'

An eventless night turned to morning. Eiichi washed his hands and stopped off at the nurses' station. He wrote 'No changes' in the night log, signed and stamped it, and left the hospital. He had a cup of 'Morning Service' coffee at a tea room and returned to the dispensary.

One after another the staff members appeared for work.

'Good morning.' Eiichi rose from his chair and greeted his superiors.

'No changes last night?'

'No. Nothing.'

'What's on the schedule for today?'

'This afternoon there's a dispensary meeting to discuss the operation on the day after tomorrow.'

Kurihara had not yet arrived. Of course no one had noticed that the tin of pipe tobacco was missing from his desk; even if they had, they would have thought nothing of it.

The dispensary chief arrived and made a number of phone calls. After he had bustled out of the room, Kurihara finally appeared. He set down his bag, straightened his desk and opened a drawer, Eiichi knew he had just discovered that the tin was missing. A look of surprise flashed across Kurihara's face, and he glanced quickly to the left and right.

'Did someone take a tin from off my desk?'

'Not me,' one worker answered lifelessly.

'I know I left it here yesterday. . . .' Kurihara tilted his head.

Eiichi put his hand into his pocket. His fingers brushed against the edge of the photograph.

What section is this nurse in?

It seemed unlikely that Kurihara would enquire about the tin if the picture meant nothing to him. Eiichi stood up and left the room.

He had certainly seen the nurse somewhere before. All that he knew for sure, however, was that she was not in Surgery.

He stole glances at the faces of the nurses who walked past him down the hall. None belonged to the woman in the picture.

Maybe I should ask Keiko? he suddenly thought. But since he had broken up with her, he decided it would be too selfish to ask her something like that.

Another typically tumultuous day was beginning at the hospital. The examination rooms had not yet opened for the day, but a number of outpatients were already seated on the sofas in the hallway, and a small queue of people stood at the reception desk. Suffering people did not disappear from this hospital for even a day. And Eiichi was one of the doctors who relieved the sufferings of these people.

'Doctor Ozu!' someone suddenly called out to him. He turned and recognized a patient from the surgery ward who had been released from the hospital about a month before.

'Ah, Mr Uno. How have you been since your operation?'

'Things are going pretty well. I'm here today for an X-ray.'

Eiichi nodded seriously. 'Now you take it easy for a good three months after your surgery.'

On the Friday of that week there was an operation to remove a lung from a patient. Three years before, the patient had undergone thoracoplasty, but it appeared that the pus cavities had not been sufficiently destroyed. Since the patient's condition had worsened this year, it had become necessary to remove the lung.

Dispensary chief Uchida was scheduled to perform the operation, assisted by three dispensary workers. Eiichi was one of them.

Adhesions in the pleura were extreme, and the operation to incise them was time-consuming. Surgery began at 10:00 a.m. and continued until almost 4:00 p.m. When the suturing was completed and the nurse wheeled the still-anaesthetized patient into the hallway on a stretcher, Eiichi and the others were overcome with exhaustion.

The three assistants washed and returned to the dispensary. As they moistened their throats with some beer that the patient's family had brought them, the dispensary chief came in.

'He seems to be getting along well. That lung should have been taken out to begin with, but since the previous hospital botched it, it made a hell of a lot of trouble for us.' He poured some beer into a cup and drank it down.

'It looked like there might be a danger of tracheal fistula,' someone said from his seat.

Tracheal fistula is a complication that easily develops during surgery to remove a lung when the tracheal tubes have been damaged by tuberculosis. Should fistula develop, treatment becomes difficult. In such an event, it is common sense to revert to the old technique of thoracoplasty rather than to remove the lung.

'That's why you've got to hit bronchial TB hard enough with drug therapy. He probably had a relapse because they didn't know how to use drugs properly. But we made a clean cut in the surgery today.' Doctor Uchida looked around proudly at everyone. 'Well, I think I'll go home.' He began to clear his desk. 'You can go home too, Ozu.'

Eiichi had of course been planning to go home. The doctor in charge of surgery as well as the supervising physician were permitted to go home.

'I'll do just that.'

'You're certainly looking pleased about something. A date, perhaps?'

Eiichi smiled wryly and put some books into his bag. Ever since the previous day, he had been reminding himself that this was the day of his date with Yoshiko at the golf range.

Where should we go after dinner? he wondered. Conversation together at a tea room no longer held any charm for him. And the young doctor had little interest in movies.

I'll talk it over with her on the phone.

He stopped by the pay phone in the hospital lobby and

waited patiently beside a middle-aged man glued to the receiver.

The phone was finally vacated. He dialled the number he had already memorized. Yoshiko herself answered, 'Ii residence.' Her voice sounded pleasant to his ears.

'It's Ozu. . . .' Then, 'Our date's for today, you know !' He spoke in lively tones that seemed slipshod even to him. 'Where should I meet you?'

'I can't go. . . . I'm sorry,' she answered uncomfortably.

'You can't? Has something come up?'

'Father says I have to go to dinner with him and Doctor Kurihara and his father. . . .'

At that moment, Eiichi despised the huge face and body of Kurihara from the bottom of his heart.

Eiichi hated Kurihara.

He loathed Kurihara for suddenly moving in from the sidelines and snatching from him the date with Yoshiko that he had laboured to set up and looked forward to since yesterday – no, for a whole week.

He can do this, too, he thought, because his father's the president of a pharmaceutical company.

Doctor Ii and Kurihara's father were getting together for dinner tonight and taking daughter and son along. Eiichi had no idea where they would have dinner, but he could imagine the subject of their conversation. They would discuss the research funds for the new cancer centre to be built at this university, or else the prospects for Doctor Ii carrying out further tests of the anti-cancer drug being produced by the pharmaceutical company owned by Kurihara's father. After touching on these subjects, the conversation just might turn to a discussion of a wedding between Kurihara and Yoshiko.

As Eiichi imagined these events, he clenched his fists in jealousy. It was not jealousy at losing Yoshiko. It was the jealousy of a man with no backing for one who succeeds because he has his father behind him.

And what about me . . .? If my old man had talent,

I wouldn't have to live with miserable thoughts like these.

And what about me . . .? I want to get on in the world just like you. But I've got to do everything on my own, he shouted inwardly as he thought of Kurihara's fat body and narrow eyes. For some reason, the downcast figure of Tahara appeared beside Kurihara at that moment.

Yoshiko isn't the only girl around, Eiichi told himself. I'll get her sometime, but . . . . It occurred to him that that would be the most scathing revenge he could take on Kurihara. But he knew that such a move could damage his own position. There must be a more subtle, hidden form of vengeance.

He picked up the telephone receiver once again and called the operator. 'The nurses' station in the Internal ward, please.' He felt around in the pocket of his suit. The photograph was still there. Fingering its edge with his finger, he changed his voice and asked, 'Nurses' station? Miss Imai, please. . . . How have you been?' Eiichi could tell that Keiko had caught her breath for a moment. 'I haven't seen you for a while. . . . If you're free, how about dinner?'

Still she said nothing. She seemed to be silently weighing up his intent.

'If you're busy, that can't be helped, but . . . my operation this morning went beautifully, and I'm in great spirits. . . . What about it? Will you come?'

'I'll . . . come,' Keiko answered softly.

'Okay. I'll wait for you at Roppongi. At that tea room. You're relieved at five, aren't you? Then six'll be okay, won't it?' He spoke without giving her a chance to respond and hung up.

Yoshiko isn't the only girl around, he repeated to himself. And I'm not the only bad apple around here, Mr Kurihara. You're the one that drove me to this. . . .

Keiko arrived at the Roppongi tea room at six o'clock, as promised. She stood stiffly in the doorway, staring at Eiichi, and then sat down without a word.

'It's been a while, hasn't it?' Eiichi grinned sardonically. 'But let's get out of here right away. I'm starving. The operation today was a clean cut, but I'm dead-beat from incising those pleura.'

Keiko had scarcely touched the tea the waitress set before her when Eiichi abruptly rose to go. As they stepped out onto the pavement where young men and women in fashionable clothes were strolling, thin clouds were floating in the sunset. He wished this date were with Yoshiko.

He frankly did not like this Keiko who was walking along beside him. His blood chilled each time she drew near him, acting as though they were still lovers. An unpleasant feeling welled up from the depths of his heart. Now more than ever, he regretted the stupidity that had led him to ask Keiko out. The sooner he could get away from her the better.

At a small *sushi* shop, Eiichi drank some *sake* while Keiko ate.

'You regret this, don't you?' He had said nothing, but she was sensitive enough to read his mind. 'You're sorry that you asked me out. . . .'

To himself, Eiichi muttered, 'You bet,' but with his customary smile, he said, 'You never give up, do you? You asked me the same thing a little while ago. . . .'

'Then why did you hang up on me when I called you that night?'

'I've told you over and over. You can't call me at home. My sister . . . and my mother listen in.'

'You never used to do that. That's a lie. I know it is.'

Eiichi glanced quickly towards the owner of the *sushi* shop. He was hacking away with his knife, as though he had heard nothing.

'If you know that, then why did you come here tonight?'

She clutched her teacup in both hands and said nothing. Then suddenly, 'I've had a marriage proposal from back home.'

'Oh?' His eyes lit up. 'Isn't that nice? Have you met him yet? What's he like?'

'He manages a petrol station.'

'If he's a good fellow, you ought to marry him.'

'That's what I thought you'd say,' Keiko muttered, staring into her teacup. 'You probably think you'll get off easy now. But you won't. . . .'

'Why not?'

'I won't let you be the only one who comes out of this smiling. I'll follow you everywhere!'

He tried to laugh, but couldn't. She really means that, he thought.

'Let's get out of here.' As he rose and picked up the bill, Eiichi thought, That's one more obstacle in my way. Kurihara and now this woman. Those two blocked his way like a brick wall.

Outside the restaurant, they stopped a taxi whose red light indicated it was vacant.

'To Harajuku,' Eiichi instructed the driver, folding his arms. Several times before Eiichi had taken Keiko to 'Mark', a small bath hotel in Harajuku. So she would know perfectly well what was to come when he told the driver 'To Harajuku.' But she was silent and offered no resistance.

If Yoshiko hadn't broken our date tonight, I wouldn't be going to Harajuku with this woman, Eiichi thought as he gazed absently through the window at the lights from the neon signs and shops. Since I probably won't be able to get my hands on Yoshiko, I'll sleep with Keiko here.

'Say something. I hate it when you're quiet,' Keiko whispered so the driver would not hear. She reached out to take his left hand. Recalling her threat never to let him go, Eiichi brushed her hand away.

The taxi passed by the outer gardens of the Imperial Palace, turned onto the main road to Harajuku, and then struck off down a side road. It came to a stop in front of a small hotel. Eiichi paid the fare and then, as he always did, quickly disappeared into the hotel entrance. Keiko buried her face in the collar of her raincoat and followed at a distance.

The maid escorted them to their room. Eiichi drank down a cup of insipid tea.

'Go and get into the bath.' He indicated the tiny bathroom with his chin.

'You're sure it's okay?' A thin, sarcastic smile appeared on Keiko's lips. 'You're sure you don't mind going through this with me again?'

'What's that supposed to mean?'

'You'd like to break up with me, wouldn't you?'

'It doesn't matter to me one way or the other. But if that's how you feel, why did you come here tonight? If it's going to be that painful for you, we can leave right now.' He put a cigarette to his lips and continued on the offensive. 'What we're doing tonight is no big deal. It's just like a man and woman going to dinner or to a movie together. There's all kinds of young doctors and nurses at the hospital who play around, you know.'

'I'm not like them.'

'Idiot. What do you put yourself in a special class for? Everybody's doing it. Take Kurihara in the dispensary, for one . . .' He thrust his hand into his pocket and tossed the photograph onto the tea-stained table. 'He's fooling around with this nurse here.'

Keiko peered at the photograph with eyes full of curiosity. 'Why, it's Nurse Shimada!'

'What section is she in?'

'Ear and Nose – ' She stopped herself and raised her head. 'What are you doing with this picture?'

Eiichi blew smoke from his mouth and answered

casually, 'It was stuck in a book I borrowed from Kurihara. Everybody in the dispensary is the same. I really don't understand it – you're the only one that's so damned serious. . . .'

An hour later –

There was the faint sound of a train in the distance. Just like when he arrived, Eiichi went out of the hotel first and walked ahead to the dark back street to find a taxi. He had not felt it as much when they were making love, but now that they were finished he could hardly bear to have Keiko beside him. It upset him just to have her breathe on him.

But it paid off. . . . He could hear Keiko's footsteps behind him. . . . At least I got the information I wanted from her. I guess you've got to sleep with a women before you can get her to talk. . . .

He remembered the words he had whispered in Keiko's ear as he embraced her.

They scarcely spoke in the taxi. When they reached Harajuku Station, he handed her a thousand-yen note. 'I'll take a train home. This should cover your fare to the dorm.'

She said something to him as he turned away, but he headed for the station without answering.

So it's Nobue Shimada . . . . A nurse in the Ear and Nose section. . . .

At the station, he wrote the name in his notebook so he would not forget it. He was not yet sure what use he would make of this name, but at any rate he was now in possession of one of Kurihara's secrets.

The clock on the platform read 11 o'clock. Yoshiko must have returned home with her father by now. And Kurihara would certainly be home too.

Just imagining the sort of conversation that had passed between the two and their fathers made Eiichi jealous.

They must have eaten at a stylish restaurant in Akasaka or Yanagibashi. He could almost see the four of them trading cups of *sake* beneath the bright lights. As he heard the train ease along the platform, Eiichi recalled the dim lights in the shuttered hotel room he had just left.

When he arrived home, a Corolla was parked in front of the gate. Eiichi recognized it as the car of the neighbourhood physician.

Is Mother ill . . .?

When he opened the door, the doctor was just putting his shoes back on. His mother and sister had seen him to the door.

'Oh!' his mother cried. 'Your father's sick again, and we had the doctor come over.'

The doctor was slightly embarrassed. 'I didn't think that with a doctor in the family there was any need for me to come, but . . . .'

'What happened to my father?'

The doctor softly answered Eiichi's question, 'He seems to have coughed up a little blood. I'm sure it must be from his stomach. I've taken care of the immediate problem, but I think he should have some X-rays taken at your hospital.'

'I examined him when this happened once before.'

'I don't think it's anything serious.' The doctor glanced towards Eiichi's mother and sister. 'It might be the beginnings of stomach ulcers.'

'I see.' Eiichi nodded his thanks. 'I'll take him into the hospital in the next few days.'

Some five days later, Ozu called in at his son's hospital to have some X-rays made. He had visited the hospital where his son worked several times before, but this was the first time he had gone to be examined.

He phoned the dispensary from the crowded lobby of

the hospital and Eiichi quickly came out to meet him. Eiichi took care of all the formalities for his father and said, 'I'll have them take the X-rays right away.'

'Don't I need to have a doctor look at me?'

Eiichi seemed irritated at his father's question. 'I happen to be one of the doctors at this hospital. Please do what I tell you.'

As they walked down the hall where outpatients were waiting, Ozu watched his white-smocked son, who occasionally bowed his head slightly, and tasted a measure of satisfaction and pleasure. Eiichi's way of thinking is different from mine no matter what the subject, Ozu thought, but in his own way he's doing something to help people out.

'It's crowded, isn't it? In every section.'

Eiichi seemed to misunderstand the remark. 'I've asked them to take you in right away.'

'Will you be there?'

'I plan to be.'

Outside the X-ray Room, which was indicated by a red lamp, five or six patients sat with drooping heads.

'I could wait my turn. . . .'

'I'm very busy. Please go in right now.'

In the darkened room stood two men wearing protectors that looked like the ones worn by baseball catchers.

'Doctor Tazu, this is my father,' Eiichi introduced Ozu.

Ozo stood surrounded by the photographic equipment and bowed in greeting. 'I appreciate everything you do for my son.'

He stripped to the waist and stood on the X-ray platform. Eiichi handed his father a cup of white liquid and a tiny, bean-like pill resting on a sheet of paper. 'Please drink this when Doctor Tazu tells you to, Dad.'

'Take a drink.'

The liquid was thick and had an unpleasant taste. Doctor Tazu pressed Ozu's ribs with his fingers.

'Take another drink. Then hold your breath,' he said.

He had to close his eyes and drink the liquid down several times. His son and the doctor whispered German medical terms to each other.

'We're going to lower the platform, so please lie down in a comfortable position.'

Maybe I have cancer. The thought suddenly clouded Ozu's mind.

'Hold your breath. We'll take just one more picture.'

If it's cancer, then fine. I've lived a long life. I really might have died during the war, Ozu thought. Like Flatfish. Just as Flatfish died then. . . .

'All finished.' At Doctor Tazu's words, Ozu climbed off the X-ray platform and reached into a basket for his underwear.

'Is it . . . bad?'

'There's really nothing to worry about. There's a scar on the duodenum from some old injury. But nothing serious to be concerned about.'

Along with a sense of relief, an oppressive feeling of melancholy that he had to go on living flashed through Ozu's heart.

Walking out of the dark X-ray Room with Eiichi, Ozu wiped the traces of the white liquid from his lips with a handkerchief.

'Thank you.' He nodded to his son. 'I feel more at ease now, thanks to you.'

'I'll get your medicine from the pharmacy a little later. If you're going into the office today, don't have anything more than a bowl of noodles for lunch. And no *sake* for a while.'

'All right.' Ozu put great trust in his son. 'What will you do now?'

'I'm going to the surgical ward. The rooms I supervise are there.'

'Would it be all right if I had a look?'

Eiichi smiled faintly at his father's unexpected, embarrassed request.

'Of course. But please don't stare into the rooms.'

Ozu had no idea what sort of work his son did in the ward each day. Eiichi himself never talked about it when he came home. But, having come all the way to the hospital today, Ozu wanted to have a look at the ward where his son's patients stayed.

They crossed the long hallway and entered the elevator.

'This is the Radium Treatment Room,' or 'In that room they carefully examine all the urine and blood and secretion samples from all over the hospital,' Eiichi explained, and Ozu nodded, 'I see. I see.'

Outside, the sun was shining, but in the surgery ward, with rooms on both sides, the hallway was dark.

'Do you spend all your time here?'

'No. I'm usually in the dispensary.'

'Quiet, isn't it?'

'Uh-huh. It's always like this.' Eiichi put his hand into the pocket of his smock and said wearily, 'Well, I've got to look at my patients.' Leaving his father standing there, he disappeared into a room.

Ozu stood at the door to the hallway for a moment. A cleaning woman was mopping the hall.

The elevator doors opposite opened and a gowned woman lying on a stretcher came out accompanied by a nurse. Ozu caught a brief glimpse of her profile and felt he had seen her somewhere before.

She looked a little like Aiko Azuma.

But the Aiko he had last seen some thirty years before had been younger. And there was no reason why Aiko should be hospitalized here.

The patient and her nurse disappeared into a room on the right-hand side of the hall. Ozu lowered his eyes and went down the nearby staircase.

After leaving his father in the hallway, Eiichi examined two of his patients and then poked his head into Aiko Nagayama's room.

'We've just finished the tests,' the nurse said as she

pushed the stretcher out into the hall. 'She felt ill twice.

'Tests? What tests?'

'The liver tissue test.'

'No one's said anything to me about it. . . .'

'But Doctor Kurihara ordered it yesterday.'

Eiichi said nothing and went over to his patient. She had obviously felt sick during the tests and her face and lips were pallid.

'Was it hard?'

'Yes,' Aiko answered listlessly, still exhausted from the tests.

'As I told you before, you may develop a fever after the tests, but it's nothing to worry about.'

'What were the results?'

'I haven't spoken to Doctor Kurihara yet, but . . . I imagine they were checking for problems with the liver. If we have to operate, we have to make sure it doesn't affect the liver.'

'Then . . .' Aiko hesitated. 'You're going to have to operate?'

'It's the best way. Then we can cut out all the bad parts,' Eiichi lied, smiling. They would probably go through the motions of opening her up, and then quickly sew her up again. It was the unanimous consensus at the dispensary meeting the previous day that the cancer cells had spread throughout her body.

The patients were told that the doctors were operating for stomach ulcers. During the operation, once they had confirmed their suspicion that it was too late to stop the spreading cancer, they would cut out one portion and then sew the patient up again. After that, the only recourse was to use anti-cancer drugs, radium treatments and injections and transfusions to alleviate the pain. Finally the patient would suffer a relapse and die.

'How soon after the operation can I go home?'

'Well, let's see.' Eiichi cocked his head slightly. 'Maybe two months. If all goes well, a month and a half.'

'That long . . .?' Aiko looked surprised.

'The period *after* the operation is the most crucial.'

'There are several matters . . . if I don't go home soon . . .'

Eiichi pretended not to hear. He had not been lying when he said a month and a half or two months. But this woman would probably be readmitted to the hospital in another six months.

'Since you had tests today, we'll forgo the examination. I'll bring something for the fever later. You can take it if you need it.'

They had already ascertained from blood tests that her liver was malfunctioning. But why had Kurihara gone so far as to have a portion of her liver cut out for a tissue examination today?

He phoned the dispensary from the nurses' station.

'Yes, we ran some tests. I didn't say anything to you about it. . . .'

'Why not?'

'Well,' Kurihara replied, 'I think Doctor Uchida would like to talk that over with you.'

10 The War

1942 was a busy year. At the beginning of the year the Japanese, having occupied Manila, sent troops into Burma and made a triumphal entry into Singapore. Batavia and Rangoon also fell into Japanese hands.

The streets buzzed with excitement as news reports of the conquests poured in one after another. When evening fell, lantern processions were held in various locations. And in Europe, Japan's ally Germany had opened up a war front against the Soviet Union. No Japanese doubted they would be victorious.

However, the inconveniences of daily life multiplied swiftly. Compared with two or three years before, when articles could be obtained with little difficulty, it seemed like a dream now to have so many items vanish from the store shelves. Posted prominently in the stations at Sannomiya and Umeda were massive signs bearing the strange slogan, 'We Don't Want Anything Until We Win!'

In response to the times, the periods of military drill and labour service were expanded at Ozu's P. University, and a decree from the administration to the students proclaimed that no student would be promoted without participating in military drill twice each week.

In the classrooms, the teachers were divided into two factions – those who viewed these activities with loathing, and those who actively supported them. The presence of these two factions made Ozu and his fellow students uneasy. They wanted the war to end quickly, but at the same time they felt overwhelmed by the awesomeness of the Japanese army as it displayed its might to the United States. Since student draft deferments were still recognized, they rested easy in the knowledge that they would not be drafted, but this privilege could be taken away from them if conditions changed. A sense of apprehension hung over the students.

When Ozu returned home from school one drizzling day in June, his mother hurried to the entranceway and cried, 'Call up Flatfish right away!'

'What's happened?'

'He's been drafted.'

'Who? Flatfish?!'

'Yes. He rang a while ago from Akō.'

He kicked off his shoes and scampered to the phone in the parlour. He asked the operator for Akō, and as the phone was ringing Ozu felt uneasy, just as though something he himself had dreaded had finally come to pass.

The call finally got through to Akō, and Flatfish answered, 'Hello?'

'Hey! That's terrible . . .' Ozu could think of nothing else to say.

'Yeah. I'm coming back to Kobe tonight. I've got to see my mum and my sister.' Flatfish's voice was unexpectedly calm. It sounded as drowsy as ever. Ozu could all but see that fish-like face and the bleary eyes as Flatfish gripped the receiver.

'Where do you enlist?'

'The Kakogawa squadron.'

'What time do you get in tonight? I'll meet you at the station.'

Flatfish was silent for a moment. 'No. I don't know which train I'm taking. I'll get hold of you tomorrow.'

Ozu could think of nothing to say. One usually offered congratulations to a man going into the army, but he could not bring himself to utter words he did not truly mean.

It's because he doesn't have a draft deferment, he thought, feeling himself without excuse. 'Well, then, be sure to call me tomorrow.'

He replaced the receiver. Thought after thought came into his head – will he be able to survive the rough life of a soldier with that body of his? Aw, he's shrewd. He'll be all right!

The following evening Ozu was invited to the farewell party for Flatfish. Food and *sake* were brought in from the little restaurant right next to Flatfish's house, but still for such a small event there were quite a few people in attendance. Among the guests were the chairman of the neighbourhood association, a representative from the veterans' league, and the president and several employees from the company where Flatfish worked. Flatfish's mother and sister sat deferentially in one corner. Ozu sat beside them.

'In times such as these, with our difficulties mounting, we can scarcely contain our delight that Flatfish, from our very own neighbourhood, is going into the army.' The address by the chairman of the neighbourhood association was as long as a cow's piss. He commented on the times, offered counsel, and urged determination just as if he had been made Prime Minister. When he finished speaking, it was the turn of the representative from the veterans' league. His remarks were along the same lines, as though he were the Army Minister.

Ozu endured the cramp in his legs, glancing occasionally at the strange expression on Flatfish's face. He was not sure whether Flatfish was listening to the addresses or not, but seeing the ever bleary-eyed expression Ozu thought of sleepy afternoons in the classrooms at Nada Middle School.

After the speeches, Flatfish's sister went around pouring *sake* for everyone.

'Let's drink to Flatfish's enlistment. . . .' The president of Flatfish's company proposed the toast. So this is the miserly president that Flatfish has patterned himself after, Ozu thought, gazing at the bald head and the square body reminiscent of a heavy tank.

Confusion reigned as the *sake* was passed around the room.

'When I was a soldier,' the chairman of the neighbourhood association was loudly proclaiming, 'it was during the last war in Europe. I was never sent to the front, but . . . the money I hung onto from those days really came in handy the day I was discharged.'

'Oh, what did you use it – '

The association president whispered something in his neighbour's ear and then guffawed loudly.

The company president called across the table to Flatfish, who was thoroughly drunk from the cups of *sake* that had been passed to him from the left and the right. 'We generally don't have *sake* or sweets, but we can forget about that just for tonight. . . . While you're in the army, we'll be sure to deposit your salary every month. So you go out and serve your country and don't worry yourself about that.'

'Yes, sir.'

'He's an admirable young man!' the company president said loudly enough for everyone to hear. 'At my company, I bring up my new employees strictly, but he's always listened carefully to what I tell him.'

Flatfish looked at Ozu with tired eyes. While the president was praising him, Flatfish stuck his tongue out so that only Ozu could see.

This guy'll make out okay even as a soldier, Ozu thought, nodding.

When Flatfish stood to go to the bathroom, Ozu followed him out into the hallway.

'Hey. Are you okay?'

'Yeah. Just sleepy.'

'You shouldn't drink too much. It doesn't suit a soldier.'

Flatfish suddenly grasped Ozu's hand. 'You work hard now!' he said.

Ozu was embarrassed. 'What do you mean?'

'And I'm taking her fountain pen with me. If you happen to run into her, would you tell her that?'

'Sure,' Ozu nodded.

The next morning Flatfish set off for a station on the Hanshin line, accompanied by members of the Women's National Defence League and people from his neighbourhood. He was draped in a Rising Sun flag inscribed with parting phrases from everyone at the party the previous evening.

Ozu followed along behind the procession, remembering the time he and Flatfish had observed a similar scene from the coffee shop at Sannomiya.

My day to enlist will come, too, Ozu thought. Images of barracks and battlegrounds that once seemed so distant now flashed before his eyes.

'*Banzai!*'

'Flatfish – *Banzai!*'

Surrounded by the aproned members of the Women's National Defence League, Flatfish bowed his closely-cropped head to the right and left. The train finally pulled in, and as the passengers looked on, he boarded with his aunt, his mother and his sister. The carriage door closed.

One month, then two passed, but still no word came from Flatfish. Undoubtedly as a new recruit in the Kakogawa squadron he was so busy every day that he had no time to write letters.

Ozu too spent his days in military drill and labour service twice a week. The outlook for the war, which had begun so magnificently, became uncertain after the turning-point in June at the naval battle of Midway. The Imperial Headquarters continued to send out reports of successful military exploits, but after August, when the

Americans invaded Guadalcanal, a rumour began to circulate that Japan was on the road to defeat.

At the end of the year, a single postcard finally arrived from Flatfish. An ink stamp indicated that it had been passed by the censors. On the back, in those familiar scrawled characters, Flatfish reported that he was in Korea and diligently applying himself to his military duties and that there was no cause for concern. 'I'm writing this postcard with the pen that you gave me,' he had written.

Ozu was surprised to learn that Flatfish had been sent to Korea. He was apparently not allowed to say when he had left or where he was stationed in Korea, since there was not a word about that. Holding the postcard in his hand, Ozu recalled a scene from Korea he had once seen in a picture : endless stretches of bald mountains.

'I'm writing this postcard with the pen that you gave me.' He knew what Flatfish was trying to say with those words.

Is he . . . *still* . . .?

He wished he could relate those words to Aiko. But he reconsidered. It might lead to an unfortunate misunderstanding.

The following year at the P. University prep school, the only classes deserving of the name were held but briefly, after which the students were put to work in the munitions factories, working one semester in Amagasaki and the next in Kobe.

A severe food shortage developed. At the factories where Ozu was assigned to assemble airplane parts, many machines could not be operated, perhaps because of the shortage of materials. The students had lunch at noon, concealing their meals of soy beans from their comrades. Ozu could have brought along a much better lunch if he were still living at home, but for the dormitory dwellers lunch was over as soon as they had put one or two small rice balls into their mouths.

At 3 p.m. an orderly rationed out porridge from a bucket. It looked like steaming white water. But no one turned it down.

When is the war going to end? No one said it aloud, but the thought was vaguely present in every mind.

If it doesn't end soon, we'll be drafted too!

But it seemed as though the gloomy war would go on forever. . . .

Ozu remembered that a letter had come from Flatfish a short time later.

A photograph was included in the letter of thanks acknowledging receipt of the comfort bag Ozu had sent. In the photograph about ten soldiers stood in two rows. Flatfish stood dreamily in the back row. 'Stood dreamily' is an unusual expression, but that was just the feeling Ozu had as he looked at the picture. The other soldiers smiled, their arms around each other's shoulders. Ozu looked closely at the picture and could tell from the two- or three-star insignias that these soldiers were privates and privates first-class. Only Flatfish and one other soldier wore the single star of a buck private.

Flatfish's face appeared swollen. Ozu imagined from that swollen face that Flatfish must be totally exhausted.

Ozu had heard about the treatment that buck privates received in the army. No matter how crafty the frail Flatfish had been in training camp, his swollen face told how much more worn than the others he was now.

'I'm doing well and applying myself to my military duties, so don't worry about me.' Ozu could not believe that those words in the letter had come from Flatfish's heart. He must have written that to get past the censors.

Hey, please understand the way things really are, he could almost hear his friend saying between the lines of his letter. Once again, Flatfish had written with Aiko's fountain pen.

Feet thrust into the quicksands of war were sucked down at an ever-mounting speed. In Europe, the Allied forces invaded Italy; *Il Duce* Mussolini was forced from office and the country capitulated. Even in Japan, only the military authorities and reports in the newspapers maintained an air of optimism. It was clear to all observers that America had moved from the defensive to the offensive.

At the beginning of their second semester after the summer break, the event that Ozu and his classmates dreaded at last came about. Military deferments for liberal art students in the universities and prep schools were abolished.

'Your time to rise up has finally come. When soon the day arrives that you take leave of these school grounds and proceed to the battlefield, do not forget the pride you have felt as a student at P. University,' the dean of students loudly addressed the prep school students assembled on the athletics field. But such sentiments were out of the question. It was the students who were being conscripted into the army, not the dean of students or the teachers.

Ozu returned to his family residence in Kurayoshi, Tottori Prefecture to receive his induction examination.

He was accompanied by two old men from the village office of the town where his father was born. As he stood in the lecture hall of the elementary school among the other young men clad only in loincloths, receiving one examination after another, he thought of the day he had accompanied Flatfish to take the naval academy examination.

When he was examined for venereal disease and haemorrhoids, he had to take off his loincloth and get down on all fours like a dog.

He supposed he would be classified Second Grade. The

physiques of the young men around him were imposing. But when he stood motionlessly at attention as the classifications were read off, the examiner announced loudly, 'First Class!'

'Congratulations!' He was greeted warmly by the old men from the village office who had accompanied him.

Ozu still remembered the day of his induction with great clarity.

A flock of pigeons had gathered on the black roof of the barracks and they were cooing softly. Placards indicating the prefecture of birth were set up on the parade ground, and Ozu and the other recruits were lined up in four columns behind them.

'We will now announce the names of the squadrons to which you will be attached. When your squadron has been announced, line up directly in front of your squadron commander.'

When the squadrons had been determined, Ozu and the others followed their squadron commanders into the barracks for the first time. As they entered the barracks, again they heard the 'coo-coo' of the pigeons clustered on the roof.

Did Flatfish hear the cries of these pigeons . . . , Ozu wondered, . . . just like I'm hearing them now?

There was a long table in the middle of the barracks room, which smelled of oil and body odour. Beds with straw matting were ranged along either side of the table.

'I am Uchida, your squadron commander.' The tanned staff sergeant clasped his hands behind his back and began to speak. 'Your squadron commander is your mother, so you should come to me about any and all matters.'

Suddenly a tall corporal standing beside Uchida barked, 'Listen! Some of you ain't standing at attention while the squadron commander is speaking! Maybe we ain't been to the university like you, but even before we enlisted we knew the proper stance to take with our superiors. In the army, when you listen to orders or instructions from an officer, you stand at attention!'

When Staff Sergeant Uchida had wearily ended his hackneyed address, the corporal added, 'Now we'll issue you your uniforms. Fold your civvies up right now and stick them in the corner of your foot lockers. When you finish dressing, go out onto the parade ground. There you'll be given your weapons!'

A banquet was set before them that evening. Besides the rice and red beans and pork stew that could seldom be had back home, sweet bean jelly was brought out. But . . .

They'll only treat you well on the first day. The next day it's all over! their predecessors had told them. So the food did not slip down their throats so easily.

'After you've finished eating, each of you face towards your hometown and bow your head,' the squadron commander instructed them quietly. 'After that, consider all connections with that world as broken!'

That night, as they closed their eyes for their first night's sleep upon the straw matting, they heard the long, plaintive call of the lights-out trumpet far in the distance.

> The brand-new soldiers
> How cute they are
> As they lie there –
> Do they cry there?

As he inhaled the odours of oil, of sweat, and of the barracks themselves and listened to the sound of the trumpet, Ozu thought of the expression on Flatfish's face in the company photograph he had sent.

Every night now for a long time, he's been listening to the sound of this trumpet. . . .

Then the white road along the Ashiya River floated up before his eyes. Aiko Azuma, dressed in a sailor suit, was walking down that road with her friend. They stopped from time to time, laughing together about something.

I've got to get to sleep. With a mighty effort, he sought to drive his memories away – these memories now so far from his grasp. . . .

As they had feared, the intangibly fabricated atmosphere that prevailed on the first day of their induction disappeared on the second day. Ozu and the other new soldiers were run around, worked around, shouted at and beaten, and they were not given a moment to themselves. The only times they could rest were when they went to the toilet and after the mournful call of the lights-out trumpet.

They were beaten every single day. They were beaten during drills and then beaten when they returned to their barracks. On the first day, the staff sergeant had told them that the squadron commander would be their mother, but instead of laying hands on them himself, he was the sort of mother who sat on his straw mat and looked on as the sergeants and privates first-class inflicted their own personal forms of torture on the new recruits.

'We ain't been to college, and we ain't got no learning. But even if we 'adn't been to college, we weren't lazy and insubordinate like you guys!' the senior soldiers invariably announced each time they gave Ozu or any of the other student soldiers a beating. And when the new recruits had reached the end of their tether and went to consult with the squadron commander after their chopsticks and washing were stolen –

'We-e-e-ll . . . I'm not sure what I should do about it, since I ain't been to college.' Even the staff sergeant looked the other way.

The new recruits could not stick up for one another. They could not even afford to help someone else out. So with time, the feelings of friendship so often discussed in their schooldays, and the desire to sacrifice themselves for others were stripped away from Ozu and his contemporaries. If someone blundered, he was not the only one punished. The entire group of new recruits was lined up in two rows, and after a long tirade each had to turn and beat the man beside him.

At this point it finally dawned on Ozu. The photo of Flatfish's swollen face that had been sent from Korea. That face was not simply swollen. It was puffed up from being beaten.

So Flatfish's getting it every day, too. Ozu realized what had happened to Flatfish by observing a fellow named Yamamoto, who shared barracks with Ozu and had been at a university in Tokyo.

Yamamoto tired quickly during their morning sprints, perhaps because he was not as strong as the others. He trailed behind, panting heavily, and the distance between him and the others progressively widened.

'What're you doing, you son of a bitch?' The squadron commander whacked Yamamoto across the cheek when he finally struggled in. 'D'you think you can fight a war like that? Do another lap by yourself,' he screamed. So Yamamoto ended up running further than any of the others.

Once in the middle of the night, Ozu and the others heard wild shouting near the barracks exit. 'Did you go to the can without reporting it?'

They heard Yamamoto apologize profusely for his mistake. Then came the sound of Yamamoto being knocked down.

'What is it? What's happened?' The squadron commander thrust on his overshoes and went to the door.

'I see. I'll make it very clear to him, leave him to me.'

The negotiations complete, the sounds finally ceased.

He won't get off unpunished, Ozu and the others thought, burying their chins beneath their blankets.

Their fears were realized. The next day, Yamamoto had two teeth knocked out by a couple of senior officers. His face swelled up like a pomegranate.

About four months after their induction, a rumour raced through the barracks that they were going to be sent overseas.

The rumour became reality one night when they were transported in full military dress on a train and then loaded aboard cargo ships. To avoid being intercepted by enemy submarines, they were not allowed to tell any outsiders the date of departure or their destination. They were sent abruptly on their way, without even a chance to see their families.

The boat bounced up and down upon the black ocean. And a cold rain was falling. The hold of the ship reeked with the smell of paint and the body odour of the soldiers.

From the portholes the ocean seemed to be tilting. Gazing at it, Ozu dozed off to sleep. As he slept, the athletics ground at Nada Middle School and the white bed of the Sumiyoshi River appeared.

'Turner, you see . . .,' the Shadow muttered as he paced about the classroom. 'Turner, you see. He was a great man, you see.'

Then bleary-eyed Flatfish was standing before the mathematics teacher.

'What kind of answers are these? Read the answers you wrote to these test problems?' the teacher shouted at the bewildered Flatfish. 'Aren't you going to read it?'

'Yes, sir.'

'Not "Yes, sir"! How did you answer the question!'

'All right then, I'll read it. I . . . I answered: "That's right. That's exactly right. I think so, too." '

An explosion of laughter rocked the classroom. The laughter awakened Ozu.

The dull pounding of the engine. The ocean still rising and falling through the porthole. Senior officers asleep. Ozu closed his eyes again.

The ocean. Thunderhead clouds floating. Flatfish and

Ozu were swimming in the sea at Ashiya. With the feeling of liberation that summer vacation brings, they splashed water at each other, dived, and spat the salty water from their mouths.

'Don't pee in the water!' Flatfish said. 'Have you ever farted while you're swimming?'

'Nope.'

'Try it! It's just like a rocket. Poo, poo, poo, and it makes you swim faster!'

All the things that were lost. The memories of his youth seemed memories no longer. They were part of another world he could never again take hold of.

'Are you thinking about the same things?' Ozu asked Flatfish, who appeared before his eyes.

'Yeah,' Flatfish answered sadly. 'Nothing we can do about it. Keep pluggin' away.'

'Are you pulling a lot of stunts?'

'Can't. They do nothing but beat me every day.'

'Me, too. But we've got to hold on. We've got to make it back alive.'

'I . . . I'm not sure about that. . . . Whether I'll make it back alive or not. . . .'

Why had Flatfish said that? Even after Ozu opened his eyes and realized it had been a dream, the expression of sorrow he had seen on his friend's face remained with him. Not just the face. Even the voice echoed in his ears.

'I'm not sure about that. . . . Whether I'll make it back alive or not. . . .'

Ozu's regiment was unexpectedly put ashore at Dairen. Later Ozu and the other student soldiers learned that they had been sent to Manchuria as replacement troops to allow the infantry to pour one division of crack troops from the Kantō Army into the south.

Disembarking from the cargo ship that had moored alongside the rainy Dairen wharf, Ozu and his fellow soldiers looked about in wonder at the unfamiliar foreign landscape. On the dock, where coal was piled up like a mountain, a large group of coolies laboured with gigantic sacks on their backs. Japanese military police supervised their activities.

The regiment lined up in formation and marched into Dairen city. Unlike the demolished streets of Japan, here rows of acacia trees grew luxuriantly green, and the streets were lined with clean, Western-style buildings.

Here the troops regrouped into three columns. One was to be stationed in Port Arthur and Dairen; the other two were to patrol the border of Northern Manchuria.

In the depths of his heart, Ozu hoped he would remain in Port Arthur or Dairen. Fortunately his column stayed in Dairen as he wished.

But training there became even more severe. The senior officers of the elite Kantō Army squeezed them dry, as though they had just been waiting for some puny student soldiers to arrive.

Ozu thought less and less about Flatfish. With the severe training and barracks life to occupy his mind he had no time to sink into reveries about the past. The student soldiers not only had to endure the training to make them fully-fledged soldiers; at night they had to prepare on their own to become officer trainees.

Letters from Japan finally arrived some two months later.

Ozu received a letter from his mother. While she was relating news about his father and friends, she seemed to be concealing something else that she wanted to say. Then Ozu turned to the second page of the letter and froze in horror.

'And yesterday we learned that Flatfish has died from an illness he contracted on the battlefield. His sister phoned us about it. We don't know any of the details yet. I knew you'd be shocked at this, and I couldn't decide whether to write you about it or not. But since you two were friends for such a long time, I decided to go ahead and tell you. Please take care of your health and do your best for your country. Now . . .'

In the dim light of the barracks, Ozu read that portion of the letter time after time.

The news was so unexpected that he felt no emotion at all. He seemed to be reading and rereading the letter in order to produce some sort of emotional response.

Flatfish? . . . Dead?

He felt no shock or surprise. Everything was being swept away in the dismal fortunes of this dismal age. He himself might be one of those swept away.

'Hey, Ozu!' a private first-class beside him called out. 'How come you're looking so down-in-the-mouth over a letter? Did something happen?'

'Yes. I just got word that one of my friends died of an illness at the front.'

'Oh?' The private's voice was milder than usual. 'Well, don't let it get to you. Everybody's gotta die sometime.'

Ozu announced he was going to the latrine and stepped out into the hallway. In these barracks, the toilet was the only place one could be alone. There in the bathroom, Ozu shed his first tears. . . .

11 *The Experiment*

Kurihara himself would say nothing about the liver examination on Aiko Nagayama. Not only did he refuse to discuss it, he commented that the dispensary chief would probably want to discuss it with Eiichi.

What's going on? Suspicious, Eiichi returned to the dispensary.

The dispensary was deserted. Even Kurihara, to whom he had just spoken on the phone, had vanished. The dusty afternoon sun shone through the unwashed windows and onto the desks and books and beakers.

Eiichi sat in a chair and wrote out a prescription for his father.

The phone rang. His cigarette still dangled from his mouth as he picked up the receiver.

'Ah, is that you?' It was the voice of the dispensary chief. 'I guess you've heard from Kurihara. There's nobody in the dispensary now? That's perfect. Would you mind waiting there?'

As he waited for the dispensary chief, Eiichi stared at the cigarette smoke that rose from his fingertips. He had a slightly uneasy feeling in the pit of his stomach.

Just then he noticed a postcard tacked to the small blackboard that hung next to the door.

It was a postcard from Tahara. It was addressed to everyone in the dispensary.

'It's been over two weeks since I arrived here. I wasn't used to anything at first, and I felt really lost, but now I think I've finally settled down. I'm very glad I came here. I'm beginning to think that it was my mission in life to come here and do my best for patients who haven't been fortunate enough to receive good medical treatment. Thank you for everything while I was at the hospital. . . .'

Eiichi recalled Tahara's ungainly appearance. It was unlikely he would ever be recalled to the dispensary. He had deviated from the path to success and gone off in some other direction. Even the young co-workers who had sympathized with Tahara at the time no longer discussed him. A fellow finally forgotten . . .

Maybe . . . A pain shot through Eiichi's chest. Maybe the reason the chief wants to talk to me . . . is because I'm going to be packed off somewhere like Tahara. . . .

He tossed the cigarette that had shrunk in his fingers into an empty medicine tin. As he sought to drive the malignant thoughts from his mind, Doctor Uchida came in quietly.

'Sorry to keep you waiting. Boy, those people at the Ministry of Welfare are hard-headed. You can't even talk to them. When we played golf the other day, they talked like everything was all set, but now it's all up in the air again!' When he finished grumbling about these matters that Eiichi could not comprehend, he said, 'Well . . . sit down. Now, the reason we did those liver tissue tests on the patient Nagayama today . . .' He paused and glanced at the door. 'Actually, no one knows about this but Doctor Ii and I, and Kurihara. So for the time being, don't discuss this with anyone in the dispensary.'

'Yes, sir.'

'When Doctor Ii had dinner with Kurihara's father the other day, they discussed several aspects of our Cancer Centre. And Kurihara's father asked us to perform some additional tests on a new anti-cancer drug they've been developing. We can expect a high degree of effectiveness on the experimental level, but the problem is that it affects the liver.'

Eiichi thought back. Yoshiko had told him that she and her father were going to have dinner with Kurihara and his father. This discussion must have taken place then.

'And, er, we're thinking of testing out this cancer-controlling drug on the patient Nagayama.' The dispensary chief glanced up at Eiichi. 'Frankly, and I'm sure you know this, it's too late to do anything for Mrs Nagayama. In fact, we also considered the lung cancer patient you're working with, Mr Tajima – er, the executive – but his liver is probably pretty well shot already.' Doctor Uchida looked quickly at his wrist-watch. 'Well, that's what I wanted to tell you. We shouldn't have done the liver cell tests without telling you, but you understand. If this new drug is effective, we want to have our surgical section announce the findings in medical circles. Were going to have Kurihara and you do that. Kurihara's father says he'll provide us with sufficient research funds. . . .'

He rose from his chair. 'Anyway, for now this is all secret. You understand that, don't you?'

'I understand.' Eiichi bowed his head and watched as the dispensary chief left the room.

So that's what it is.

He was delighted to be included in the reigning clique in the dispensary. If they did not intend to include him, there was no reason for the dispensary chief to reveal a secret like this to a young worker like Eiichi.

'If this new drug is effective, we want to have our surgical section announce the findings in medical circles. We're going to have Kurihara and you do that.' The chief's voice still rang deep in his ears. Eiichi imagined himself standing in front of a blackboard and a projection screen, announcing the experimental data.

Then his eyes shifted involuntarily to Tahara's post-card on the blackboard. He felt as if Tahara's mournful face were accusing him.

Are you so eager to make it in the world that you'll even go this far?

Eiichi tried to laugh derisively. Tahara's mournful face went on:

What you're thinking of doing now is no different from using that worthless Bethion.

The circumstances are different. This drug we're going to test is a *new* drug.

But aren't you just experimenting on human guinea pigs?

You show me a doctor that wouldn't like to experiment on a human being! If we didn't try out new operative techniques and new drugs on humans, there wouldn't be any advances in medicine!

But what happens if the patient becomes a victim for the sake of the experiments?

Tahara stared at him mercilessly. As if to drive the face away, Eiichi snatched the postcard from the blackboard and threw it into the wastebasket, muttering, 'You're a coward! As long as people like you are doctors, there'll never be any advances in medicine!'

When Eiichi returned home that evening, his father was reading the evening paper in high spirits.

'Welcome home! Thanks again for this morning. Have you had dinner?'

'I've already eaten.' He looked at his father with rare affection. The things Doctor Uchida had said to him today had cheered him considerably.

'Here's your medicine.' Eiichi took the medicine for his father from his case. 'Take it thirty minutes after each meal.' He started to get up.

'Say, listen. Why don't you have some tea with me?' his father stopped him.

His mother and sister came in from the kitchen.

'Your father says he even had a look at your hospital

ward today.' His mother tilted the teapot. 'That's all he's talked about all evening.'

'There's a doting parent for you,' his sister stuck out her tongue and laughed.

'Listen, Eiichi is an important man at the hospital. When I was walking down the hall with him, one of the patients came right up and thanked him for all his help'.

'Oh, that fellow had a lung removed in our ward.'

How many years had it been since Eiichi had chatted so comfortably with his family? We still got together like this as a family when Eiichi was in high school, Ozu thought.

'Medicine is a good profession. I'll bet you get a lot of satisfaction out of it. Seeing suffering people healed by your hands . . .'

Eiichi grimaced faintly. His old man considered everything in such an optimistic, sentimental light. That was the unbearable 'humanism' of his dad's generation.

'I don't cure illnesses by my hands. Those days have passed. Medicine is more methodical now.'

'But the happiness of a patient who's been cured is the same now as then.'

'Sure. But patients come and go. There's no time to get sentimentally attached to each one. We aren't like the doctors in the movies or on TV.'

Ozu started to speak, but he caught himself. He did not want to spoil the evening by another argument with his son.

'I suppose not. But . . . today when I looked in at your ward, there was a woman patient in a wheelchair being pushed out of the elevator by a nurse. Her colouring was really bad.'

The slightly angry expression on Eiichi's face returned to normal when Ozu changed the subject.

'Ah, that was a patient who had some tests today. She's being operated on soon.'

'Is she one of your patients?'

'Yes, but I'm not the only doctor that looks after her. She's a widow, named Aiko Nagayama. Said she lost her husband in the war or something.'

Eiichi sensed his father staring into his face.

'Is something wrong?'

'What did you say . . . that patient's name was?'

'The patient's name? It's Aiko Nagayama. Do you know her?'

'No.' Ozu shook his head.

There was no doubt about it. It must be her. But the woman he had seen at the far end of the hall this morning was so wasted away. The young girl who swam in the sea at Ashiya. He could no longer remember what the woman he had seen today looked like.

'This woman . . .,' his mother asked Eiichi, 'what's wrong with her?'

'Er . . . it's cancer. Stomach cancer.'

'If it's stomach cancer, it can be cured, can't it?' his sister interjected.

'If it's in the early stages. It's all right if we find it in the mucous membranes, but when it spreads it makes it very difficult.'

'Has it spread with this Mrs Nagayama?'

'Yes.'

'Then an operation wouldn't do much good?'

'We won't know until we open her up.'

Eiichi was no longer interested in this discussion. He drank down the tea in his cup, picked up the paper his father had finished reading, and said to his mother, 'Is the bathtub ready?'

'You can get in. I'll turn on the gas if it's cool.'

As he stood up and started out of the room, his father suddenly called to him, 'I want you to cure that woman.'

Eiichi turned around in surprise.

'You see that she's cured.'

'Dad, there's cancer that can be cured and cancer that can't be helped no matter what. A doctor never knows until he opens the patient up.'

Ozu listened as his son went upstairs, then came back downstairs and opened the glass door to the bath.

'Say. . . ,' Ozu's wife looked up at him and asked, 'do you . . . know that woman?'

'Why?'

'No reason. I just all of a sudden felt that you did. . . .'

Ozu said nothing and switched on the television set. A singer with a professional smile was performing on the screen.

Flatfish has summoned her again, Ozu thought. He had not thought he would ever see Aiko again, but perhaps she had turned up again because Flatfish from that other realm had made her do so. But for what reason? For what reason?

'I like this song,' his daughter Yumi muttered as she stared at the television screen. 'Maybe I'll buy the record.'

'Are you going to take your medicine?' His wife filled a glass with water and brought it in. 'Eiichi said thirty minutes after eating.'

The medicine tasted bitter on his tongue. He took another drink of water.

If Flatfish were still alive, would he be sitting like this, surrounded by his family, watching television and chatting idly?

He had been the same age as Ozu, but he had died in the war. And that sort of life was not granted those who died of illnesses on the battleground. But were the survivors happy?

One afternoon several days later, the dispensary chief, Kurihara and Eiichi waited in a conference room of the hospital for a man to arrive. The man was a researcher from the pharmaceutical company owned by Kurihara's father. He was to explain the new drug.

'And I'd like to perform Mrs Aiko Nagayama's operation next week. . . ,' Kurihara, gripping the back of a chair, was explaining to the dispensary chief. 'And in order to study the effectiveness of the new drug after the operation, I'd like to cease administering FU-5 and Mytomycin about five days before the operation.'

'Yes.' Doctor Uchida, who had his little finger in his ear, nodded. 'I'll leave that sort of thing up to you two. You discuss it and then go ahead with it. He's late, isn't he? Our appointment was for 4 o'clock, wasn't it?'

'Yes. They said he'd already left, but the traffic may be heavy.'

'I suppose so.'

'Isn't Doctor Ii coming?' Eiichi asked.

Doctor Uchida smiled wryly. 'It's the Welfare Ministry again. They grabbed him. But Kurihara, I hear you went golfing with Doctor Ii's daughter.'

'Yes.' Kurihara's large face turned slightly red, and he glanced quickly towards Eiichi. 'She asked me to, so I joined her on the course.'

'That was her first time on a course, wasn't it?'

'Yes. But she seems to have spent a lot of time on the practice range.'

'How's her form?'

'Not bad.'

The dispensary chief stood up, put his hands in front of him, and demonstrated his golf form for Kurihara.

The faint evening light shone through the somewhat dirty windows of the conference room, throwing shadows on the large desk and chairs.

Eiichi turned his face and gazed stiffly out of the window, trying to control the violent jealousy and rage that welled up within him because Yoshiko had grown even more intimate with Kurihara than before.

They're probably . . . planning to get engaged.

But I won't let you get away with that so easily, he muttered to himself. I've got a certain photograph in my drawer. The engagement won't come off so smoothly if Yoshiko finds out about the relationship between Kurihara and the nurse Shimada in the photograph. But the problem is when and how to break it to her. . . .

The door opened. A partially balding man came in carrying a briefcase. Perspiration bathed his forehead as he bowed. He was the researcher from the pharmaceutical company.

'Sorry I'm late. The roads were awfully crowded.'

'That's what we figured,' the dispensary chief smiled amiably. 'Well, well, please sit down.'

After he was seated, the researcher busily piled documents and slides on the table.

'This new drug is a further development of the Adliamycin D that you're all familiar with. . . ,' he began to explain. 'But the loss of hair, the inflammation of the mouth, and the decrease in white blood cells caused by Adliamycin are absent here. . . .' He fiddled with the projector and then went on with his explanation. 'These are of our tests with animals. . . .' Illustrating the changes in the tumours after two weeks, three weeks, then one month, he went on, 'We believe that this new drug is more effective than Adliamycin, FU–5, or Z–4828.'

'Have you given this new drug a name yet?'

'No, not yet. In the laboratory, we call it Blaliamycin.'

'That sounds like a cross between Blaomycin and Adliamycin,' Doctor Uchida chuckled. But the researcher's face remained serious.

'In the prevention of the outbreak of cancer, it's more effective than FU–5 in our tests on animals.'

'But what about humans?'

'The problem is the effect on the liver. . . .' Switching on the lights, the researcher again wiped the perspiration from his forehead with a handkerchief.

Questioning continued for almost an hour.

'It seems like it would be best to use it in conjunction with MMC and FU,' Doctor Uchida said, gazing at

Kurihara. He felt it was more effective to use anti-cancer drugs together rather than singly.

'But if we use them together, won't that leave the effectiveness of this new drug open to question?' Kurihara shook his head. 'I'd like to try using just this drug alone on Mrs Nagayama.'

If this drug were used in conjunction with others, they would have no data on this drug alone to report to the medical conventions.

The faint evening sun that earlier had poured into the conference room had now gone completely from the window.

'Well, shall we call it a day?' Patting Eiichi on the shoulder with his right hand, the dispensary chief said, 'We'll get together again and go over your research announcement in detail.'

Eiichi rose and opened the door to the conference room for the researcher, who had gathered up all of his materials ready to leave.

'What are you two doing now? Will you come and have a drink with us?' the dispensary chief invited Kurihara and Eiichi. But Kurihara bowed and replied, 'Sorry, I have to get back early tonight. . . .'

'A date?'

'No, it's not that . . .'

'There's no need to hide it from us.'

The three men walked out into the hallway. When they reached the end of the deserted hall, Kurihara again apologized to Doctor Uchida. The dispensary chief watched as Kurihara's massive, frocked body disappeared down the corridor to the surgical ward. 'He's got a date. I'm sure it's a date.' He stuck his tongue out a bit.

As they left the elevator, Eiichi remarked that he had some work of his own to do and returned to the dispensary. For several minutes he had been stifling the urge to tail Kurihara. He concurred with the dispensary chief's feeling that Kurihara was meeting Yoshiko.

He picked up the telephone in the dispensary and called the nurses' station in the surgery ward.

'Hello? Has Doctor Kurihara been by there?'

'He's just left,' the nurse answered innocently.

'Oh?' Shoes in hand, Eiichi flipped off the lights in the dispensary. He scurried down the dusty hall and headed for the entrance.

He caught sight of Kurihara about fifty feet ahead of him, passing through the main entrance. Kurihara walked with his head slightly bowed, holding onto his shoes just as Eiichi was.

Eiichi stopped. Kurihara was heading for the bus stop in front of the hospital.

'Damn!' thought Eiichi. Kurihara knew that Eiichi always took a train and not a bus. He would think something was going on if Eiichi stood at the same bus stop. 'What am I doing this for, anyway?' Eiichi chided himself. 'It'll just upset me if I see Kurihara with Yoshiko.'

He knew it would upset him. It would wound his pride deeply to see Yoshiko greet Kurihara with a cheerful look or smile. Then what impelled him to follow the two of them?

After Kurihara had stood at the bus stop for a few moments, he suddenly walked away, heading for the taxi stand by the railway station. Eiichi quickened his pace when he saw Kurihara get into a taxi.

'Would you follow them, please?' Eiichi asked when the driver rolled down his window.

'Forget something?' the driver asked.

'Huh?'

'Did the fellow in the taxi up there forget something?'

'Yeah.'

The taxi headed toward Aoyama. They'll probably have dinner for two in some swank restaurant at Aoyama, Eiichi thought. Having no acquaintance with such places, he felt shabby and miserable. His chest prickled with jealousy.

But in the outer gardens of the Meiji Shrine, Kurihara's taxi turned right and drove straight down the road lined with gingko trees.

'Stop!' Eiichi shouted to the driver.

'You wanna stop?'

Eiichi paid the driver and pretended to be strolling along the tree-lined road. He kept an eye on Kurihara's taxi, which had drawn up by an art gallery.

The taxi stopped, but Kurihara did not get out. Instead, a woman who had been standing by the stone steps of the gallery ran quickly up to the taxi.

It was not Yoshiko.

When the woman climbed into the taxi, it sped off towards Harajuku.

If that wasn't Yoshiko . . . maybe it was Shimada?

He couldn't know for sure. But Eiichi was pleased with the result of his pursuit, having observed Kurihara in company with a woman other than Yoshiko.

In the nurses' station there was a blackboard on which the scheduled dates for surgery and the patients' names were recorded in chalk. The following day, the name Aiko Nagayama was entered there.

The life of a patient becomes hectic once surgery is decided upon. Cardiographs and lung capacity tests are repeated, and the central research lab takes another blood test from the ear. This is done not only to determine blood-type, but also to observe the amount of time required for the blood to coagulate once the patient begins to bleed. The blood that comes from the ear is absorbed on a long strip of paper until the flow stops.

The report from the central research lab on Aiko Nagayama concluded that, though there was a slight chance of difficulty with her heart, her overall physical condition would allow for surgery.

'Doctor.'

When Eiichi visited her room four days before the operation, Aiko was sitting up in bed writing a letter. When she noticed him, she put down her pen and note-paper.

'They've stopped giving me my medicine,' she said with a puzzled look.

'Uh-huh,' Eiichi nodded casually. 'We're going to use a new medication. So we've stopped your other medicine for now.'

'A new medication?'

'Yes. We'll use it after the operation. Hasn't Doctor Kurihara talked to you about it?'

Aiko shook her head. But she did not seem particularly suspicious about the change in her medication.

'They tell me I'll be dying for a drink of water after the operation,' she said with a smile.

'That's what everyone says. But everyone else has been able to bear with it, so you can, too.'

'Oh, I'm not worried about that.'

'Are you worried about the operation?'

'Not when I think about the war. We were so used to suffering then. An operation seems like nothing at all.'

The number of potted plants in her room had increased. She seemed to like flowers, and Eiichi had often seen her watering them.

'Will your family be coming for the operation?'

'I haven't a husband or children.' She smiled again. 'But I have some close friends who'll be here.'

'Oh, that's right. Your husband was killed in the war, wasn't he?'

'Yes. He was killed in the navy.'

And you've been alone since then? Eiichi started to ask, but he stopped himself.

'Er . . . ,' she said with an imploring look, 'do you think I could leave the hospital for about three hours before the operation?'

'Leave the hospital? That's a critical period. It would create all kinds of problems if you caught cold. Do you have some important errand?'

'I wanted to set my husband's grave in order before my operation.'

Eiichi gazed at her face in surprise. Set her husband's grave in order before the operation? The action seemed futile and meaningless to him.

The morning of the operation came.

A nurse gave Aiko a light sedative and an injection.

'Now, don't get up. We've had patients take this and think that they're in perfect control of themselves and then when they get up they fall right down again.'

Aiko smiled and nodded, pulling the blanket up to her chin. She was to be operated on soon, but she did not seem especially nervous.

'Are you getting drowsy?' The two friends beside her pillow peered into her face.

'No. Not yet.' Still smiling, she blinked her eyes. 'It was so funny yesterday. This young anaesthetist came and examined me . . .'

' Yes?'

'And with a straight face he asked, "How much *sake* do you drink?" '

'I've heard that anaesthetics don't work well on heavy drinkers.'

Aiko nodded. 'Then the anaesthetic should have taken effect on me right away . . . but it hasn't yet!'

'I don't think that was an anaesthetic. I'm sure they'll give you the real thing in the operating room. Did you sleep well?'

'Yes. . . . And I dreamed about our days at Kōnan.'

Aiko and her two friends began to talk about their days at the girls' school.

'There was that dilapidated old train that ran down the highway. The one we rode on with the boys from Nada Middle School. They always smelled of sweat . . .'

'I wonder what's happened to all our classmates? They're probably all married with children.'

'Those boys used to tail us all the time.'

'They certainly did. But they never were able to find much to say to us.'

'And if we said anything to them, they'd flush bright red and wouldn't be able to say a word. Naïve, weren't we? Back when we were at school?'

'There's no comparison with the high-school students nowadays. Like my son – he'll talk on the phone to his girl friends for hours on end and think nothing of it – even when we're sitting right there!'

'I'm starting to get sleepy.' When Aiko closed her eyes, her two friends went over to the window and looked up at the sky. The day was overcast. In the distance, they could hear the faint rumble of cars and trucks.

'I told her it was a pity she couldn't visit her husband's grave,' one of the friends whispered to the other.

'I don't like the way this hospital has to stick rigidly to the rule book. It wouldn't have hurt to let her just do that.'

'That's right.'

They heard footsteps in the hall. The nurse who had been there earlier came in with another pushing a bed on wheels.

'Well, Mrs Nagayama, let's go to the operating room,' the nurse said, standing by Aiko's pillow. 'Just relax. We'll move you over to this bed.'

Aiko smiled at her friends. 'See you in a while!'

'Good luck! We're going to wait here in your room. Can we do anything for you?'

'Nothing,' Aiko started to say, but then she glanced from her bed at the flower pots that lined the room. 'Well, would you mind watering my flowers?'

In the operating room she could hear the sound of flowing water. The water continuously washed away the dust of the floor and the blood of the patients. The scalpels and tweezers made shrill noises on the glass table. Behind the table stood a nurse clad in a blue surgical robe and wearing a large mask.

The anaesthetist spoke to Aiko. 'There's nothing to worry about. You'll be asleep before long. When you wake up the operation will all be over.' He instructed Aiko to begin counting.

'One. Two. Three,' she muttered in a weak, languorous voice. She quickly fell into a deep sleep.

The operating room was silent again. The flowing water, which reflected the light of the astral lamps, served only to deepen the stillness.

Some ten minutes later, Doctor Uchida, the chief surgeon, and his two assistants, Kurihara and Eiichi, appeared. They wore their white smocks open over rubber aprons, and sandals on their feet. After the nurses placed sterilized gloves on their hands, they lined up beside the sleeping patient.

'Well, now,' the dispensary chief said in a low voice, 'we'll begin the operation. Have all the preparations been made?'

'Blood pressure gauges and intravenous tubes are all set,' Eiichi replied.

The nurse picked up a piece of cotton with her tweezers, soaked it in tincture of iodine, and silently daubed it on Aiko's body.

'Scalpel.'

Taking the electric scalpel in his gloved right hand, Doctor Uchida bent forward slightly. There was a sizzling sound. A line of white fat shot up, and in that instant Eiichi saw the murky blood gush forth. With a rattling sound, Kurihara quickly clamped off the veins and Eiichi tied them off with thread.

An intravenous needle was inserted in Aiko's leg, and

through the rubber tube a liquid containing cardiacs, vitamins and adrenalin surged continually into her body.

'Blood pressure?'

'Normal.'

He had already cut the xiphisternum open. The doctor brought the scalpel to a stop slightly to the left of Aiko's inverted navel. He proceeded to open up her peritoneum.

'Blood pressure and heart?'

'No change.'

The sky was overcast. In the hospital, the outpatients sat as always in the waiting-room with weary expressions on their faces. There were audible cries of children and infants. In Aiko's room, her two friends continued to chatter in low voices.

'And then he started to drown. That student from Nada. . . .'

'Couldn't he swim?'

'I guess not. It caused a big scene. . . . He really seemed to like her. . . .'

'Didn't he know that Aiko already had a fiancé?'

'I don't think so. Why, she hardly knew anything about him, after all.'

'Of course. When you consider the way students at Nada Middle School were in those days. . .' She looked at her wrist watch. 'It hasn't even been two hours yet.'

12 The Pen

Half a year after the end of the war.

Ozu returned to Japan, crossing back over the same black ocean he had seen through the rain when he was sent to the battle front. The filthy cargo ship was crammed with Japanese soldiers, the same crestfallen expression on every face. Deprived of their weapons and stripped even of the collar insignias that indicated their ranks, they had had all dignity and pride wiped from their faces. The exhausted soldiers squatted here and there on the deck of the ship, clasping their knees.

Still, they could take comfort in the fact that they had been captured by the communist Chinese armies. Those from the same barracks who had been sent to Northern Manchuria were captured by Soviet troops and transported to Siberia.

They arrived in Maizuru on a rainy day. After they were inspected at the demobilization headquarters, the soldiers were placed on trains that resembled cattle cars and sent to their respective homes.

The landscape in all directions was a charred wasteland. From the station where their crowded train screeched to a halt, the soldiers could see burned-out ruins and the figures of men and women bearing knapsacks on their backs.

'I never thought we'd come to this,' a friend whispered to Ozu, laughter and tears blended on his face.

Ozu said farewell to his friend and returned to his home from Osaka Station.

His own house had been lucky enough to survive the bombing, but it was in a far worse state of deterioration than he had ever imagined as he sat in his barracks.

The garden plot his father had once acquired was now a field. The air-raid shelters were still standing. The wall around his house had crumbled in places. He was told it had been damaged by blast winds when the nearby aircraft factory was bombed the previous year.

'We were scared out of our wits that day,' his mother said, looking out over the field still covered with lingering snow. 'I heard a sound like an express train going over a steel bridge, and then the house started to shake like there was an earthquake, and the wall collapsed right before my eyes. Your father had gone out and I was all alone. I couldn't even run for the air-raid shelter.'

Even though Ozu had been a soldier, because he had been stationed in Dairen he had had no direct contact with actual battles or air raids. Dairen was momentarily occupied by Soviet forces, but they later turned it over to the Chinese communists. He could say that he had been lucky in many respects.

Classes had not yet started up again at the university, as over half the school buildings had been burned.

Black market operations began to line the streets of Osaka and Kobe. There men like Ozu, dressed in their repatriate uniforms, loitered about with sacks of food slung over their shoulders. Exhaustion, hopelessness and futility were etched on each of their faces.

One day, on the spur of the moment, Ozu visited Flatfish's home. But the neighbourhood of the little house he remembered so well was now a wilderness of ashes. The winter wind blew up debris from among the rubble.

He sat down on a pile of rubble and thought about each of the things he had lost.

Flatfish. That bleary-eyed friend of his. Remembering that his friend was no longer alive, Ozu suddenly could not control the tears that spilled from his eyes.

He hadn't been a bad fellow. He hadn't been brilliant or outstanding, but he had been one of Ozu's closest friends. No. He was my only friend, Ozu thought as he wiped away the tears with the palm of his hand.

Ozu could hardly loaf about until school started.

Many of his repatriated comrades had had their homes burned to the ground. Ozu heard that they had got part-time jobs, and he followed suit.

Many kinds of jobs were available. They joined together and formed a Students' Co-operative Union. They stocked up on unusual soaps, tea kettles and bread ovens from factories in Osaka and Amagasaki, and walked around the streets selling them. Any available goods could be sold in those days, so their items were in stunningly high demand.

Ozu joined in with his friends. With a knapsack slung over his back, he delivered their wares to the black markets. They packaged their fish-oil soap in wrapping paper imprinted with foreign words, and wrote 'MADE IN USA' on the packages. This was easily mistaken for 'MADE IN U.S.A.,' so the soap sold well.

Ozu became a familiar face in the black markets, and he picked up the habit of drinking *sake* with his friends. Reed-screened bars lined the alleyways behind the black markets, and there the uniformed repatriates piled fried whale meat on their plates and guzzled cups of cheap *sake*.

When evening came, Ozu could be found sitting with his friends in the reed-screened bars, watching the noisy crowds go by as he sipped the strong-smelling *sake*. And he thought of Flatfish and Aiko. From time to time, MPs in white metal helmets appeared in the black markets or the bars. They were on the lookout for street walkers.

It was one day in March.

Finished with their part-time jobs for the day, Ozu and a friend were, as usual, standing in one of the reed-screened bars having a drink. Suddenly there was a clamour of voices and the sound of footsteps.

'We can't help it – there's nothing to eat!'

The patter of footsteps mingled with the shouts of a man and the shrieks of women. Two women scampered into the bar.

'A raid?' the old barkeeper asked. 'Is it the Americans? Or the Japanese cops?'

'The cops,' one of the women answered. 'They found out we were hiding some black-market rice.'

There were occasional raids on the black markets. Ozu and the other students were safe, since they did not deal in rice. But people who carried black-market rice from the farms in knapsacks or kerchiefs were raided and carted off by the police.

The faces of the two women were bound in kerchiefs. They squatted in one corner of the reed-screened bar with their backs to the customers. Ozu and his friend stood to their side to shield them from view and ate their fried bean sprouts.

Two policemen tramped from bar to bar for a while, but then they seemed to give up and disappeared.

'It's all right now.'

'Thanks, mister.'

The two kerchiefed women brushed off the knees of their trousers. They gave the barkeeper twenty yen to thank him for hiding them and made for the door.

Just then, the eyes of one of the women met Ozu's.

'Oh!' she cried, stopping in her tracks. 'Mr Ozu!'

It was Flatfish's older sister. . . .

'To think that you've seen me like this!' She removed the kerchief from her face. Flatfish's sister was self-conscious about the men's trousers she was wearing. But Ozu himself was wearing a threadbare repatriate uniform. 'I didn't think I'd ever see you again.'

'I went to your home. But the whole area's burned out. Is your mother all right?'

'She's fine. She lives with me now.'

Ozu's friend and the woman with Flatfish's sister stood

at the front of the bar and listened as these two talked.

'This is a friend of my brother's from his middle-school days. I'm sorry, Toshi, but why don't you go on ahead?' Flatfish's sister said. When the two of them were alone, she said to Ozu, 'It's filthy, but . . . would you like to come over to my place? There's something of my brother's that I'd like you to have.'

A train rumbled across the elevated tracks. Below, a murky stream of water flowed along a cement wall. A tramp was leaning against the wall, gazing absently at the passers-by.

'If my brother was still alive, he'd probably give me a tongue-lashing, but . . . I can't give any thought to the way I look when there's only me to take care of mother.'

Flatfish's sister still felt uncomfortable about her attire and the fact that she was a peddler. Ozu remembered the way she had looked the night she served *sake* at the going-away party when Flatfish was drafted.

'I heard that he died of an illness at the front. . . . What kind of illness was it?' Ozu asked.

'It was pneumonia. We got a letter from a man in the same regiment. . . . He said that Flatfish died two days after they put him in the army hospital.'

'So it was . . . pneumonia.'

He imagined Flatfish's feeble body. The young soldiers ran around outside in the cold while the senior officers warmed themselves by the stoves in the barracks.

'The winter in Korea must've been cold,' Ozu sighed involuntarily. The winters had also been severe in Dairen, which was much like Korea. The chill there was not simply 'cold' – it was actually physically painful.

'He really put his whole heart into it.' He had no other words of comfort for Flatfish's sister. As they walked along, she held a corner of her kerchief to her mouth to stifle her sobs.

Crossing over a burned-out area, Flatfish's sister led him to a faintly-lit shack. The shack was assembled from the walls of a burned-out garage, with a tin roof.

'Mother!' she called out at the front. 'Mother!'

Ozu recognized the face of Flatfish's mother that appeared at the window, but her hair had turned snow-white.

'I remember you, Mr Ozu! It's Mr Ozu, isn't it?' Her composure crumbled and tears flooded her eyes.

Flatfish's sister led Ozu inside.

'I'm ashamed of the place. It's so filthy. . . .' She hurriedly gathered up the teacups and chopsticks on the low tea table and moved away the charcoal brazier set beside it. A framed photograph of Flatfish was tacked to a wooden panel on the wall.

'If that boy were alive now . . . I don't think we'd have come to this . . .,' Flatfish's mother, seated beside Ozu, lamented.

'Mother, how many times do I have to tell you to stop repeating nonsense like that?' Flatfish's sister said loudly. 'Mr Ozu. Here are the things my brother left behind.'

The knot on the faded checker kerchief bundle she produced was tightly fastened. When she untied it in the dim light, a wallet, and the suit and necktie that Flatfish had worn on the day of his induction appeared.

'Then there's some other things that one of his army friends brought us.'

Ozu instinctively brought his palms together reverently over Flatfish's suit. He could see his friend, proudly wearing this suit when he got off the train on the platform at Sannomiya Station.

'His army friend brought us the pen and notebook that he used.'

'His pen? Could I see it?'

'Sure.' She stood and opened a box on top of the small desk in the corner. 'Here it is.'

It was the fountain pen he remembered. It was a fountain pen he could not have forgotten even had he tried.

'Ah,' he said softly. 'Flatfish used this . . . a lot.'

'Please take it.' Flatfish's sister stared intently at Ozu's profile. 'We have nothing else to give you to remember him by. . . . Please take this, Mr Ozu.'

'You don't have to . . .'

'It's all right. I think it would please my brother for you to use it.'

Ozu raised the pen reverently to his forehead and then put it in his inside pocket. 'Then I'll accept it.'

'Why don't you take his notebook, too?'

Ozu shook his head. He could hardly take away two of the few remaining articles that still had the smell of Flatfish about them.

But Flatfish's sister said, 'No, really. It's painful for us to have the notebook around to remind us of him.'

In the faint light, Ozu thumbed through the notebook.

It was mostly blank pages, but in the address section, the names and address of his acquaintances were written. There were also several pages that seemed to be something like a diary.

Then on one page Ozu noticed a sort of map drawn in Flatfish's hand.

It was the Ashiya River area. Ozu deciphered some scribbled characters that said, 'Pine Trees'; 'Bridge'; and then : 'Aiko's House'.

Ozu put the notebook down.

It was already pitch black outside when he left Flatfish's home, taking the pen and notebook with him. The wind was blowing across the burned-out ruins. When he looked up at the sky, the winter stars were shining brightly. An indescribable feeling of despair clutched at Ozu's chest. He could not imagine what had brought on this wave of despair.

Why do good guys like Flatfish have to die? He was stifled by feelings of anger he could not vent. But that was not all there was to his anger.

Why do pure and simple people like Flatfish have to

die? But these feelings were not the source of his despair.

A plain, unassuming fellow. A fellow maybe a little cunning, but one who, somewhere in his heart, embraced a purity that made him treasure the first love of his youth. Fellows like that probably existed everywhere in the world. But this particular fellow died in the war, leaving behind him only the suit he wore, a pen and a notebook.

Doesn't that . . . make you . . . sad? Ozu felt like shouting to the stars in the sky.

I don't feel sad when a strong man or a hero dies. But I mourn when a fellow like Flatfish dies. It's unbearably sad precisely because he was the sort of fellow you can find anywhere.

The tramp, leaning just as before against the cement wall by the trickle of murky water that flowed beneath the railway overpass, had fallen asleep. Just beyond the overpass, a soldier dressed in white leaned on a pinewood cane and pumped an accordion.

> 'The apple doesn't say a word,
> But I know how the apple feels.'

With that weary voice echoing behind him, Ozu hurried to the station. In the dim lights of the platform he took out the pen. Its colour had not faded, and it looked just the way it had the day he received it from Aiko. Except that traces of black ink were caked on the nib.

He turned first to the address section as he flipped through the notebook. Flatfish had written Ozu's name and address in a clumsy scrawl. He looked for Aiko's name, but for some reason he could not find it.

Announcements from PFC Uchiyama after manoeuvres.
Assembled at 2 :30 p.m.
Gist of instructions : strict regulations and a fighting
   spirit.

Indecipherable scribblings of this sort were scattered throughout the pages.

The platform was almost deserted. A single station attendant came down the stairs and walked to the front of the platform.

'AMUZAOKIA.'

The letters suddenly caught Ozu's eye. He cocked his head at the unknown word. It was like telegraphic code. But he soon unravelled the mystery.

Aiko Azuma. With loving care, Flatfish had written her name backwards. He must have considered the possibility that his squadron leader or a senior officer might discover his notebook.

You idiot. . . .

Ozu suddenly felt impelled to return the pen to Aiko, no matter how much effort it took. AMUZAOKIA. He had to convey to Aiko the pain that Flatfish had endured, stealthily copying down those nine letters as he sat in his barracks, another beating from his senior officers imminent.

He had not got off the train at Nigawa for three years. But the station and the surrounding area had not changed much in those three years. The small white river flowing in front of the station, the cream-coloured houses that lined the river, and the round Mount Kabuto opposite the river were just as they had been.

He still remembered the way. After walking a short way through the pine grove he would come to a pond. He remembered that someone at the bakery shop in front of the station had told him the Nagayama home was just beside the pond.

There were no boats visible on the winter-wasted pond. It appeared to have been neglected during the war. The sign reading 'Benten Pond' and the house beside it were in a shambles.

And the name on Aiko's house was different. He could

not determine whether there was any relationship between the Nagayama family and the Uchiboris whose name now appeared on the door.

He roamed around the neighbourhood for a few minutes and then decided to ring the bell. He pushed the doorbell several times, but no one answered. There appeared to be no one at home.

He returned to the station and slid open the glass door of the bakery.

'Who is it?' A weak voice, perhaps that of someone who had been sleeping, answered from within. Ozu glanced around the shop, but there was no bread to be seen. There was only a bicycle parked in the entranceway.

A middle-aged woman came out. 'We don't run the bakery any more,' she explained with regret, opening the glass a little. 'We still can't get any of the ingredients.'

'No, you see, there used to be a house belonging to the Nagayamas over by the pond, didn't there? Do you know where they've moved to?'

He thought of a children's story called 'Searching for Mother' that he had read when he was a boy. A boy separated from his mother wanders from place to place searching for her. But each time he reaches a city, his mother has moved on to another place. . . .

'Nagayama? Killed in the war, I heard. . . .'

'Killed in the war?'

'Yes. In the navy, wasn't he?'

Ozu remembered the tanned face of the naval cadet dressed in a white uniform and carrying a short sword on the bridge over the Ashiya River that day.

'Then his wife has been widowed?'

'That's right. Sad, isn't it?'

'Where did his wife go?'

'To wherever she was evacuated, I suppose.'

'She was evacuated?'

Now I've got to set off somewhere else far away, he thought. On his way back from visiting her here once before, he had muttered to himself, This is it. I'm not doing anything else for him!

Yet even now he seemed to hear the bleary-eyed Flatfish pleading from behind him, 'Hey, please don't say that. Please take the pen to where she's been evacuated.'

The woman at the bakery went inside to look for a postcard she had received from Aiko. She remembered that Aiko's evacuation address had been written on the card which had arrived a year and a half before. It turned out to be a tiny village named Shūzan to the north of Kyoto.

One afternoon several days later, Ozu boarded a bus that crossed over the Northern Hills from Kyoto. His destination was the village of Shūzan, where Aiko was still living with her parents since the evacuation.

The sky was veiled with thick clouds. From time to time the weak winter sun shone upon the mountains. When the bus left the northern outskirts of Kyoto and finally entered a ravine, it was already dark. Hills densely grown with Kitayama cypress pressed in on either side. Blackened snows still clung to the hillsides.

It was cold on the bus. The handful of passengers sat with gloomy expressions, abandoning themselves to the violent motions of the bus. The meandering road was narrow and rough. They felt they were moving into mountainous country.

Ozu turned up the collar of his worn overcoat and peered intently at the ice-covered valley streams and the forests of slender Kitayama cypress that were visible from time to time.

They passed through several tiny mountain villages. There were lumber mills resembling cattle sheds between the houses roofed with straw or shingles. Women were working there alongside the men.

After panting slowly up the mountain road for almost

an hour, the bus finally reached the summit. Ozu still found it hard to believe that Aiko was now living in these dark, desolate mountain recesses. Every so often he reached into his pocket and ran his fingers across the fountain pen.

When the bus crossed over the summit and started downhill again, he saw a village lying in a basin bathed with faint sunlight. This was the Shūzan Basin where Aiko lived.

The bus drove through the basin and along a road surrounded by hills in such a way that it resembled the mouth of a valley. If the address he had received from the woman at the Nigawa bakery was not mistaken, Aiko was living along this road near the Jōshōkō Temple.

The old bus left Ozu there alone and started off, trailing dust behind it. Ozu climbed up a sloping road, wading through the frozen snow that still clung to both its banks.

The main gate of the Jōshōkō Temple came into view. The stone steps of the temple were sporadically visible on a slope enclosed with trees. Ozu knew nothing about the history of this temple.

He looked at his watch when he finally reached a farmhouse with a gate to one side. If he missed the return bus at four o'clock, he would not be able to get back to Kyoto.

Hearing his footsteps, a black dog tied up in the garden barked viciously.

At the sound of the barking, the glass door of the farmhouse opened and an old woman wearing an apron came out.

'Is this the Nagayama home?' Ozu asked.

"Mrs Nagayama lives behind here. Are you looking for the missus? She went up to the temple a little while ago. She's copying the sutras.'

Ozu thanked the woman and climbed the stone steps to the temple. The cold air was stretched like a bowstring between the trees in the grove. There was the shrill cry of a bird from time to time.

When he reached the top, he saw a pond and a small statue of Kannon enshrined there. The roof of the temple was visible still further up.

As he started up towards the temple, a woman appeared at the top of the steps.

It was Aiko. She was wearing plain pantaloons and carrying a cloth bundle in her hand.

'Ah!' Ozu cried. She stopped and looked down at him warily. A blush of surprise flashed across her face as she stood there motionless.

The two faced each other across the stone steps in silence for a moment.

'I'm Ozu. Do you remember me?' he shouted.

'Yes,' she nodded.

'I looked for you at your house, and I was told that you were at this temple. . . . I have to go back on the four o'clock bus. There's something I'd like to give you.'

He reached into his pocket and slowly climbed the steps.

'It's been a long time,' Aiko said, bowing politely.

Standing there in her shabby pantaloons, she bore no resemblance to her youthful self. The invisible anguish of her life seemed to ooze from her face and from the hands that held the bundle.

'This is . . .' Ozu started to say, but he swallowed his words. 'I heard that your husband passed away.'

'Yes.'

'And you've been here . . . ever since . . .?'

'Yes. This has been my home since before the war ended.'

The faint sun once again shone from between the clouds. A tiny snowflake drifted down from somewhere. Aiko lifted her head as though to catch the snowflake and looked up at the sky.

'You work in the fields?' he asked on impulse, noticing the scars on her fingers.

'My father and mother are so old, you see. But you've come back from the war, too, haven't you?' She lowered her gaze to Ozu's army boots.

They went down the stairs and sat on a bench beside the pond. Caught by the wind, another tiny snowflake blew past them.

'It's cold here, isn't it?' Ozu muttered.

'It is. The basin is surrounded by mountains.'

'You've changed, haven't you, Aiko?'

'It's not just me. It was a long war.'

'When I was in the army, I thought a lot about Nada Middle School.'

She smiled and was silent for a moment. Then she muttered, 'I wonder if that train on the highway's still running?'

'It's running! It's older and slower than ever.'

'I miss that train, and the neighbourhood around the school.'

'We never thought we'd end up like this, did we? We were so carefree.'

'Mmm.'

'How's your child doing?'

Aiko shook her head sadly at Ozu's question.

'He died of pneumonia. . . .'

'Pneumonia?'

'Mmm.'

It seemed to Ozu that every source of human happiness had vanished during the war. There was not a single Japanese who had not lost something. All had seen homes burned, parents killed, and relatives vanish.

'Do you remember . . . Flatfish?'

'Yes. What's he doing now?'

'He's dead. Him, too.'

'Oh, no!' Surprise and sorrow flashed across her eyes.

'He died of an illness on the battlefield in Korea.' Ozu reached into his pocket and took out the paper-wrapped pen. 'Do you remember this. . . ?'

She was staring with hollow eyes at the surface of the lake. Word of Flatfish's death must have reminded her of the day her husband was killed.

'Do you remember this?' Ozu repeated, and she finally collected herself. 'It's the pen. The one you once gave to Flatfish. He prized it until the day he died. . . .'

Her brow clouded over, and she listened carefully to Ozu's broken words.

'He . . . in his notebook . . . he drew a map of the Ashiya River area. The rows of pine trees. And the bridge. And your house. Do you understand why? He was an idiot. Every painful day he spent as a green soldier, that's how he consoled himself. By drawing maps of Ashiya with the pen you gave him. . . .'

A thin snowflake grazed the shoulder of Ozu's worn overcoat and landed on Aiko's cheek. The sky, faintly illuminated for a brief moment, was once more darkly veiled with clouds.

'This . . . used to belong to you. . . . Now it's a remembrance of him.'

Silently she took the small package.

'I feel better about this now. . . .' Ozu forced a smile.

This tiny little pen had passed from Aiko to Flatfish, crossed over from Japan to Korea, returned again to Japan, and now came back to Aiko.

'A lot has happened, hasn't it?' Ozu looked at his watch. 'It's time for the bus. I have to go.'

'Thank you very much.' Aiko bowed unexpectedly. 'Thank you for coming all this way up into the mountains.'

Together they descended the steps, passed through the temple gate, and walked to the bus stop.

Beyond the fields and hills still covered with snow, they could make out the cold and desolate Northern Hills. The only way to return to Kyoto was to cross those peaks shrouded with dark cypress.

'Won't you be coming back to the Hanshin area?'

'I really don't know.'

They caught sight of the bus moving slowly towards them from the distance. I'll never see her again, Ozu thought. He would not be seeing her again, just as he could never see Flatfish again.

'Take care of yourself,' Ozu said as the bus came to a stop.

'You too,' Aiko answered.

He boarded the bus, which was empty but for two passengers, and it moved quickly away. Beyond the grimy window, Aiko in her pantaloons was smiling sadly. She soon disappeared from sight. . . .

13 The New Drug

The doors to the operating theatre opened, and a stretcher surrounded by four nurses came out. The transfusion bottles and oxygen tubes made Aiko's sleeping figure seem part of a machine.

The stretcher moved silently down the long, lighted hallway. Here and there, visitors to the hospital pressed against the walls, as though some fearsome being were passing by.

Aiko's two friends were waiting anxiously at the door to her room.

'Thank you very much,' one of them bowed to the nurses.

'Aiko's all right, isn't she?'

'She'll be just fine now.'

But Aiko's pale face did not move a muscle. Beneath the vinyl tent that covered the bed, a nurse busily wrapped the strap of a blood-pressure gauge around the patient's arm. A new tank of oxygen was brought in.

After removing his surgical uniform and showering, Eiichi visited her room. He listened to her heartbeat with his stethoscope and then lightly slapped her cheeks with his hand.

'Mrs Nagayama. Mrs Nagayama!'

Aiko drowsily opened her eyes a crack.

'The operation is over.'

'Thank you. . . ,' she muttered, moving her parched lips. 'Thank you . . . very much.'

Aiko drifted back into unconsciousness. Eiichi injected a cardiac and the anti-cancer drug Blaliamycin into her arm. Instructions from the research lab at the pharmaceutical company stated that an intravenous injection of 100 to 200 milligrams of this drug daily would be effective.

Work, damn it! Eiichi thought earnestly as he inserted the hypodermic into her thin, white arm. This just had to be more effective than Blaomycin or Adliamycin. Then I'll be remembered in medical circles . . . as the first one to use this drug!

Once again he imagined the massive lecture hall where their announcement would be made. The audience packed into the tiered classroom. At the front is a row of doctors from various universities. There are audible exclamations of surprise as he and Kurihara present their findings. From that moment on, his name would be engraved in the memories of each of these doctors.

'I'll be here in the hospital all night.' Handing the hypodermic to a nurse, he turned to Aiko's friends. 'There's nothing at all to worry about, so you might as well go home. A veteran nurse will be in to look at her every thirty minutes.'

'But we've already decided to take turns staying with her.'

'You have? Well then, if there's the slightest change in her condition, push that button there. And, just as a precaution, don't give her any water to drink.'

'All right.'

Eiichi and the nurse went out.

'Isn't he terrific?' one of Aiko's friends sighed. 'He's so young, but he's so confident and dependable. . . . I wish I'd married a doctor.'

'Yes, I know. It's such a relief to hear him say there's nothing to worry about.'

That night, Eiichi looked in on Aiko twice every three hours. Near midnight, she awoke from her anaesthetic once again, but there seemed to be nothing abnormal. Injections of camphor and glucose were administered according to schedule.

'Why don't you get some rest now?' Eiichi cordially encouraged Aiko's friends again before he returned to the night shift room. As he rolled up the sleeves on his white shirt and was washing his hands, the phone rang.

It was Kurihara.

'How's she coming along? I haven't heard a peep from you, so I figured there weren't any problems.' Kurihara chided Eiichi for not keeping in touch with him, then asked for details of Aiko's condition. 'I see. That's good news. You didn't forget to give her the new drug, did you?'

'Of course not!'

'Good work.' Kurihara uttered his first words of praise to Eiichi. Then, as though he had suddenly remembered something, 'Did you know Tahara's coming to town today?'

'Tahara?'

'Yeah. I understand that's what he told Doctor Uchida in a postcard.'

'I wonder what he's coming for?'

'Who knows? To report on his work up there, maybe.'

Eiichi was no longer interested in Tahara. Even the news that Tahara was returning to Tokyo after a long absence evoked no feelings of nostalgia in Eiichi. Tahara no longer had anything to do with Eiichi's life. But it incensed him to be coerced into working the night shift and then forced to give progress reports over the phone to the condescending Kurihara. But that was standard procedure at the dispensary, so he had no choice.

When he awoke in the night shift room after a short nap, it was already morning. To a patient who has just been through an operation, and to her friends who have endured a long, painful night, nothing is more welcome than the first flickers of light at the windows as day breaks.

When Eiichi entered the room, Aiko's two friends stood up as though greatly relieved.

'Doctor!'

'She's had a fever all night.'

'It's all right. It's a fever that occurs after surgery.' Eiichi read the charts hanging on the bed. 'She's making good progress,' he comforted them. 'Has she wanted any water?'

'No. Not at all. She seems to have borne up well.'

This is a persevering woman, Eiichi thought. Most patients crave water after an operation. Men especially were insistent. But the nurse reported that Aiko had requested neither water nor an injection to relieve the pain.

Eiichi left the room. Aiko, who had been lying with her eyes closed, spoke softly to her friends. 'Thank you.'

'Were you awake? You're doing just fine, so don't worry.'

'I had a dream. About my husband.'

In her dream, Aiko had seen her husband standing alone on the deck of a cruiser crossing the rough sea. He wore his pure white uniform and stood with his hands on his hips. With a stern face, he stared far off into the distance. Aiko called to him, but he did not turn towards her.

He was walking down the congested hall on his way back to the dispensary.

In the crowd of nurses and patients, Eiichi caught sight of Tahara walking towards him.

Eiichi had not seen him for some time. Tahara was still wearing the same shabby clothes and carrying the same battered shoes in his right hand. But there was a somehow cheerful expression on his face that had not been there when he was banished from the city.

Tahara advanced without noticing Eiichi until Eiichi

shouted, 'Hey!' Tahara blinked in surprise and smiled, revealing a missing tooth.

'It's been a while.' Eiichi held out his hand. 'I heard last night from Kurihara that you were coming in. But I didn't think I'd run into you so soon.'

'I took the night train and got into Ueno at six this morning. I just dropped by the dispensary, but they said you'd had an operation yesterday.'

'Yeah. Stomach,' Eiichi answered vaguely. 'How long'll you be in Tokyo?'

'Four or five days. I've got several things to take care of. Our head nurse walked out on us and I've got to find a replacement for her. And I have to get my hands on an X-ray machine. . . .' Tahara's voice was filled with animation. From his lively tone it was clear that the hospital in the North-east, although small, had entrusted Tahara with work requiring responsibility and that he felt a real sense of purpose in performing it.

'Can't you find a head nurse up there?'

'We'd really like a veteran from Tokyo. To make matters worse, there's a real shortage of doctors and nurses in the provinces.'

'We're even short of nurses here. Have you found someone?'

'Kurihara tells me there's a good person here. She's in Ear and Nose now, but she's worked in both Internal Medicine and Surgery. Her name's Shimada. . . . Do you know her?' Tahara asked innocently. In his innocence, he did not detect the spark of surprise that flickered in Eiichi's eyes.

'Shimada!' Eiichi cried.

'That's right. Do you know her?'

'No, I . . . don't know her.'

'She's supposed to be a veteran. According to Kurihara.'

Eiichi recalled every word of Kurihara's phone call the previous night. He had acted as though he knew nothing about Tahara's purpose for coming to Tokyo or about their discussion about nurses.

So that's what was going on. The bastard . . . now that she's in his way, he's driving Nurse Shimada out of the hospital!

Under the pretext of recommending her as a head nurse, Kurihara was adroitly whisking Nurse Shimada out of the hospital. Because she'd got in the way. Because she was an obstacle to his marriage with Yoshiko.

He's got that boyish face . . . but he's more cunning than I thought.

You won't get away with this, Eiichi thought, swallowing and lowering his eyes. He quickly pondered the best course of action. At that moment an ingenious plan sprang into his head.

Since he had been on night shift the previous evening, and since there was nothing abnormal about Aiko's progress, he invited Tahara to an *oden* shop near the hospital that evening.

The good-natured Tahara's face reddened after two or three cups of *sake*.

'To tell you the truth, I was miserable at the time, but now I'm glad I went to the North-east.' Tahara tediously repeated these words several times during the conversation. Eiichi realized he was speaking honestly, and that this was not the sour grapes of a loser.

'It's true that "Fortune waits beyond the hills of home." ' Tahara poured himself another cup of *sake* that he could not hope to down. 'The countryside suits me to a tee. Of course, when you go out to a place where there aren't many doctors, you've got the old women and the complaining brides to put up with. But – what can I say? – there's something there that lets two hearts reach out and touch each other.'

Eiichi nodded in assent, painfully conscious of the time.

'Listen,' he said to Tahara, who was licking his chopsticks, 'shall we try a change of scenery?'

'Huh?'

'There's no atmosphere in this *oden* place. I hear they've opened up a great snack shop just down the road. Let's go there.'

'I feel out of place in high-class places like that.'

'Don't worry about it. You've come all the way to Tokyo, and I've just finished up an operation. Let's call up a nurse, and the three of us'll go and have a drink.' He glanced at his watch and decided that Keiko would still be in the internal medicine ward. His real reason for asking Tahara out was so that he could bring Keiko here.

He telephoned, and Keiko was at the nurses' station in the internal medicine ward, just as he had thought.

'Hurry over here. You remember Tahara, don't you? We're having a drink together, and we're thinking of going over to the snack shop now.'

Keiko uttered an exclamation of surprise at the invitation from Eiichi, but she agreed to join them right away. Eiichi returned to his seat.

'Who'd you call?' Tahara asked.

'Imai in Internal. Do you know her?'

'Let's see. I'd probably recognize her if I saw her. . . .'

When Keiko arrived, the three hurried out of the *oden* shop and walked towards the newly-opened snack shop.

'Tahara here . . . .' As they walked along shoulder to shoulder, Eiichi abruptly spoke up in a deliberately cheerful voice. 'He's come to Tokyo to find a head nurse for his hospital.'

'It's rather like looking for a wife.' Tahara had no inkling why Eiichi had brought the subject up.

'Wouldn't you like to go?' Eiichi taunted Keiko.

'You mean you'd be kind enough to recommend me?' Keiko answered acidly. Eiichi could read her thoughts clearly.

'I give up!' Eiichi shook his head exaggeratedly. "'Cause Kurihara's recommended Miss Shimada. I think it's already decided.' He paused for a moment. 'Rumour has it that Kurihara might be marrying Doctor Ii's daughter,' he added off-handedly. Keiko's face turned sharply towards him.

How's my luck going to run on this little gamble? He prayed that things would turn out as he hoped.

Eiichi said nothing further on the subject. Keiko as usual pretended that nothing had happened.

'You have all kinds of different experiences in the provinces.' Even at the snack shop. Tahara evinced no interest in the modish surroundings and continued to gabble about his hospital. 'Now say you put an old woman with TB in the prefectural hospital. The treatment she gets there will be impeccable, but her recovery, on the other hand, will be slower. That's because old women get so upset spending every day in a big, impressive, antiseptic hospital that it wears them out. So when you send them back to the countryside, they get better right away!'

'Could be,' Eiichi nodded, stifling a yawn. He had no more use for Tahara. He had brought this fellow along only so that he could say what he had said to Keiko. . . .

'It's true! That's why it's always seemed to me that medicine isn't just a matter of drugs and technical skill. It concerns the heart! Lately I've decided that a good doctor is one who can help a hopeless patient to die happily. We've got good doctors like that at our hospital in Fukushima. None of the big-wigs in the intellectual circles know about them, but I have to bow in respect when I see them dealing with their patients.'

'What do you mean?'

'It's . . . because they have sympathy. If he's got a doctor like that working on him and there's *still* no hope, a patient feels like it doesn't matter if he dies.'

Eiichi suddenly thought of Aiko Nagayama. This new

drug *has* to be effective. Then in the medical circles he . . .

'Well, I'd better be going.'

When they left the snack shop Tahara got on a bus, leaving Eiichi and Keiko alone together.

'The right man in the right place – that's Tahara for you,' Eiichi muttered. 'I'll bet that bored you, didn't it?'

'Oh, not at all!' Keiko answered caustically. 'I wasn't the least bit bored. I figured out right away why you'd asked me to come.'

Eiichi feigned ignorance and put a cigarette in his mouth. A taxi stopped beside them, then drove off again when they did not get in.

'You wanted me to tell Nurse Shimada about Kurihara and Doctor Ii's daughter, didn't you?'

'I don't know what you're talking about.'

'You're terrible. You stalk your prey just like a viper. You hate Doctor Kurihara, don't you? You want to kick him out of your way. You'd like to upset his marriage plans, wouldn't you?'

'That's not funny. Don't let your absurd delusions make me into a villain.'

'You really did want to ship me off to the North-east, didn't you? Like Doctor Kurihara is doing with Nurse Shimada. . . .'

'Oh, honestly. That really makes me cross!'

Keiko stopped and peered into Eiichi's face. 'Women are such fools. I can't give you up, even knowing how rotten you are.'

'If you loved me. . . ,' Eiichi muttered half to himself as he crushed out his cigarette with his shoe, 'you'd help me make a name for myself.'

'Fine. I'll tell Nurse Shimada all about it. In return, I want . . .'

On the afternoon of the third day after the operation, Aiko developed a slight nausea. Her eyes had not turned yellow, so they could not yet be certain whether it was a symptom of jaundice. Eiichi felt sure it was a reaction to the new anti-cancer drug.

'What should we do?' Eiichi consulted with Kurihara to see if they should continue injections of the new drug or not.

'Let's see,' Kurihara cocked his head uncertainly. 'The Old Man makes his rounds tomorrow, doesn't he?'

'Yes.'

'Well then, continue the injections for the rest of today. If she still seems nauseated, we'll report it to the Old Man when he comes around and let him decide.'

Eiichi could understand how Kurihara felt. Like Eiichi Kurihara wanted to see this new drug succeed. He wanted to continue the injections even though the patient had some reaction to them, choosing to regard the reaction as an unrelated matter.

Doctor Ii made his rounds the following day. With one hand thrust into the pocket of his white smock, he followed his usual pattern, walking ahead of the dispensary chief and the staff workers, visiting each room and calming the anxieties of the women patients and sharply scolding the young patients who lacked the right attitude to their convalescence. Meanwhile the supervising interns stood nervously at attention.

When he entered Aiko's room, Doctor Ii stopped and purposely praised the flowers in pots around her bed. 'They're opening up beautifully!'

'She loves flowers,' one of Aiko's friends answered.

'Don't you have trouble breathing when the scent of the flowers is so strong? You ought to put them out in the hallway at night,' he said gently. He slowly took out his stethoscope and opened the neck of Aiko's robe.

'Are you administering the new medication?'

'Yes.' Eiichi reported the amount and frequency of the injections.

'What about post-operative symptoms?'

'The post-operative fever has broken. But yesterday she complained of a slight nausea.'

'Oh?' He nodded broadly, as if to indicate that this was nothing to be concerned about. 'Well, you're coming along just fine, ma'am,' the doctor comforted Aiko and her friends. 'The nausea is nothing to worry about.'

Smiling and bowing his head slightly, the Old Man went out. Doctor Uchida and the staff workers followed.

'Kurihara.' Out in the hallway, the doctor spoke not to Eiichi but to Kurihara. 'How severe is this nausea she's experiencing?'

'It still seems rather mild. But if it's a reaction to the new drug, there's not much room for optimism . . .'

'I'm not especially optimistic.'

'Yes, sir. Then shall we continue the injections?'

'Continue. We still don't know whether her nausea is caused by the new drug. It could be hepatitis as a result of the transfusions. . . . Run a liver examination and give her some glucose intravenously.'

'Yes, sir.'

Eiichi felt that he had been ignored. He had been the one who had examined the patient after the operation and on the day following. He had been the one who had recognized her symptoms. But Kurihara replied to the doctor just as though he had done it all himself, and not once did he mention Eiichi's name.

That afternoon, an even more intense nausea swept over Aiko. But in line with the doctor's instructions, Eiichi gave her the intravenous glucose, along with another injection of the new drug.

On Sunday, Ozu went to a department store to buy some paper, a brush and black ink. Several days earlier, the managing director of his company had shown him a book on calligraphy and he suddenly made up his mind to try his hand at it.

His wife and daughter laughed at him when he mentioned his plan to them. 'You never stick to anything. You got all worked up about rock collecting once, but you gave that up before long.'

The department store was crowded with young men and women. In the Exhibition Hall on the seventh floor there was a one-woman display by the painter Naomi Sekiya, who had just returned from France. Ozu stood in front of paintings of the stone steps of Montmartre and cafés, and he was filled with envy for the young. At the age when they could have been travelling abroad and soaking up all sorts of experiences, he and Flatfish had been in the army, washing floors, polishing rifles and getting beatings. The young woman in white pantaloons who sat to the side of the reception desk talking to a visitor was probably the artist herself. Her profile, with her long, dark hair, was beautiful.

Besides the brush and ink, Ozu bought Sun Kuo-t'ing's *Notes on Calligraphy*. Ozu was attracted to his simple, unaffected characters. He sat by himself in the crowded department store restaurant and sipped black tea as he looked over the characters. He had not spent such a relaxing Sunday in a long while.

The afternoon sky was still clear. An advertising balloon was floating across the clear sky. As Ozu walked towards his bus, he even felt a tinge of regret that he had to set off home.

Where could I go?

An idea popped into his head. He could visit his son's hospital.

He's off today, but . . .

Ozu knew that Eiichi had gone out for the day, but that he was not going to the hospital. Even though his son would not be there, he wanted to go to the hospital because he was concerned about Aiko since her operation.

'Did her operation go well?' he had asked Eiichi three days earlier, feigning unconcern.

'She's doing fine,' he remembered Eiichi answering with some irritation.

If her operation had gone well, then by now, a week or so later, she might already be walking around the halls. She might even pass him in the hall. So many years had passed, she probably wouldn't even recognize him. He had not seen her since that day at the Jōshōkō Temple.

It doesn't matter, Ozu thought as he sat on the bus. It doesn't matter even if she's forgotten all about me and Flatfish and the pen. He would slip quietly into the hospital, and even if he did not get to see her, or just pass her in the hall, he would slip quietly out again.

He got off the bus and went into the hospital. The courtyard and the entranceway, which were usually filled with the comings and goings of patients and nurses, were deserted. An occasional taxi drove up, let out a visitor, and drove away again.

Ozu's heels clicked as he walked down the long hallway and got in the elevator. He remembered the ward where his son worked.

He went into the ward and approached Aiko's room. Somewhere a television was showing a baseball game. Otherwise it was silent.

Suddenly a nurse darted out of Aiko's room. She raced towards the nurses' station, alarm written on her face.

Oblivious to the emergency in the hallway, the television in the large room blithely continued its broadcast.

Two nurses seemed to come tumbling from the office. Behind them, a young collegiate-type doctor clutching a stethoscope ran into Aiko's room. Ozu was sure now that there had been a sudden change in Aiko's condition.

He staggered back against the wall. When he came out of the department store and suddenly decided to visit the hospital, he never dreamed he would encounter a situation of this sort.

What is Eiichi doing? . . . Eiichi . . .!

He felt he had to get word to his son who was somewhere else and knew nothing about what was happening. He rushed to the pay phone at the end of the hallway and called his home.

'What's happened to Eiichi? Has he come home?'

'No, not yet.' His daughter Yumi was alarmed by the frantic tone of her father's voice. 'Where are you, Dad?'

'It doesn't matter. If Eiichi comes home, tell him to contact the hospital right away!' He hung up and took a handkerchief from his pocket to wipe the perspiration from his face.

'Doctor!' Another nurse came out of the office and called to the young, collegiate-type intern who had just stepped out of Aiko's room. 'Doctor Tahara is at the nurses' station in Internal.'

'Doctor Tahara?'

'Yes. The Doctor Tahara who went to the hospital up in the North-east.'

'Please ask him to come right away. Tell him I'm an intern and can't handle it.'

'Okay.'

Ozu sat down on a nearby sofa and again wiped the perspiration from his brow.

Help her! Help her! he prayed, placing both hands on his knees. What is Eiichi doing? . . . Eiichi . . .!

Soon the doors of the elevator next to the nurses' station opened, and a nondescript man slightly older than Eiichi got out. Ozu knew this would be Doctor Tahara.

The doctor. who was not even wearing an examination smock, disappeared into Aiko's room. Several minutes later a nurse walked slowly out of the room. Ozu sensed from her slow pace that matters had finally been brought under control.

'Get a blood sample a little later and send it down for a liver test,' Doctor Tahara ordered another nurse as he came out from the room. 'We've got it under control now, but there's no telling when she might have another attack. Get hold of Kurihara and Ozu right away. Her

225

heart is quite weak. It looks to me more like a violent reaction to some medication. What are you giving her?'

'It's a new drug.'

'A new drug? What's it called?'

'I don't know. Doctor Kurihara and Doctor Ozu sent it over to be given to the patient.'

'Can I see her charts?' The nurse hesitated, and Tahara glared at her. 'I'll take full responsibility.'

Ozu waited a few moments while Tahara went in to look at Aiko's charts. He was not related to Aiko, so it might be improper for him to ask about her condition, but he could not bring himself to leave without doing so.

It seemed, judging from what he had heard Doctor Tahara say, that the deterioration in Aiko's condition was a result of some drug his son was administering to her. Yet at this very moment his son was out somewhere playing around, neglecting his patient. As he sat waiting on the sofa, Ozu felt like apologizing to Aiko and throttling Eiichi.

He heard Doctor Tahara's voice.

'Well, I'll stay downstairs until Doctor Kurihara and the others come. Call if you need me.'

'Thank you so much, Doctor.'

As the nondescript doctor started down the hall, Ozu found himself chasing after him.

'Excuse me!' Having said that much, Ozu was at a loss for words. 'Is she all right . . . the woman in there?'

Surprised, Tahara turned towards Ozu.

'Is she all right?'

'Her heart is quite weak, and her liver is swollen. . . . But I'm not with this hospital. . . .' He blinked his eyes, as though the words were difficult for him to speak. 'The doctor in charge will be here right away. So please wait over there, and don't worry.'

After Tahara left, Ozu walked down the stairs. There were several empty sofas in front of the deserted dispensary this Sunday afternoon. He sat down as though to hide himself in one of them.

He waited almost an hour before a taxi finally pulled up at the glass door at the entrance. Eiichi hurriedly stepped out. He must have received the message and rushed to the hospital. Ozu watched as his son entered the elevator. Then he breathed a sigh of relief and left the hospital, wiping the perspiration from his face. Deep inside, his stomach began to ache for the first time in weeks.

When he left the elevator, Eiichi stepped into the nurses' station. The two nurses cried, 'Oh!' and then were silent for a moment. 'We tried to reach you at several places.'

'It is Sunday, you know.'

'Doctor Tahara took care of her. She seems to have settled down a bit now, but she threw up several times. There's a chance it might be hepatitis.'

'How would you know it's hepatitis?' Eiichi's voice was unexpectedly biting.

'That's what Doctor Tahara said. He looked at her charts and . . .'

'Tahara looked at her charts!' Eiichi's colour changed. 'You know Tahara isn't associated with this hospital any more. You have no right to show him a patient's charts without permission!' Eiichi glared at the nurses with reproachful eyes.

'We had no other choice!' one of the nurses replied hysterically. 'An intern – Doctor Hori – sent for Doctor Tahara. And Doctor Tahara said he'd take responsibility for seeing the charts. Call him up and ask him about it!'

Eiichi left the nurses' station without another word. He looked into Aiko's room. His pale patient was asleep, the needle of an intravenous bottle inserted in her thin white arm. The room still smelled of alcohol, and a blood-stained piece of cotton was lying on the floor.

When Eiichi came out of the room, Tahara was standing across the hallway, looking at him.

Eiichi controlled his emotions and forced a smile. 'I
understand we've caused you some trouble. She's all right
now, thanks to you.'

Tahara looked unflinchingly into Eiichi's eyes. 'I only
took some stopgap measures. I had the nurses show me
her charts.'

'So I hear,' Eiichi nodded calmly. 'It's all right now.
We'll handle everything from here. . . . I didn't know
you were still in Tokyo.'

'We're taking the train back the day after tomorrow.'

'You're taking Nurse Shimada back with you?'

'Yeah, she'll be going with me. We've got patients
there waiting for us.'

'Is that right? Well, take care.' Eiichi held his hand
out lightly to Tahara, as though nothing had happened.
But Tahara stood motionless in the hallway.

As Eiichi started into the nurses' station, Tahara called
out to him, 'Hey! What's the new drug you're using on
that patient?'

'Huh?' Eiichi's face was expressionless. 'New drug? Oh,
that. It's nothing at all.'

'What's it called?'

'Ask the dispensary chief or Kurihara. I'm acting on
orders from the top.'

'That patient . . . from what I could see, it's the reaction
to that drug that's done so much damage to her liver.
Have you been running tests on her liver?'

'None of your business!' At last Eiichi showed anger.
'You have nothing to do with the dispensary here any
more! I'm not interested in taking orders from you. . . .'

Eiichi's retort would have silenced the old Tahara.
Eiichi had always argued Tahara into silence on questions
of medicine in the past.

But now Tahara shook his head. He answered in a low
voice. 'I'm not asking you as a member of this dispensary.

I'm asking you as a physician.'

'Well then,' Eiichi rebutted, 'I'd like to see a little respect shown towards another physician's position and method of treatment.'

'You call that a "treatment"? You're experimenting on a human being with your new drug!'

'Doctor Ii and Doctor Uchida have approved the treatment.'

'Is that so? Even a quack like me knows better than to try out a dangerous new drug on a patient whose liver is so weak.'

'The deterioration of her liver could be a result of blood serum hepatitis. We've been giving her transfusions.'

'But according to the charts, you've . . . Oh, what the hell. It doesn't matter. After all, I'm the one who was booted out of this dispensary that uses worthless drugs like Bethion on its patients. I know how you write up the charts here. You may be able to fool others, but you can't pull the wool over my eyes.'

The two nurses in the nurses' station were straining to hear what Eiichi and Tahara were saying.

'Listen, Tahara. Let's go over there and talk.' Eiichi's voice was accommodating as he yielded to his uncommonly determined opponent. 'The patients might overhear us.'

Together Eiichi and Tahara walked over and got into the elevator. They waited in chilled silence while the elevator descended to the first floor.

'You just can't talk like that upstairs,' Eiichi muttered as they walked down the hallway.

'I'm sorry. I was excited.'

'Anyway, think of my position. When Doctor Uchida or Kurihara tell me to use a new drug, I can't very well say no. I'm on the bottom rung of the dispensary staff. . . .' His chief goal was to placate Tahara and lead him outside. 'When the doctor made his rounds the other day, I told him and Kurihara about her liver. But . . .,' he sought Tahara's sympathy with his voice, 'both Kurihara and the Old Man told me to keep using the new drug for the time being and see how she does.'

'Has this new drug already been tested at other hospitals?'

'I don't know anything about it.'

'So you're using it without any data whatsoever.'

'Of course we've studied the data from the pharmaceutical company.'

Tahara stopped in his tracks. 'Ah, the pharmaceutical company. I suppose that's the pharmaceutical company that Kurihara's father owns?'

'Uh-huh.'

'Then . . . this patient is the very first test case, isn't she?'

'I can't comment about that.'

'You can't comment! Well, what if this patient was a relative of yours – would you still give her this test drug? What if she was your mother? Or your sister?'

'I probably would,' Eiichi replied desperately, after a moment of silence. 'No matter what kind of drug you're talking about, you've got to have a patient to use it on for the first time so you can improve it and judge its effectiveness.'

'We're not like Jenner discovering vaccination. When we try out a new drug, it's either got to be because another drug is no longer effective, or when we have the patient's voluntary consent. One or the other. Do you have her consent?'

'This is hardly the time for you to put the screws on me. In America they test out new drugs on convicts. . . .'

Tahara stared at Eiichi in surprise. Then a look of sadness washed slowly across his eyes. 'Do you really believe that?'

'I don't want to talk about it any more.' Eiichi shook his head and smiled grimly. There was no point in continuing this discussion any further. Their ways of thinking were different, and they would never agree however long they talked.

'We're doctors. Since we're human, we have ambition, and we want to be recognized . . . but a doctor . . .,' Tahara spoke softly, as though to himself, '. . . a doctor is above all else a doctor! Someone who claims to help other people.'

'Yeah. I've got work to do, I must be going.'

'I suppose I won't be seeing you again,' Tahara muttered sadly as Eiichi glanced back at him.

'No,' Eiichi shook his head and turned his back on his friend since schooldays. 'There's nothing I can do about it. Not if that's the way you feel.'

14 Whistling

Aiko had a dream.

She was visiting her husband's grave. Ever since she had entered the hospital, her greatest wish had been to set her husband's grave in order before her operation.

She bought some flowers at the office and borrowed a bucket and a small broom. She walked through the silent graveyard.

For some reason the season in her dream was autumn. She noticed chrysanthemums decorating graves here and there. Around others cosmos bloomed in profusion.

I should have planted some cosmos for him, she thought. Cosmos had grown thick in the garden of her husband's family home in Nigawa. That garden had been filled with pink and white flowers in the autumn. Tiny droning bees had flown from flower to flower in search of nectar.

Her husband sometimes returned from the naval base at Kure. He had been very fond of cosmos.

'We didn't really plant them at the house. . . . The wind just blew the seeds in from somewhere, and this is what they've turned into,' her husband told her. In fact, every house in the neighbourhood had cosmos in its garden. The weightless seeds floated upon the wind, producing blossoms from place to place down the road.

She pulled up the tiny weeds that surrounded the grave, swept it, and poured some water on the gravestone.

'I won't be able to come for a while. I'm having an operation,' she whispered to her husband, both hands joined in front of her. 'So please forgive me.'

'You're having an operation?' Her husband answered in her ear. The voice was that of a young man, just the way he had spoken before he was killed.

'Yes.'

'Once in everyone's life there's a time when they have to do battle. Your time to go to war has come now. You have to stick with it and win, no matter how much it hurts!'

'Yes.' She had faith in her own ability to persevere, to endure, to withstand. 'I can do it. I did everything by myself when I was evacuated to Shūzan.'

'Yes, you did, didn't you?'

Her husband's face appeared. The tanned, manly face smiled and nodded. The whiteness of his teeth when he smiled was dazzling.

'I was so good at working in the fields, even the farmers complimented me. The vegetables I grew were so good, I wanted you to try them.'

She thought of herself wielding a hoe. She had never used a hoe before in her life, but with her strong will she was able to endure the experience. As she thought of her dead husband and spoke with him, she recalled each day she had spent, cultivating the fields with stroke after stroke of her hoe. She drove herself to exhaustion until the evening sun set over the Northern Hills. It was the best way to forget her sorrow.

'Was my death the hardest time for you?' her husband asked.

'Yes. That and when we waited too long to do anything for the baby's pneumonia. I don't know how to apologize to you. . . . '

'It's all right. It was because the doctor wouldn't come.'

Aiko shook her head, trying not to remember that day of grief. . . .

Aiko sensed the presence of someone and opened her eyes a fraction. A nurse was standing at the door of her room. She was holding a basket of flowers in her right hand.

'How are you, Mrs Nagayama?'

Aiko smiled feebly, an effort that required all her strength.

'Someone sent you these flowers. Shall I leave them in the hall?'

All the potted plants that had lined her room had been taken out into the hallway when Aiko's condition deteriorated. The aroma of the flowers made it difficult for her to breathe.

'Yes,' she answered faintly. 'Who are they from?'

The nurse reached into the flower basket and pulled out a small envelope.

'How do you read this? Heimoku? That's the way it's written, anyway. Heimoku. . . . I'll put them in the hall. The doctor will be here soon. If you need anything, just press the buzzer. . . .'

Heimoku . . .? No. It was Flatfish.* A memory from the far-distant past took shape in her mind. Flatfish. The Nada student. That young man who was always following her and the other girls.

Why would Flatfish . . . ?

Drowsily she remembered the day one of Flatfish's friends had visited her. She remembered the friend telling her that Flatfish had died in the war. Then he had taken a pen from his pocket.

Why would someone who died in the war . . . send me a basket of flowers . . . ?

But she was too listless to search for reasons. She was no longer able to distinguish between the living and the dead. Death was already beginning to veil Aiko's face,

Translator's note: The Chinese characters for 'Flatfish', a strange and uncommon name, read 'Hirame' in Japanese. Because of their rarity, the two characters would be practically unreadable to the average person. 'Heimoku' is just a guess based on other readings of the same characters.

like a shadow cast through the window of her hospital room.

She had another dream. It was the night she lost her child in Shūzan.

The doctor still had not come. The man they sent to find him came back and reported that the doctor was now making a house call in another village and would not arrive for another two hours.

Her child was asleep in his tiny bed, his face flushed and the whites of his eyes exposed. He gasped frantically for breath. Aiko placed wet towels on his forehead, replacing one with another as soon as she had placed it there.

The tin of medicine on top of the brazier made a thin sound. Aiko's father-in-law stood at the glass door in the hallway.

'It's snowing,' he muttered painfully.

A grey evening haze had risen. Aiko could see the large white snowflakes dancing in it.

'What's happened to the doctor?' her father-in-law muttered meaninglessly over and over again.

In her dream, Aiko felt her left arm being lifted, and she opened her eyes again.

Doctor Uchida and Doctor Kurihara were standing beside her pillow. They seemed to think that Aiko was still asleep.

'Stop the injections.'

'Yes, sir.'

'Did you give her an antipyretic?'

'Two hours ago.'

'Well, the worst may come in the next couple of days.'

Aiko's exhausted senses picked up fragments of their conversation.

Again that evening, Eiichi returned home quite late. Ozu watched as his son wearily washed his hands at the sink. He sensed that Aiko's condition was not good.

'Good evening.' Eiichi opened the *fusuma* to the living-room a crack and poked his head in. Ozu called to his son as he started up the stairs.

'Won't you have some tea?'

'No. I've got things to do.'

'Oh, come on.'

Eiichi glanced at his family with a degree of displeasure in his eyes, and then stepped into the living-room.

'You look tired.'

'I am.' Eiichi took the teacup his mother held out and noisily sipped his tea.

Ozu's eyes were riveted on his son. 'How is your patient?'

'My patient?'

'Is it bad?'

Eiichi set down his teacup. 'I guess so. It looks to me like terminal cancer.'

'That's so sad,' his mother sighed. 'Can't you operate on her?'

'We did operate. But even an operation won't help when the patient is this far advanced.'

Eiichi's manner of speaking normally did not irritate Ozu. But now he was upset by the irresponsible tone in his son's voice. 'If you knew it wouldn't help, why did you operate?' he asked.

'Because it puts the patient's mind at rest, at least for a while. And we can determine how far the disease has advanced much easier by opening them up than by using X-rays and instruments. And it gives us much better research data.'

'So . . . you operated on her to get research data?' Ozu could sense the anger in his own voice.

Eiichi looked at his father suspiciously. 'This patient . . . Aiko Nagayama. Do you know her?'

Ozu realized that not only his son, but his wife and

daughter were all looking at him. It was too late.

'Yes, I know her,' he answered softly. 'When I was at Nada Middle School, she was going to Kōnan Girls' School. . . .'

'How did you know she was a patient at Eiichi's hospital?' Nobuko asked her husband incredulously.

'The time I went to Eiichi's hospital, I just happened to notice her name on the door. That's all.'

'Are you sure?'

Ozu grimaced and picked up his teacup. 'Mrs Nagamaya's husband was a big officer in the navy. He was killed in battle, and she suffered a great deal after that.'

'This is the first I've heard anything about it.'

'There wasn't any real need to tell you about it.'

Nobuko was somehow misjudging the situation. Some people think that when a man and woman are acquainted, there must be something shady about their relationship. Nobuko seemed to be one of those people.

The telephone rang. Eiichi got up and went out into the hall.

From the living-room, they heard him answering briefly 'Yes' and 'Really?', and soon he came back into the room.

'I've got to go out. I'll be back later.'

'You're leaving now?' His mother looked up at him in surprise. In dismay, she followed him to the door, where he was putting on his shoes. 'What's happened?'

'I've got to see Kurihara.'

'At a time like this? It's already after ten!'

Eiichi opened the door without answering. He walked out to the main road and after a few moments hailed a taxi.

'Listen, we're in big trouble!' He could still hear Kurihara's worried voice over the phone.

'What's the matter?' The name of Nurse Shimada popped into Eiichi's head. But it was a different matter that was troubling Kurihara.

'Can you come over right away? The newspapers have got word of our new cancer drug.'

'How did they find out?'

'I don't know. But get over here quick!' Kurihara gave Eiichi the name of his apartment building in Azabu. It was a private apartment, away from his parents, where he could enjoy his carefree bachelor life.

Eiichi followed Kurihara's instructions and rode past the Tōyō English-Japanese School. He found the apartment building on the right-hand side at the foot of the hill. It was a posh building of the sort someone like Eiichi could never hope to live in no matter how many years passed.

He got out of the taxi and walked through the automatic doors at the entrance. Kurihara was seated in the lobby with another man at his left. This man must be the newspaper reporter.

When Kurihara caught sight of Eiichi, he stiffly introduced him to the man. 'This is Ozu of the same dispensary.' The reporter took a card from his pocket and held it out to Eiichi. The name on the card was Yuke.

'Actually, I've just been asking about this new cancer drug you've been using on a patient named Nagayama,' Yuke remarked, looking directly into Eiichi's face. 'We've heard that you're the first ones to use this new drug on a patient.'

Eiichi glanced quickly at Kurihara. 'Yes,' he replied.

'I understand that this drug was manufactured at a company owned by Doctor Kurihara's father?'

'Yes.'

'And did this patient know beforehand that you would be using this drug?'

'I'm sorry,' Eiichi said, 'but have you talked with Doctor Uchida?'

'No. I'm planning to see him later.'

'Oh. Well, as you know, this is a new drug, and since we're only staff workers at the dispensary, we can't say anything about it without the dispensary director's permission. . . .'

Eiichi did a swift mental calculation and decided it would be best to adopt the position of a low-ranking member of the dispensary staff having no responsibility in the matter.

'But,' the reporter persisted, 'you two are Mrs Aiko Nagayama's supervising physicians, aren't you?'

'Yes, we are.'

'I understand that Mrs Nagayama's condition has worsened because of this drug.'

'What?' Eiichi feigned ignorance. 'Because of the drug? Who told you that?'

'I can't disclose my sources.' After a moment of silence, the reporter continued, 'Well, I'll talk to Doctor Uchida. If he gives you permission, would you be willing to offer an explanation of all this?'

'Yes, of course,' Kurihara nodded. 'Just let me make one thing clear. We used this new anti-cancer drug because we felt it would be beneficial in treating this patient. I hope there'll be no misunderstanding on that point.'

'Then are you saying that you expect Mrs Nagayama to recover?'

'Yes.'

The reporter looked somewhat puzzled. 'I see. Well, that's an entirely different matter. To tell you the truth, the information we received indicated that Mrs Nagayama was beyond help, and that that was why you were experimenting on her with this new drug. . . .' He put his memo pad into his pocket and stood. 'I'm sorry to have troubled you this late in the evening. My job forces me to ask some irritating questions at times. Please forgive me. I hope Mrs Nagayama recovers soon.' He bowed to them.

Kurihara accompanied the reporter as far as the automatic doors. He returned to the lobby with a scowl.

'Do you have any idea who blabbed this to the papers?'

'No idea at all.' Eiichi shook his head. 'What are we going to do? I don't think you should have told him that she'll recover . . .'

'But there wasn't anything else I could say!' he blurted out. He began to chew his fingernails nervously.

Eiichi stood up. 'Should we call Doctor Uchida and tell him what's happened?'

'Yes.'

Eiichi went to the pay phone in one corner of the lobby and lifted the receiver. Just then the thought that a nurse might have given that information to the papers clouded his mind.

'Just a moment, please.' When Doctor Uchida's wife answered, Eiichi called Kurihara over and handed the receiver to him.

'We've got a real problem.' Kurihara looked down glumly as he gripped the receiver. His body was massive, but when a crisis occurred all his timidity seemed to be revealed in that particular pose.

The lobby was dark and deserted. Eiichi puffed on a cigarette as he waited for Kurihara to finish the call.

If this comes out in the papers, he thought, the ones who'll get blasted the most will probably be Kurihara's father's company and Doctor Ii. I'm a mere staff worker, so I'm not responsible. I can get by with saying that I was acting on orders from above. That's how I'll have to handle it.

But if that drug really is no good, does that mean I won't be able to make my announcement to the medical world?

That was regrettable. Every single day he had imagined how he would look as he stood before representatives of all the medical schools seated in the great tiered lecture hall and announced the data on the new drug.

While Eiichi and Kurihara discussed their problem in the dark hallway, a night train for the North-east was about to depart from a platform at Ueno Station.

'Here's something for dinner.' Keiko handed a meal box and some tea to Nurse Shimada. 'Doctor Tahara's late, isn't he?' she muttered. The clock on the platform showed three minutes to departure time. 'You'll write to me when you get there, won't you?'

'Yes.' Nurse Shimada, who seldom had much to say, nodded.

'Forget about everything else and work hard,' Keiko said, looking at her watch. 'Can you forget what's happened in Tokyo?'

Just then, the nondescript Tahara appeared, carrying a suitcase. He must have scrambled up the stairs, because perspiration soaked his forehead.

'Ah, I'm sorry I'm late. Sorry!' he apologized, panting for breath.

'Doctor, please take good care of Nurse Shimada.'

Tahara grunted in compliance. 'It's reassuring to have a trustworthy head nurse at your side – for both the doctors and the patients.'

'She'll do a great job.'

The departure bell rang. Tahara let Nurse Shimada go ahead of him and then climbed onto the step of the train.

'Give my best to everyone.'

'Who's "everyone"?'

'The dispensary staff, of course.'

The train slowly started forward. Keiko walked along for four or five steps, waving her hand and smiling at Nurse Shimada, who stood on the platform between the carriages and looked back sadly at her friend. Before long, her sad face and the figure of Doctor Tahara had disappeared from sight.

'You won't see Tokyo again for a while,' the doctor told the nurse as she stared at the lights of Ueno. 'I felt lonely when I left Tokyo, too. It was very painful. I felt discouraged. But when we arrive up there, you'll soon make the same discovery I did. The people there have a real need for doctors and nurses.'

'Mmm.'

One by one the neon lights were vanishing. The tall advertising tower, the neon sign of the cabaret, the electric newsboard. The train sped on, like the cellophane strip peeled from the top of a box of chocolates.

'Would you like a drink?' Tahara took a small flask of whisky from his pocket. 'I'm not having any, but one drink is a good substitute for sleeping pills when you're on a train.'

'Doctor . . .'

'Yes?'

'Have you heard all the fuss about the new cancer drug in the Surgical dispensary?' Nurse Shimada suddenly lifted her head and muttered. 'The newspapers are calling it an experiment on human guinea pigs . . .'

'That's what I hear. But I'd rather not say anything about it. After all, that's the dispensary where I got all my training.'

'The person that told the newspapers . . .,' the nurse looked steadily into Tahara's eyes and whispered, 'it was me.'

Tahara's eyes opened wide. His hand froze in mid-air, holding the cup of whisky he was about to bring to his lips.

'Why . . .?'

An oppressive atmosphere hung over the dispensary. The staff workers did not discuss the topic openly, but all were interested in how the situation would develop.

The new anti-cancer drug was no longer administered to Aiko Nagayama, but her condition did not improve in the least. Injections of morphine were initiated to relieve her pain. She slept in a coma-like state most of the day as a result of these injections.

The plants and flowers at the door of her room gradually withered and were discarded by the cleaning women. The flowers in a basket that Ozu had sent secretly in Flatfish's name also faded and were flung onto the refuse dump at the hospital. One day rain began to fall on the remains of the discarded blooms.

'You seem to be feeling well today,' a nurse said as she took Aiko's blood pressure before giving her an injection.

'Yes, I am.' The flesh was gone from Aiko's cheeks. 'A lot better than yesterday.'

'That's wonderful. Today you take your first step on the road to recovery.'

'That would be nice,' Aiko smiled feebly. 'Um . . . I'd like to ask a favour.'

'What is it?'

'Do you think you could wash my hair? It's so filthy I can't stand it.'

'Of course,' the nurse nodded. She helped Aiko sit up in bed and put a pillow behind her back. Then she combed out Aiko's hair. 'I'll bring some shampoo and water in just a minute.'

As the nurse left the room, she remembered something else she had to do. Her thirty-minute errand turned into an hour.

At last she prepared everything for Aiko's shampoo and went back to her room. Aiko was asleep, her eyes shut tightly in her pale face.

'Mrs Nagayama. Mrs Nagayama!' the nurse called. But there was no answer.

When the call came from the nurses' station, Kurihara and Eiichi rushed from the dispensary to the ward.

Kurihara glanced at the patient's face and angrily ordered the nurse, 'Prepare an oxygen tent!' Eiichi injected a hypodermic of camphor into her thin arm.

'Is she going to make it?' Eiichi asked Kurihara, who stood beside him listening with his stethoscope.

'I don't know.'

'Should we contact her home?'

Kurihara nodded silently. This outcome was inevitable, but if Aiko died today it would be more than the death of just another patient. The reporter Yuke would undoubtedly link her death with the new drug.

After Eiichi hurried from the room, Kurihara walked over to the window and stared out at the misty rain that was sprinkling the courtyard.

The rain was falling softly on the roof of the ward and on the flower garden in the courtyard. The courtyard was deserted.

When that moment comes . . ., Kurihara thought absently, I'd better resign. If I stay at the hospital, this will follow me around for the rest of my life. . . .

On that day of misty rain, Ozu stopped off at a flower shop near his office. He had bought flowers for Aiko in Flatfish's name at the same shop a few days earlier.

'Good afternoon.' The shop clerk greeted him with a cordial smile, perhaps remembering his face. 'We have some lovely roses.'

'No, I think I'd like to get a potted plant today.' Ozu crouched down and examined the potted flowers lined up on the floor. Since they were for a sick person, he decided against bright-coloured flowers.

On the card the clerk handed him, he wrote, 'Never say die. Flatfish.' For Ozu, this was a supreme attempt at humour.

'The same hospital as before, isn't it?' the clerk said knowingly. 'I'll have them there in two hours. As a special service to you.'

Ozu got on a bus and returned home. He still had a little time before dinner, so he began to practise calligraphy with the brush he had purchased.

His wife Nobuko made her usual racket in the kitchen as she prepared dinner. His daughter Yumi had gone out and had not yet returned home.

'Yumi says she wants a stereo,' his wife called from the kitchen.

'A stereo? To listen to records?'

'Mmm. She's been pestering me for some time to get her one.'

'We've already got a record player in the house!'

'She says she wants one of her own.'

'And I suppose she'll play that nonsensical jazz all day long?'

Ozu was in high spirits. Yumi returned home just as dinner was ready. Ozu teased her and eventually promised to buy her a record player for her birthday.

'When you get married,' Nobuko told her daughter, 'your father'll be more sorry to see you go than anyone.'

The phone rang. Those mysteriously silent phone calls had ceased.

'Can you take that, Yumi. It might be from Eiichi.'

Yumi got up when her mother called and went out into the hall.

'Uh-huh . . . uh-huh . . . okay,' she answered briefly and returned to the living-room.

'That was Eiichi. He's not on night shift tonight, but he says he might be staying at the hospital all night.'

'What for?'

'He says that Mrs Nagayama is in a critical condition.'

Ozu rose abruptly from the table. Then, realizing what he had done, he sat down again.

'Eiichi said she was . . . critical?'

'Yes.'

He was silent and went on with his meal. Yumi turned on the television, and a quiz programme came on.

'When it's summer in Tokyo, is it spring, summer, autumn or winter in Melbourne?'

Nobuko gazed at her husband's sombre face. 'Go to the hospital.'

Ozu set down his chopsticks and nodded.

He rose silently from the table. Nobuko followed him into the next room. She opened the wardrobe and took out a white shirt. Ozu dressed without a word.

'Here's your wallet.'

'Thanks.'

Those were the first words they spoke to each other.

'You'll be late, won't you?'

'Maybe,' Ozu nodded, looking at Nobuko. 'I'm sorry,' he apologized softly. He had not told her the details of his relationship with Aiko. But as he looked at Nobuko's face now, he felt sure that she would understand everything when he told her about it.

Nobuko saw him to the door. As he walked to the main road, he looked up at the sky. One, two, then three stars were shining, an occurrence unusual in Tokyo. Ozu stopped and gazed intently at the stars. The realm where Flatfish dwelled. Flatfish and all the dead. He was overcome with the realization that Aiko was now leaving the earth and heading for that realm. Flatfish's brief life. Aiko's life. His own life, that had touched theirs.

Ozu hailed a taxi and got out in front of the hospital. The hospital looked like a boat floating on the sea at night. Faint lights shone from some of the windows of the still, dark building. Hearing his own footsteps, he clattered down the long, cold hallway. His mind was strangely at ease. He now felt more resignation than sadness at the knowledge that Aiko was dying. First Flatfish had gone to that world of the dead; now Aiko was approaching it, and sooner or later, he too must step into that realm. These thoughts filled his heart as he pressed the elevator button.

The ward was deserted. At this late hour, every room was darkened and asleep. The only illumination came from the dim lights in the hallway. A bright light shone from the nurses' station.

'Excuse me.' He peered into the nurses' station.

The young nurse at the desk turned towards him in surprise.

'I heard that Mrs Nagayama had . . . taken a turn for the worse.'

'Are you a relative?'

'No, a friend . . .'

The nurse rose from her chair and muttered sympathetically, 'Mrs Nagayama . . . passed away. About an hour ago. . . .'

Ozu stood at the door with a dazed look. 'She died?'

'Yes. The doctors and I tried our best, but . . .'

'She died. . . . And now . . .?'

'Her body is in the morgue. Two of her friends are there now. . . . Would you like to go down?'

Ozu nodded. The nurse gave him directions to the morgue.

'There's an attendant there. . . . Tell him you were a friend of Mrs Nagayama.'

Ozu thanked the nurse. 'Did Mrs Nagayama . . . suffer a great deal?'

'No. She was in a coma for quite a while, so I don't think she felt any pain.'

Following her directions, Ozu descended to the first floor of the deserted ward and walked out into the courtyard.

It was pitch black. The hospital rose before him like a wall. Most of the lights in the windows were out. Work went on only in the nurses' stations on each floor. This place where life is brought forth, and where life dies out. People often wonder when they will die, but they never wonder *where* they will die. When Aiko was still in good health, for instance, did she ever imagine the spot where she would die? Did she ever imagine this forlorn hospital room at night?

Ozu passed through the courtyard and approached a

square concrete building deep in a thicket of trees. It was the morgue.

The attendant was reading a book in a small room beside the entrance.

'I'm a friend of . . . Mrs Nagayama.'

The attendant looked Ozu over and then handed him a wooden token through the tiny window. 'It's on your left as you go up the stairs. Please give this back when you leave.'

The stairs smelled of cement as he climbed them. Light poured from the lamp-lit room. Two women were seated on small chairs. Beyond the candle flames was a coffin of unpainted wood. Smoke from the incense curled silently upward.

Ozu bowed to the two women. He joined his hands in prayer before the coffin and lit a stick of incense.

Aiko. It's me. Ozu, he muttered inwardly. So we meet again. The last time I saw you, over twenty years ago, I never thought we'd be meeting again like this.

He thought of Aiko in her pantaloons slowly climbing the stone steps of the Jōshōkō Temple at Shūzan. Ozu was twenty-four years old then, Aiko twenty-three.

The morgue was bare of any decoration. The walls were all plain concrete. The shadows from the candle flames were like stains on the walls. Ozu sat down near the two women, who were apparently friends of Aiko's.

He closed his eyes and scene by scene recalled the far-distant past. Aiko in her sailor uniform riding on the train along the highway. She notices Ozu and Flatfish following her on the road beide the Ashiya River and walks away with her nose in the air. Aiko in her swimsuit, splashing water on her friends in the ocean at Ashiya. Just one hour ago, her life, a patchwork of all these scenes, had come to an end.

'Excuse me.' Ozu opened his eyes at the voice. 'Will you be staying here for a while?'

It was one of Aiko's friends. She was rather old, but

Ozu had the feeling he had seen that face long ago.

'Yes.'

'We'd like to phone around and let people know that Aiko has died. We'll be back in about half an hour. . . . We'd really appreciate it.'

When Ozu rose from his chair, one of the women looked at his face in surprise.

'Excuse me, but . . . didn't you go to Nada Middle School?'

'Yes.'

'Do you remember me? I always went with Aiko to school on the train from Ashiya. My name is Nakamura.'

Ozu blinked his eyes and nodded several times. The fish-like face of Flatfish appeared before his eyes.

When the women had gone, Ozu rested his clasped hands on his knees and gazed at the incense smoke that rose in a single thread, then at the candle flame that fluttered occasionally. These were the only implements of mourning for Aiko to be had.

Soon the undertaker will come and take away the body. Maybe the deceased doesn't even remember this fellow sitting across from her remains now, Ozu thought.

No, Ozu had not been a part of her circle of friends. Yet tonight he was keeping watch over her earthly remains. This was not a mere chance of fate. Ozu sensed a meaning of life concealed somewhere there.

What did this woman mean to Flatfish and me? Ozu wondered, staring at his entwined fingers.

Some people leave no impression at all upon your heart, no matter how often you encounter them in life. But there are also people who touch your life only once whom you cannot forget for as long as you live. Aiko had been such a girl for Flatfish. And Flatfish had been that sort of friend to Ozu.

'But you were hardly aware that Flatfish and I existed, were you?' Ozu said to Aiko's remains. 'I suppose it must annoy you to have someone like that beside you here now.

But please try to put up with me.'

Ozu did not have the words to express the profound emotions that held sway in his breast.

If there hadn't been a war, Flatfish might have had a wife now, and perhaps he would have been the father of several children.

Somewhere along the way, the words he uttered to himself changed into the Kansai dialect he had spoken as a student at Nada.

If there hadn't been a war . . . you probably wouldn't have had to die all alone here like this. . . .

That's why I can't separate you and Flatfish in my mind, Ozu told Aiko. You two shared the same fate. I'm still alive, but Flatfish is dead, and now you're gone too.

'Sometime I'll be coming to your world, too.'

There was not a single flower to adorn Aiko's remains within these hollow cement walls. In the stillness, Ozu closed his eyes and tears slowly streamed from them. These were tears that Eiichi's generation would never be able to understand. They were tears that only a generation that had lost relatives and loved ones in a war could comprehend.

This room's too miserable, he said, turning to Flatfish. There's no flowers, no family . . .

Well then . . ., Flatfish whispered, his face floating up in Ozu's tears, why don't you whistle a little for us? You were great at it at Nada. Do it for her and for me.

Ozu puckered up his lips and tried to whistle. But only a faint, broken sound came from his lips.

15 *Triumph*

Doctor Uchida was seated in the conference room where they had once met with the researcher from the pharmaceutical company. Drumming on the table with his fingers, he tried to collect his thoughts, but he could not quell the uneasy feeling that was spreading throughout his breast.

There was a knock at the door.

'Come in.'

It was Kurihara and Eiichi, dressed in white smocks. They bowed and then sat down across from each other. They were silent for a few moments.

'No one . . . noticed you, did they?' the dispensary chief asked, still drumming away on the table.

'No. We slipped away.'

'Ah. . . .' There was a brief pause. 'Late, isn't he? The Old Man . . .'

'He should be here any minute.'

The doorknob turned and Doctor Ii came in, clutching a pipe in one hand. The three stood to greet him.

The dispensary chief bowed to Doctor Ii. 'We must apologize for the senseless blunder that has resulted from our carelessness.'

'It's not your fault.' The Old Man chewed on his extinguished pipe. 'But tell me how things stand.'

'I've had a number of calls from that reporter Yuke. I couldn't go on refusing him indefinitely, so I've set up a meeting with him for this evening.'

'And so . . .?'

'And so I'd like to ask your opinion about what I should say to him. . . .'

'I see.' Doctor Ii sighed and closed his eyes. 'First let me hear what you have in mind.'

'One possibility would be to keep insisting that the patient's death was not caused by the new drug. The problem with that is that it won't necessarily bring the matter to a close.'

'What do you mean?'

'The newspapers seem less concerned with the cause of death than with the fact that we used the new drug without the patient's consent.'

'Can't you tell them that we had the patient's verbal consent?'

'I thought of that,' Doctor Uchida nodded. 'But wouldn't that lead to more problems if they pursued the reasons we stopped using the other anti-cancer drugs and used only the new drug?'

'Do you think they'd pursue that?'

'This reporter Yuke thrives on controversy. . . . Apparently he's already talked with several authorities on medical care and amassed a good deal of knowledge.'

Kurihara and Eiichi listened to the exchange in silence. Doctor Ii's consternation was obvious. Noticing that his pipe had gone out, he took a lighter from his pocket and toyed with it in his hand.

'I don't suppose there's any way we can suppress the article?'

'We looked into that, but . . .' Doctor Uchida shook his head feebly. 'It's a hell of a mess.'

'Yeah . . .'

'The staff in Internal seem to have caught wind of the whole thing. They're just delighted. I suppose they think they can snatch control of our Cancer Centre away from us now.'

It was common knowledge that the Surgery and

Internal sections at the university hospital were grappling for control of the new Cancer Centre. Doctor Ii and the Surgical dispensary would of course be wounded if the present scandal were made public. That thought alone was enough to delight the staff in the Internal section. Doctor Uchida feared that the Surgical dispensary would be defeated.

The four men were silent for a few moments. The same solution had occurred to each of them. Yet each hesitated to be the first to voice it.

'Kurihara.' Doctor Uchida spoke, unable to hold back any longer. 'Do you have any ideas?' He gazed intently into Kurihara's face. It was a signal to Kurihara to voice what each of them was now thinking.

'Doctor,' Kurihara lifted his massive body from the chair and answered in a slightly shrill voice. 'If I . . . may be permitted to say this, the new drug was manufactured by my father's company. So a great portion of the crime, at it were, lies with my father's company. In that sense . . .' He looked down and swallowed, groping for words. 'In that sense, I would like to take responsibility for what has happened with this new drug.'

Neither the Old Man nor Doctor Uchida tried to interrupt Kurihara. They were fully aware of what Kurihara would say next.

'I'd like to announce publicly that I used this new drug on my own initiative, without consulting you. Let me take full responsibility as her supervising physician. I've decided that, if circumstances require it, I'll resign from the dispensary.'

'Now wait a minute . . .' Doctor Uchida shook his head. 'We don't intend to let you carry all the responsibility.'

It was apparent even to Eiichi that these words did not come from the dispensary chief's heart.

'No. Please don't worry about me. My father has asked me before to work in his company. . . .'

'He has . . .?' Doctor Uchida's response was a blend of a sigh and a gasp. 'Then would you mind handling it that way?'

'All right.'

'We'll see to it that your future is secure in any case, so you'll be patient for now, won't you?'

'Yes.'

'Thank you.' The dispensary chief placed his hands on his knees and bowed his head to Kurihara. This was all an empty charade, but the Old Man and Uchida played out their parts as if they were deeply moved.

Victory . . .! Eiichi muttered to himself. This way, I'm unscathed, and Kurihara's been booted out of the dispensary. Now the Old Man won't give another thought to marrying his daughter to Kurihara.

But Eiichi still had a bit part to play in this drama. He put on a rather tragic face. 'I don't think Kurihara should have to bear all the responsibility himself. Since I was also her supervising physician, I . . .'

Kurihara shook his head sadly. 'There's no need. There's no need.'

Eiichi awoke earlier than usual the next day. He was eager to see what sort of article would appear in the morning newspaper.

His family did not subscribe to the newspaper that Yuke worked for.

'I'm going to take a walk,' he told his mother, who was preparing breakfast, and he went out.

He went to a newsstand in the shopping mall and bought the newspaper he was looking for. He opened it hurriedly to the City News page, but there was no article. He felt at once relieved and apprehensive. He was worried that Yuke might include his own name along with Kurihara's.

When he arrived at the dispensary that day, Kurihara

had just come in. He glanced at Eiichi but said nothing.

Just after nine o'clock, Doctor Uchida gathered the staff workers together and made an announcement.

'This will probably appear in the papers tonight, so you'll all be hearing about it. It concerns a patient named Mrs Nagayama. We regret the fact that circumstances that will invite public misunderstanding have occurred. Mr Kurihara is taking responsibility for the misunderstanding and has announced that he is resigning from the dispensary. Doctor Ii and myself did our best to try to discourage him from resigning, but he is determined to do so. We were left with no choice but to accept his resignation.' The dispensary chief peered into each face to solicit sympathy. 'But each of you is in the same position as Kurihara, and I believe that you will realize that his actions did not go against his conscience as a physician. The current affair is a blow to Kurihara and to each of us at the dispensary, but we can't let it destroy the unity we have here. We believe that in the near future the day will come when Kurihara can return triumphantly to our dispensary. We look forward to applauding his return at that time.'

As he listened to the dispensary chief's speech, Eiichi suddenly remembered the going-away party for Tahara. Doctor Uchida had said the same sort of things then. He had said they believed the day would come when Tahara could return to the dispensary. But everyone had known that Tahara would never come back to this hospital.

Eternal exile . . .? Eiichi stole a glance at Kurihara's stiff profile. But Kurihara doesn't have to worry about where tomorrow's meal will come from. He's got an influential father. He's got a big pharmaceutical company to fall back on. If I'd been the one this had happened to, things wouldn't have turned out so well for me.

At this thought, the glimmer of sympathy he had felt for Kurihara in a corner of his heart vanished with uncommon speed.

'Mr Mine.' After his announcement, the dispensary chief shifted his voice to a cheerful tone and addressed a member of the staff named Mine. 'Would you be in charge of Mr Kurihara's farewell party? It ought to be done in style. In style.'

The article appeared in the evening paper. Eiichi was surprised at how accurately the article described cancer drugs and the new medication. It included the reporter's concern that using the drug without the patient's consent was a form of experimentation on human guinea pigs, as well as opinions from several doctors and experts on medical care. Comments from the dispensary chief and a defence by Kurihara also appeared in print. But Eiichi's name was not mentioned in the article.

I've climbed over one mountain; now I've got to conquer the next, Eiichi thought. As yet, he did not know how many mountains he would have to scale. But once he had conquered them all, he could look down over a vast plateau where the sun shone brilliantly. A plateau lit by the bright sun – to Eiichi, that meant a doctor's chair at this university hospital.

Kurihara was resigning from the dispensary. That was one mountain Eiichi had crossed. Now he must undertake the conquest of the next mountain.

So he looked forward to the morning of the following Saturday. He knew that Doctor Ii would be dining with officials from the Ministry of Welfare on Saturday evening.

On Saturday morning he telephoned Yoshiko. The maid called her to the phone. The voice that came over the receiver seemed drained of strength.

'It's been a long time,' she said out of courtesy. 'How are you?'

'Terrific!' Eiichi's voice was intentionally enthusiastic. 'Besides, it's Saturday. And the sky is so clear and beautiful! I see no reason to be confined indoors. Let's go out somewhere.'

She was silent for a moment. 'I . . . haven't wanted to go out much lately.'

Eiichi ignored the remark. 'I'll be waiting for you at four o'clock in the lobby of the Imperial Hotel.' He put the phone down without waiting for her reply.

There was method to his heavy-handed manner of invitation. He knew that women had a weakness for being told 'Let's go out' instead of being asked 'Would you like to go out?' There was the thrill of a gamble in it. He would be able to determine the depth of Yoshiko's interest in him by whether she showed up in the lobby of the Imperial Hotel at four o'clock.

Will she come? Or won't she?

He ambled between the hospital and the dispensary until around three o'clock. But unlike his normal routine, today he carried out his work with gusto. He was eager to know the result of his gamble.

How should I handle the conversation? he wondered as he had lunch in the cafeteria.

One of Eiichi's superiors in the dispensary, a man who prided himself on being able to get any woman he wanted, had once told Eiichi, 'Listen. When you're talking to a woman, she'll give in for sure if you whisper these words in her ear. . . .' He proceeded to whisper into Eiichi's ear two words to tickle a woman's pride. As he ate his curry rice, Eiichi suddenly remembered the words and chuckled to himself. If I get a chance, I'm going to try whispering those two words to Yoshiko today and see how she reacts, he thought.

'What are you giggling about?'

Eiichi looked up. Umemiya, a dispensary worker, was standing over him, holding a cup of coffee in his hand.

'Oh, nothing. . . .'

'Depressing, isn't it? First the business with Tahara, and now this thing with Kurihara. The dispensary's just a little place, but I guess since it's an organization you sort of have to expect this sort of thing. . . .'

Eiichi sat down on a sofa in the lobby of the Imperial Hotel, glancing back and forth from his watch to the entrance.

Will she come? Or won't she?

At the outset, he was confident. But though he had flippantly felt certain that Yoshiko would come when he first arrived, by scarcely ten minutes past four his heart was beginning to pound from fear that she would not turn up at all.

I guess she . . . really doesn't care about me.

Then, as is the wont of egotists like Eiichi, anger at Yoshiko welled up from the depths of his wounded pride.

If that's the case, she'll pay for this. I'll take her down a notch or two!

At four twenty, he started to rise.

No, I'll wait ten more minutes. I'll wait ten minutes, and if she hasn't shown by then . . .

He folded his arms again and closed his eyes. I won't wait more than ten minutes, he reassured himself.

Several minutes passed. When he opened his eyes, he saw Yoshiko standing across the lobby, wearing white pantaloons. She saw him just as he noticed her.

'I'm sorry. I was afraid you would have been furious and left. The taxi got caught in a traffic jam . . . I was so worried.'

'I didn't think you were coming.' Yet his feelings of anger quickly evaporated.

You're slipping! he chided his own sentimentality. You've got to handle everything according to plan. Eiichi again went over the plans he had made the previous evening. They were the plans he had made to bend Yoshiko's heart in his direction.

'Let's go upstairs.'

On the top floor of the Imperial Hotel was a Sky

Lounge looking out over the Imperial Palace. They would go there first. He would put on an air of sincere sympathy for her plight.

They entered the Sky Lounge on the seventeenth floor. The view from the windows that stretched out before them was made to order. The apricot-like evening sun was just beginning to set, casting its rays upon the forest around the palace, the moat, and the road encircling the moat.

'Has something unpleasant happened?' Eiichi asked, feigning ignorance. 'I can't imagine your not wanting to go out on a Saturday like this.'

'I'm worn out.'

'Have you had something in your eye again?'

'No,' she smiled forlornly. 'Emotionally worn out.'

'Well, then, as your physician, I'll start curing your exhaustion right now. The patient will please follow the course of treatment prescribed by the doctor. Okay?' He called a waiter and ordered some *sake*.

'I'd like fruit-juice or something. . . .'

'No. This is your medicine,' Eiichi shook his head and smiled. 'Didn't you agree to follow your doctor's orders? Drink this. Think of it as medicine. . . .'

It was clear from her pert, slightly flushed earlobes that the *sake* was beginning to take effect on Yoshiko.

'How old do you think you'll be when you die?' Eiichi asked soberly.

The unexpected enquiry made Yoshiko stare in amazement. 'I don't have any idea.'

'Eighty?'

'Heavens, no! I don't want to live to be such an old woman. . . .'

'Well, let's make it seventy-five. Now, I have a request. Would you do me the favour of living for seventy-five years and four hours?'

Yoshiko could not understand what he meant, and she stared at Eiichi with a quizzical look. 'You want me to live four extra hours?'

'That's right.'

'What's the point of living four extra hours? Why would you ask something like that?'

'Because I want to have those four hours today,' Eiichi laughed. 'You don't care whether you have those four hours or not, right? Since it's time you don't care anything about, why not squander it away by having fun? Think of it as four hours that isn't even part of your life. These four hours will have nothing to do with your life, so just for that long forget whatever unhappy memories or unpleasant things might be bothering you. Let's spend this Saturday as if we were somebody else.'

Yoshiko looked squarely at Eiichi. 'Are you telling me this . . . as my doctor?'

'I am. Because you're a patient.'

'Mr Ozu . . . you're a very kind man,' Yoshiko whispered, her eyes suddenly flooded with tears. 'Thank you.'

Eiichi felt his strategy progressing according to plan. He must use any and all tactics to make Yoshiko his. Gaining her trust was the most essential item.

'You know that I've broken off my engagement with Mr Kurihara, don't you?'

'Well, yes . . .'

'And the reason, too?'

'I can pretty well guess.'

'I thought so.' Her head drooped sadly. 'I never dreamed that . . . Mr Kurihara had another woman.'

'She's gone to the North-east. Kurihara sent her away so he could marry you.' Eiichi spoke casually, studying Yoshiko's expression to see the effects of his words.

'I feel sorry for her. . . .'

'So do I. But it shows how much Kurihara wanted to marry you, doesn't it?'

'I wouldn't want to get married at the expense of someone else.'

'Let's not talk about it any more. Have some more *sake*. We've got it here to make you into a different person for these four hours. . . .'

The sun slowly set. Lights were switched on in buildings, and the automobiles passing below them began turning on their headlights.

When they left the Imperial Hotel, Eiichi invited Yoshiko to a movie.

Eiichi realized it was in bad taste to ask her to a place like a cinema, but he wanted to be alone with Yoshiko in the dark.

The movie being shown at one cinema was the story of a love affair between a doctor and a married woman. It was the tale of a middle-aged man and woman who met each Saturday at a small railway station in the suburbs of London.

It was an old film, so Eiichi suggested that they see a different one. But Yoshiko said she would like to see a love story. There were few patrons inside the theatre.

'What did he say?' Eiichi whispered in her ear, pressing his shoulder lightly against hers. She did not move away, so Eiichi remained where he was.

At the scene where the two at last had to say farewell, Eiichi heard Yoshiko snuffling softly. She must be thinking about Kurihara, Eiichi thought, and he casually glanced over to see her reaction.

She quickly took a small handkerchief from her purse and wiped her nose.

'Is something wrong?' he asked.

'No. It's nothing.'

'Are you hurt by something you've remembered?'

Yoshiko did not answer. Eiichi tried to comfort her. 'Be brave.'

He placed his hand lightly on top of hers.

His move might be taken as that of an older man trying to comfort a weeping girl. But his hand remained motionless on top of hers.

There's hope. . . .

She probably would have pulled her hand away if she

disliked me. But she didn't, so she mustn't find me so bad, he thought.

When the film ended and the lights in the theatre came up, he noticed tears still shining faintly in her eyes.

'I'm sorry I brought you to this kind of movie,' he apologized. But inwardly he realized that this unplanned activity had instead worked to his advantage. 'Let's go. I'll bet you're starving.'

As they walked along the street, he said, 'It was malpractice for your doctor to take you to a movie that made you cry.'

'That's . . . not true.'

'But I took you out today to make you feel better. . . . We've taken two steps backward with that movie.'

'I'm the one that insisted. . . . I'm sorry.'

'I . . .' he started in on one of the phrases he had thought up the previous day. 'I . . . would like to heal the wounds in your heart.'

'I couldn't let you . . .'

'No. I want to. Please let me.'

Eiichi saw her home after the movie and dinner.

'Won't you come in for a few minutes?' Yoshiko invited Eiichi as she got out of the taxi.

'No. If your father found out that I had asked you out without telling him . . .' Eiichi smiled and shook his head, 'I'd get the devil at the hospital tomorrow. Please don't tell him about tonight.'

'Daddy's not that kind of person. But if you have work to do . . .'

'I do have some work. So I'll have to say goodnight. But you'll see me again?' he asked, gazing into Yoshiko's eyes. In a sense he was asking how she felt about him. 'You will see me again, won't you?'

'Yes,' Yoshiko nodded, taking Eiichi's outstretched hand.

Well done! He watched her go in through the gate and then sat back in the taxi, inwardly shouting with delight. He could still feel the touch of her hand. Yoshiko was not yet his, but he felt he had established a strong beachhead this evening. All he had to do now was push. Just push, push, push.

'Where to?' the driver asked.

He started to say 'Shinjuku Station', but he decided it was ridiculous to run up an unnecessary taxi fare when Yoshiko was not with him, so he corrected himself and said, 'No, the nearest subway station is fine.'

I wonder if she'll tell her father about tonight? Eiichi felt a bit uneasy as he hung from the subway strap. But I don't think she'll say anything that would make him angry. After all, I didn't do anything untoward. . . . There's nothing he could get angry about.

It was a little after ten when he reached home. As usual, he poked his head into the living-room, greeted his father, who was practising calligraphy alone, and started for the wash basin.

'Hey!' his father called to him.

'What is it?'

'Sit down,' Ozu ordered his son, his face unusually stern. 'Did you go to the funeral today?'

'Funeral? Whose?'

'Aiko Nagayama's funeral. She was your patient.'

Eiichi involuntarily grimaced. 'A doctor can't go to every patient's funeral.'

'I went,' Ozu said softly. 'I thought you might be there. But you weren't. Did someone from the hospital go?'

'Gee, I doubt it. But . . . you're weird, Dad. Going to a funeral like that.'

'Do you really mean that? You share the responsibility . . . for her death, you know.'

'Me! Don't be ridiculous. . . .'

Ozu gazed fiercely at his son. He had never been so infuriated with Eiichi as he was at that moment.

'I won't let you get away with saying you're not

responsible! I don't know anything about medicine, but according to the newspaper . . .'

'The newspaper? Oh, that! It's nonsense. Her death wasn't caused by the new drug.'

'If it wasn't because of the drug . . . what was it?'

'I've told you over and over again! She had terminal cancer!'

Ozu was caught without a reply. Since he was not a doctor himself, he had no way of refuting his son's contention that the drug had not been the cause of Aiko's death.

'But it said in the paper that your dispensary used that new drug on her like an experiment, without her consent. . . .'

'I don't know anything about what the paper says.'

'Are you saying you didn't use the new drug?'

'Yes, we used it! It isn't as though we gave her poison! We used a drug that was supposed to cure the patient. The ones who are irresponsible are the people who criticize us for something we did in good faith. Besides, I wasn't the one who used the drug on her. When you're at the bottom of the ladder like me, you administer drugs on orders from the directors of the dispensary. It was my superior Kurihara that used the drug on her,' Eiichi hammered away, a derisive smile on his lips. When he had argued his father into silence, he added, 'At any rate, I'd like you to stop meddling in things when you don't know anything about the circumstances. What was that woman to you, anyway?'

'Nothing at all.'

'If she was nothing to you, why did you go out of your way to attend her funeral? It makes no sense whatsoever.'

Ozu said nothing, but he was still unsatisfied. Logic was on his son's side, but something still did not fit into place for Ozu.

'I'm really upset. I come home from work exhausted,

and all of a sudden I get wiped all over the floor. What right do you have to talk to me like that? I've been wanting to tell you this for a long time, but – I just don't go along with your way of thinking. From now on, I don't want to hear anything from you about the things I do.' Eiichi spat the words out and stomped noisily out of the living-room.

Nobuko and Yumi had been listening with bated breath to this altercation from the next room. They poked their heads in stealthily.

'You shouldn't have said anything to him tonight,' Nobuko said falteringly. 'He's been so tired and excitable lately.'

'Uh-huh . . .' Ozu nodded, suppressing his agitation. He realized that an insurmountable gulf stretched between himself and his son. Eiichi has no idea why I was angry with him tonight. And he will never understand.

When Eiichi reached his room on the second floor he smothered his displeasure.

Someday I've got to move out of this house, he thought. This house, and my family, have nothing more to do with my life or my career. If anything, they're just a hindrance. . . .

It was several days after Kurihara stopped coming to the dispensary that Doctor Ii made his rounds for the first time in some while.

True to form, the dispensary staff assembled at the first-floor entrance, bowed to the Old Man and the dispensary chief beside him, formed into a group, and waited for the Old Man to board the elevator when one of the group rang for it.

On the fourth floor they went from room to room, taking careful note of the Old Man's examinations.

'Are you feeling all right?'

'Yes.'

'You're coming along well. There's nothing to worry about.'

These were the same words the staff members used, but when the Old Man spoke them they echoed like a thousand-pound weight and the patient smiled enthusiastically.

They went through several rooms and then came to the door of the room that Aiko Nagayama had occupied two weeks earlier. Eiichi studied the Old Man's expression, but his face was free of any emotion.

The room had not changed. The tiny stains on the walls, the slightly dirty windows, the bed – all were just as they had been. But the potted plants that Aiko loved had disappeared, and the patient who sat up in bed to be examined by the Old Man was a middle-aged gentleman wearing brand-new pyjamas.

'You must be bored here. Shall we run some tests on you?' The Old Man ordered Mine, the supervising physician, to perform some tests. 'There's no particular change in his condition, so I think he'll be all right.' Putting his stethoscope into his pocket, he began to chat with the patient.

It was just as if nothing had happened in this room two weeks earlier. The faces of the dispensary workers were blank, and there was no reason why this patient should know what had happened in the room he now occupied. Outside, the sky was thinly veiled with clouds, and the rumble of automobiles was audible in the distance.

'Well, take care of yourself. . . .'

The dispensary staff again meshed into a group and proceeded down the hall.

At noon, when the rounds were finished, Eiichi was on his way out of the dispensary when a messenger arrived with a Special Delivery letter.

The name on the return address was Yoshiko Ii. His heart throbbing, Eiichi tore open the envelope.

'Thank you so much for the other day. Every day was

gloomy for me but, thanks to you, I can breathe the air outside again. I'm so happy and grateful that you cheered me up when I was down.

'I promise to be a good patient. Please examine me from time to time in the future. I won't consult any other doctor.'

It was a brief letter, but Eiichi caught on to what she was trying to say. A smile of triumph involuntarily crossed his lips.

I won't consult any other doctor.

That meant she wouldn't have any other boy friends.

I promise to be a good patient. Please examine me from time to time in the future.

Let's go out together frequently, she was hinting.

Well done! Eiichi walked down the hall in high spirits. But one mountain still remained. There was the problem of what to do about Keiko Imai. If she finds out that I'm getting serious with Doctor Ii's daughter . . .

I won't screw it up like Kurihara did!

How should he deal with her? In any case, he was confident that he could handle the situation skilfully.

Several months later . . .

Ozu was in Kansai on a business trip. He spent two days meeting various people in Kobe and Osaka. When his scheduled business was completed, he still had four hours before he had to board the night bullet train on which he had a reservation. He did not feel like returning to his hotel. So he gave it some thought and an idea popped into his head.

He decided to visit his Alma Mater, Nada High School.

Many long months and years had passed since his graduation. Not once in that time had he returned to his old school, nor had he attended a single one of the reunions held in Kansai.

But he had heard that the school buildings along the

Sumiyoshi River had all been rebuilt now and had undergone a complete transformation. And he knew that, unlike his Alma Mater of former days, the school was today a gathering-place for gifted students from all over the country, ranking first or second in the number of graduates who entered Tokyo University.

But those items did not particularly interest Ozu. He wanted to visit his old school to reawaken memories of Flatfish and the others. His lost youth. With his own eyes he wanted one more look at the remains of the schoolhouse and the athletics field where he and the other backward students who never studied had spent their days.

He got into a taxi and asked the driver to take him to the Sumiyoshi River stop on the highway.

'On the highway?'

'Yes. There's a place where the train runs along the highway.'

The dilapidated brown train floated up before his eyes. The sluggish train he and Flatfish had caught every day.

Aiko and the other Kōnan girls had taken the same train.

'Oh, if you mean that train,' the driver said as he shifted gears, 'it's gone.'

'It's no longer in service?'

'Nobody'd ride on a poky old train like that!'

But the highway from Kobe to Osaka was still there. The land on either side of the highway, once vacant lots and fields, was now jammed with rows of stores and office buildings.

'The Sumiyoshi River is still there, isn't it?'

'Yep.'

He thought of the river, and of the evening primroses that had lined the white river bed. But when the Sumiyoshi River finally came into view, the river bed was nowhere to be seen. In its place was a large, insipid, cement-reinforced drainage ditch.

He caught sight of the school buildings of Nada High School. A pine forest had once encircled the space between the school and the highway. But most of the pines had been hewn down and houses built in their place.

When the taxi stopped at the gate of the school, Ozu asked the driver to wait about ten minutes and stepped inside the gate. The building in the foreground, which had housed the faculty room and the judo hall, was blackened and aged, but it was just as it had once been. As he stood before it, Ozu's chest ached, as though a massive hand was choking him.

Flatfish. This is the only place that hasn't changed, he muttered, just as though Flatfish was standing at his side.

Two or three students in black uniforms came out of the building. They all looked highly intelligent. None of them had the moronic but kind-hearted expression that students had worn in his day.

He went quietly into the building. The door of the faculty room opened and a man who seemed to be a teacher walked out.

The teacher's hair, combed straight back, was white. His jacket shone like that of an artist.

A younger replica of this teacher was filed in Ozu's memory. Yes . . . it was his Japanese teacher. Ozu remembered that this man had liked the novel *The Silver Spoon* and had talked to his students about it.

But his name was stuck somewhere in Ozu's mind and would not come loose. His nickname was . . .

Ethiopia . . . !

That was all he could remember. This teacher had been given that nickname because in those days his face had been coal-black.

'Are you a father of one of our students?' the teacher asked Ozu.

'No.' Caught off guard, Ozu quickly shook his head. 'I went to Nada Middle School a long time ago. . . . I was in town on business.'

'Well . . . that brings back old memories!' The teacher peered into Ozu's face, as if to recall his youth. 'What class were you in?'

'The ninth class at Nada. My name is Ozu.'

But the teacher did not seem to remember his name.

They could hear the voices of students exercising in the distance. From the window, Ozu could see the unfamiliar new buildings of the school.

'The school has changed a lot, too, hasn't it?'

'It has indeed,' the teacher nodded. 'It's nothing like the old Middle School. It's different because now the students study voluntarily. And the buildings have been renovated. . . . Do you remember me?'

'Yes. But I can't recall your name.'

'It's Hashimoto. Right now Mr Katsuyama, the principal, and I have been here the longest.'

Mr Hashimoto led the appreciative Ozu into the courtyard. Ozu remembered this courtyard. In his day, there had been an aviary and a platform for gymnastics bars here.

'The students today study well, but they're also involved in club activities and athletics,' Mr Hashimoto said happily. 'Times have changed, you know.'

'Yes . . . ,' Ozu muttered, a flood of emotions coursing through him. 'Times have changed.'

He thanked the teacher and returned to the gate of the school. The taxi was still waiting patiently.

'Where to next?'

'There's a girls' school called Kōnan, isn't there?'

'Yep. You wanna go there? Are you with the Ministry of Education?'

The taxi climbed a hill, passed down a residential street, and started up another hill.

'Oh, no. Kōnan isn't up here!'

'They moved it. Look, you can see it. It's that big white building.'

They were approaching a white, hotel-like building with a green lawn. A group of girl students came down the hill in a car. They commuted to and from school in a family automobile.

Ozu made the taxi stop. He gazed at the wide lawn beyond the gate marked 'Kōnan Girls' University'. A group of girls, laughing brightly, were on their way home from school. They wore lively dresses of all colours, nothing like the sailor suits that Aiko and her friends had worn. This was a generation that had not known war.

'To Ashiya next,' Ozu told the driver.

The railway had fallen into disuse, but Ozu recognized the highway leading to Ashiya. The vacant lots and fields once visible on either side were now buried under shops and petrol stations. But the station notices still remained, evoking a fathomless nostalgia and sadness in Ozu's breast.

Flatfish, he muttered, pressing his face against the window of the taxi. Do you remember this station? The name is just the way it was.

Yes – this road, and the names of the stations were just as they had been then. But the young men and women who had made their way to school on the dilapidated train were not as they had been.

Flatfish. So many things have happened.

Then the young, bleary-eyed Flatfish muttered in his ear. What did those days mean to us? Those days at Nada Middle School . . .?

The taxi was slowly climbing a gentle slope. When the old highway train had reached this point, it had creaked and panted as it climbed the hill.

The pine forest. Indescribable emotions filled Ozu's heart as the pines growing along the Ashiya River came into view.

'Where in Ashiya do you want to go?' the driver asked.

'The beach.'

'The beach?'

'Yes.'

'There's nothing there.'

Ozu said nothing, staring intently at the houses on either side of the highway. The great mansions with their black roofs and black fences were gone. In their place stood cheerful Western-style houses and high-class apartment buildings. A small tennis court had been built in the pine forest. Several young men were playing tennis.

They came to a bridge. It was *that* bridge.

'Cross over the bridge!' Ozu cried impulsively. 'Okay. Straight ahead on this road!'

Aiko Azuma's house. The house where he and Flatfish had loitered about, running their fingers along the fence. The house was gone. A stark-white apartment building stood in its place.

Ozu made the driver stop. He stared vacantly at the apartment house. Two foreign children were playing badminton.

'That's enough,' he told the driver sadly. 'Take me to the beach.'

The sea. The sea at Ashiya. Summer vacation. Great thunderhead clouds floating overhead as they swam in the blue sea. The sea. The sea at Ashiya.

'This is it.' The driver stepped on the brakes, stopping the taxi in front of an ugly concrete embankment.

'Here? There's no sea here!'

'I know. I told you they'd filled it in.'

No ocean breezes were blowing. There was none of the aroma of the sea. Ozu climbed up on the concrete embankment and gave a cry of surprise.

Far into the distance, the sea had been filled in like a desert. Two cement mixers were driving along the desolate stretch of reclaimed land. Beyond that there was nothing. Where was the spot where Flatfish, tossed about by the waves, had pursued Aiko and her friends that day? Where was the beach that Aiko and her friends had raced along, shrieking with laughter? The sea was gone now.

The white beach was gone. But it was not just here. Beautiful things, things from the treasured past were now disappearing all over Japan. Flatfish and Aiko were no longer in this world. Only Ozu was still alive. Ozu felt now that he understood what Aiko and Flatfish had meant in his life. Now, when all was lost, he felt he understood the meaning they had given to his life. . . .